The Doors Examined

by Jim Cherry

BENNION KEARNY

Published in 2013 by Bennion Kearny Limited.

ISBN: 978-1-909125-12-4

Published by Bennion Kearny Limited
6 Victory House
64 Trafalgar Road
Birmingham
B13 8BU

www.BennionKearny.com

Cover image: Shutterstock jolly_photo

Jim Morrison, Ray Manzarek, Robby Krieger and John Densmore. Welcome to the known, the unknown, and the in between.

Welcome to The Doors Examined.

The Doors remain one of the most influential and exciting bands in rock 'n' roll history, and The Doors Examined offers a unique, expressive insight into the history of the band, their influence on culture, and the group's journey following the death of Jim Morrison in Paris in 1971. It starts at the beginning, on a Venice Beach rooftop, and takes the reader on an invigorating journey, from The Whisky a Go-Go to the Dinner Key Auditorium, The Ed Sullivan Show to Père Lachaise Cemetery.

Comprised of selected acclaimed articles from The Doors Examiner, The Doors Examined also serves up original content that assesses seminal albums, how the group's music has influenced other artists, and key people in the band's history; people like Jac Holzman, Paul Rothchild, Bruce Botnick, and Pam Courson.

The Doors Examined is a must read investigation into one of the greatest rock 'n' roll bands of all time.

"The Doors Examined is an astonishingly insightful page-turner. Jim Cherry deconstructs the story of The Doors, examining all facets from every angle, exploring their history and contextualizing their achievements. He not only takes the reader back to the sixties to understand the world in which they were created, but also brings us up to the present day, showing their ongoing reverberations four decades after Jim Morrison checked out. This is a must-read for hardcores and newbies alike; maybe even for the doubters of a band that still compels people to choose sides." *Robert Rodriguez - author of Fab Four FAQ 2.0 and Revolver: How the Beatles Reimagined Rock 'N' Roll*

"A rich and wide-ranging set of articles from a writer who knows his stuff. Illuminating and informative throughout. An excellent addition to any Doors collection." *Michael Anthony, author of Words and Music: Excursions in the Art of Rock Fandom*

"A true Doors expert, Jim Cherry has crafted a remarkable book in The Doors Examined that provides fresh insights into the fascinating saga of The Doors. It's all here - from the early days on Venice Beach and at the Whisky a Go-Go to a stirring first person account of a visit to Jim Morrison's grave on the 40th anniversary of his death and everything inbetween. Through it all, Cherry provides irrefutable evidence to show why The Doors are just as relevant today as when Light My Fire skyrocketed up the charts in 1967. Eclectic, informative and eminently enjoyable, The Doors Examined is a must-read for any Doors fan." *Rich Weidman, author of The Doors FAQ*

To The Doors and their fans,
without whom none of this would be possible.

Foreword

I am looking forward to publication of this book, for the Perspective & "Filtering" it promises. In the wake of Rampant, Hysterical, Hyper-Supposition in the years since Jim died, I have SUFFERED through Endless Pontificating Volumes of everything from A through Z-Squared, & Jim Cherry has been the ONLY person to check the facts I could provide as a result of my years with Doors Music, Inc.

Given that The Doors are (seemingly) more popular Now than they were Then is largely due to the Internet, the Mysterious Persona they effortlessly achieved, and that Most Perfect Marriage of Words & Music, which, in TOTAL, IS The GENIUS Of The Doors.

Jim Morrison cannot be separated FROM the Music of The Doors with any more success than Time & Space could be extracted from Einstein's Theories; They ARE One. Were it not FOR The Doors, Jim's Poetry may not have EVER seen The Light Of Day ... Who Knows ... Neither myself or anyone else.

I celebrate Jim Cherry's inclusion of SO MANY "Ancillary" people, who had a part in the making of this Legendary Quartet; It DOES take a Village to go from unknown & "odd experiment" to Timeless International Superstars; Agents, Managers, Office Staff, Roadies, Press/PR, Promoters, etc., etc., etc. (& Maybe a moonlighting Security/Bodyguard while doubling as a Student Body President in College) ...

While we ALL have "Flaws" that we convince ourselves don't exist, Jim's "flaws" were discernible from a distance spanning dimensions & light years, which he found to be "Interesting & amusing" ... I did too!

Cheers & Hardcore Jollies

Tony Funches

About the Author

Jim Cherry was born and raised in Chicago, and spent his 20's in the pursuit of experience as research in the name of art, visiting places such as New Orleans, Los Angeles, Germany, France and Mexico.

He now resides in the western suburbs of Chicago. He's formerly a columnist for, and appeared on, The Rants, Raves and Rock 'n' Roll Magazine and radio show.

He currently writes The Doors Examiner, and has written the novels *Becoming Angel*, *The Last Stage*, and the book of short stories *Stranger Souls*.

More information is available at www.jymsbooks.com

Table of Contents

Introduction **i**
Chapter 1 - Doors Pre-history **1**
The Whisky a Go-Go Opens its Doors 1
Jim Morrison in FSU Promotional Film 3
Jim Morrison Sound Man 3
Rick and The Ravens: Doors Pre-history 4
Jim Morrison 'bumps' into Ray Manzarek on Venice Beach 5
The Doors Cut a Demo 7
John Densmore Joins The Doors 7
The Doors at The London Fog 8
The Doors Start at The Whisky a Go-Go 9
Chapter 2 - Doors History **11**
The Doors and Them 11
Paul Rothchild Sees The Doors at The Whisky 12
The Doors Get Fired 13
The Doors Debut 14
The Doors Play The Matrix 16
Jim Morrison's Missing Time 17
Jim Morrison Meets Patricia Kennealy 19
Rock is Dead 20
Jim Morrison Marries Patricia Kennealy 21
Were The Doors Trying to Replace Jim Morrison? 22
Jim Morrison Dead in Paris at Age 27 23
Chapter 3 - Doors Releases **27**
Light My Fire Released as a Single 27
The Doors release *Strange Days* 29
The Doors Record *Waiting for the Sun* 30

The Unknown Soldier 33
The Soft Parade 34
The Doors' Tribute to Jim Morrison, *An American Prayer* 35
The 40th Anniversary of *L.A. Woman* 36
Chapter 4 - Music Reviews **39**
Live in New York 39
When You're Strange Soundtrack 41
Robby Krieger's *Singularity* 42
The Doors *Live in Vancouver* 43
Ray Manzarek and Roy Rogers at the Crossroads of Rock and The Blues 45
Acoustic Tribute to The Doors 46
Ray Manzarek and Michael McClure's Symbiosis and Synergy 47
Would Have Made a Great Live Album in 68! 47
Chapter 5 - On the Road **51**
The Doors at the Roundhouse 51
The Doors in Amsterdam 52
The Doors in Toronto, 1969 53
The Doors at the Northern California Rock and Folk Festival 55
The Doors, riot at the Singer Bowl 56
The Doors Show that Created Iggy Pop 57
The Chicago Coliseum May 10, 1968 58
The Doors Play the Chicago Auditorium 59
The Doors at the Aquarius Theater 60
The Doors Play Madison Square Garden 61
The Doors in Mexico City 62
The Doors at the Isle of Wight 63
The Doors Live in NY, January 1970 64
Dallas 1970, The Doors Second from Last Show with Jim Morrison 65
The Doors Come to the End in New Orleans 66
Chapter 6 - People in the Doors' World **69**
The Work of Paul Rothchild 69
Pam Courson 71
The Doors enthrall Danny Sugerman 72
Robert Gover 75
Jim Morrison's Father Dies 76
An Actor Out On Loan: Tom Baker 78
Harrison Ford and The Doors 80
Patti Smith Meets Jim Morrison 81
Happy Birthday Jac Holzman 81
Chapter 7 - The Doors' Influences **85**
Weldon Kees, the Lost Literary Influence of Jim Morrison 85
Jim Morrison and Jack Kerouac Part 1 90
Jim Morrison and Jack Kerouac Part 2 91
Did Jim Morrison Name Alice Cooper? 92
The Doors and Elvis 93
JFK's Assassination and Jim Morrison 94

William Blake in Doors History 95
Gene Vincent 97
The Story of Bo Diddley 98
Chapter 8 - The Doors at the Movies **101**
The Doors Film Feast of Friends 101
Jim Morrison Films HWY 102
Feast of Friends Wins at Atlanta International Film Festival 104
The Jim Morrison Film Festival 104
The Doors and Apocalypse Now 106
Oliver Stone's The Doors Reconsidered 106
The Doors in the Movies 109
When You're Strange 110
Role Cast in Fictional Jim Morrison Film 111
Casting The Last Beat Nears Completion 112
Cyndi Lauper Cast in The Last Beat 112
Ray Manzarek's The Poet in Exile to be Made into Movie 113
Mr. Mojo Risin' 114
The Doors at the Hollywood Bowl Classic Restored! 115
Chapter 9 - Jim Morrison's Arrests **117**
Jim Morrison's First Arrest 117
The 'Murder of Phil O'Leno' 118
Jim Morrison vs. New Haven 120
Flight to Phoenix 121
Jim Arrested in Clearwater, Florida 123
Chapter 10 - Miami: From Incident to Pardon **125**
The Living Theatre Opens in L.A. 125
The Miami Incident 126
Jim Morrison's Obscenity Trial 128
Crist to Pardon Jim Morrison? 130
Florida Governor to Submit Doors Lead Singer for Pardon 131
Jim Morrison Still Provoking the Establishment? 131
Crist has The Last Word on Jim Morrison 132
Morrison Pardon a Done Deal? 132
Jim Morrison Pardoned 133
Patricia Kennealy Weighs in on Jim Morrison Pardon 133
The Doors Issue Statement on Jim Morrison Pardon 134
Chapter 11 - Book Reviews (Non-Fiction) **137**
Canyon of Dreams 137
Ray, Jim, John, Robby and Doug? 138
I Remember Jim Morrison 139
Forever Changes, Arthur Lee and the Book of Love 141
Jac Holzman's Adventures in Recordland 142
The Doors FAQ 144
The Doors, Greil Marcus' Lifetime 145
Dennis Jakob's Summer With Morrison 146
Jerry Scheff, Bass Player for a Classic Age 147

Jim Morrison, The Living Theatre and the FBI 148
Chapter 12 - The Doors on Television **151**
The Doors Play The End on Toronto TV Show 151
The Doors on Ed Sullivan 152
The Doors on the Murray the K TV Show 153
The Doors Appear on the Jonathan Winters Show 154
The Doors on The Smothers Brothers Show 155
The Doors on PBS' Critique 156
The Doors VH-1 157
The Doors on Cold Case 157
The Doors on Glee 158
Jim Morrison's Dark Skies 159
Brett Lowenstern Takes the Sex Out of Light My Fire 160
Strange Days Have Found The Simpsons 161
Chapter 13 - Jim Morrison's Ghost **163**
Jim Morrison's Ghost Appears… Again 163
The Return of Jim Morrison's Ghost 164
Now Appearing in Arlington, VA, The Ghost of Jim Morrison 165
Is Jim Morrison as Big as Jesus or John Lennon? 165
Chapter 14 - The Doors' Photographers **167**
Bobby Klein: The Doors Through the Lens 167
Jim Marshall Rock Photographer 168
Henry Diltz Photographer of Morrison Hotel 169
Linda McCartney: Band Member with a Camera 170
O. Bisogno Scotti: Morrison Hotel Today 172
Chapter 15 - The Doors in Fiction **175**
Lewis Shiner's Glimpses 175
Turn the Page: The Lost Letters of Jim Morrison 176
Anthology Features Jim Morrison in Story 177
Jim Morrison Jesus Complex 178
Mr. Mojo Risin' (Ain't Dead) 179
Chapter 16 - The Doors Take the Rap **181**
Cypress Hill Samples The Doors 181
Did The Doors Reunite in the Studio? 182
The Doors in the Studio with Skrillex 183
Would Jim Morrison 'Love' Skrillex? 183
The Doors and Tech N9ne 184
L.A. Woman Meets Dog Town 184
The Doors Takin' the Rap? 185
Chapter 17 - The Doors in the News **187**
The Doors Name on Trial 187
Palestinian Group Asks Manzarek-Krieger to Cancel 188
John Densmore Occupies L.A. 189
Jim Morrison's 'Love Street' House Damaged in L.A. Fires 190
'Love Street' Arsonist Arrested 191
Will Jim Morrison Play with The Doors Again? 191

The Doors Welcome the Digital Resurrection? 193
Jim Morrison 'Resurrection' Coming Soon? 194
John Densmore on the Death of Vaclav Havel 194
Chapter 18 - Fans-cination with The Doors **197**
Jim Morrison in the Theatre 197
Jim Morrison in the Ballet 198
Jim Morrison's Bust 199
L.A. Woman Tours 200
Stephen Beauvais' Doors Portraits 201
The Quest to Find Jim Morrison's Long Lost Cobra 201
A Night to Remember 202
Jim Morrison, Poet? 204
Chapter 19 - Not Quite The End **207**
Ray and Robby Music Producers 207
John Densmore in the Twenty-First Century 208
Père Lachaise July 3, 2011 210
The Classical Music of the Future 211
Acknowledgements **213**

Introducing The Doors Examined

Its Origin Story

Every good heroic tale needs an origin story, and The Doors Examiner has been a heroic tale in a lot of ways. The first article of The Doors Examiner was published August 29, 2009. I published the article and went off to dinner, not having even one subscriber, and not being very experienced in social media, I posted a message on my Myspace page and The Doors message board, not knowing what would happen.

But The Doors Examiner tale started about a week and half earlier. A woman I knew, who was already writing Examiner articles, knew I was a writer and a Doors fan. She suggested I write about The Doors for the Examiner. I was hesitant at first just "knowing" that the assignment would be filled because there were a lot of people that have better access to The Doors, were more versed in Doors history, and had more perspicacity about The Doors than I. I checked The Examiner site trying to keep in mind what other subjects I could write about when I discovered The Doors wasn't taken. Just as my friend had said, they had The Doors as a subject, and to my surprise, no one had taken it! The next step was to write a sample article and five headlines for potential stories that I did easily. I sent them in, and waited…

Introducing The Doors Examined

About five days later I got word from the Examiner that they had accepted my application and I could start publishing articles! Instantly forgetting about the five sample headlines I had to write (and never again even thinking about them as subjects for an article) I ploughed ahead and wrote the first article and went to the aforementioned dinner.

One of the concerns I had in writing The Doors Examiner was what do you write about a band that officially broke up almost 40 years before? I knew I could write about the history of The Doors and about the people in and around The Doors, but I was worried that everything would be in the past tense and what happens after that? I shouldn't have worried. A few weeks after that first article, The Doors announced the release of their *Live in New York* CD, which was quickly followed by the documentary *When You're Strange*. The Doors themselves continue to follow their artistic and personal destinies. The individual members of The Doors continue performing, writing books, creating new CDs (formerly called albums), contributing their time and energies to charitable events and causes, giving interviews, and in their capacity as rock legends lending their talents to a new generation of performers. The Doors Examiner is there to review those releases, report on their concert performances, and inform fans of appearances.

Another reason I wanted to write The Doors Examiner was because some ideas about The Doors were being missed and I thought it was an opportunity to present those ideas. These articles aren't without a point of view and you may read things in this book you've seen in no other book about The Doors. Those theories are based on the personalities of the band members and what I've read and researched about them and I hope those theories have enough evidence to make the case. At the very least they're ideas for your consideration (when it comes right down to it that's all any writer has to offer… ideas).

In the three and half years I've been writing The Doors Examiner, from those virtual humble beginnings, The Doors Examiner has built a niche for itself in The Doors world as well as the larger world. From that first article with no subscribers and little exposure The Doors Examiner has built up a solid base of subscribers and supporters. Within The Examiner purview, The Doors Examiner has become one of the most highly rated and read of The Examiner's music columnists, consistently being rated in the top ten percent of music and entertainment writers. The Doors Examiner has also been noticed outside of the circle of Doors and rock fans and has made its way out to the mainstream world with radio stations, websites, newspapers, and even The Doors themselves having reprinted, reposted, and/or linked to The Doors Examiner articles.

During the tenure of The Doors Examiner, I've written about every aspect of The Doors possible; past, present and even future. The Doors Examined captures those aspects of The Doors, and presents them in microcosm. Like all journalistic writing it is sometimes done under the gun, to get a story off while it's still timely. The articles contained in this book are the "perfect" versions of the articles which have been corrected, and in some cases, articles may have been combined to make the best articles (primarily The Doors history articles), but the subject and thrust, and certainly the opinions haven't changed.

Impressions of The Doors

The Doors Examined isn't a linear history of The Doors from 1964-1971, neither is it a biography of either the band or any of its members. It's not a critical assessment of the band, its works, or the times they're from. So, what is this book? The Doors Examined is a mélange of elements from the above types of books from The Doors history, to reviews of their work, to their influences, latter day trials and current works. The Doors Examined is a collage of pictures, that when you pull away you see the larger picture as a whole, or image upon image in quick succession to reveal the story within the ongoing film of life. I hope the impressions of The Doors stack up on each other to form a picture in your mind. As with any book that is a compilation, the articles can be read in a linear fashion (the articles are presented chronologically not only from the early days of The Doors but in the order they were published in The Doors Examiner). They can be read out of order, the reader's mind creating its own context.

The Doors Examiner treats The Doors as a living entity that is not quite finished, an organism that is still shaping and creating itself. The Doors are a legendary band, but they're not yet set in marble; the temple not yet finished. What does the future hold for The Doors Examiner? I don't know. A lot of that is up to The Doors and what the future holds for them. However, what is past is worth taking a fresh look at, from angles previously unexplored. This book is The Doors Examined…

To read future Doors Examiner articles and keep abreast of the latest Doors news subscribe at *http://www.examiner.com/the-doors-in-national/jim-cherry*

1

Doors Pre-history

It's a cliché to say something doesn't exist in a vacuum, nothing does. As we look back we see the concatenation that needed to occur, that certain things had to be in place. People and lives are in motion swirling around each other and places, events, and people need to align to bring actors and their stages together. So it was with The Doors. Before there was The Doors, there was Jim Morrison, Ray Manzarek, UCLA, The Sunset Strip, and myriad other factors that conspired to bring The Doors together. Now, looking back, it all seems pre-ordained. However, back in the Doors pre-history nothing was certain, nothing was pre-ordained. It was those swirling elements that finally brought about The Doors.

The Whisky a Go-Go Opens its Doors

While Jim Morrison and Ray Manzarek were making their way to the UCLA film school, on January 11, 1964, the Whisky a-Go-Go opened its doors and plunged into rock history. The Whisky, as it came to be known, very quickly rose in prominence on the Sunset Strip, and within the music industry, and was a model and influence for discotheques across the USA.

Founded by Elmer Valentine, Mario Maglieri, and Phil Tanzini - The Whisky had to spell its name without the 'e' in whiskey because Los Angeles city zoning laws didn't allow clubs to be named after alcohol (The Whisky constantly had problems with the city and for a while had the name "The Whisk?"). The Whisky quickly gained a reputation for having high profile acts such as Johnny Rivers whose breakthrough hit was *Secret Agent Man* (the theme song for the TV series

Secret Agent). In between Rivers' sets, a DJ named Joanie Labine, the first DJ at The Whisky, played records in a booth that was suspended to the right of the stage. During one of Rivers' sets, Labine was moved to dancing and the concept of the go-go dancer was born. Soon a 'uniform' of the go-go dancer also evolved: a girl wearing a short, fringed skirt, and high, white boots. Go-go dancers began appearing in nightclubs and discotheques across the country. During his tenure at The Whisky (a one year contract), Rivers recorded the album, *Johnny Rivers Live at The Whisky a Go-Go*, and The Miracles' song *Going to a Go-Go* soon gave the nightclub a national reputation.

Drawn by Rivers' success The Whisky became a destination for up and coming bands to try to make a name for themselves. Groups such as The Paul Butterfield Blues Band, The Rascals, The Byrds, The Turtles, Otis Redding, Love, Captain Beefheart, The Mothers of Invention, and Alice Cooper were soon performing at The Whisky. The Whisky was also the destination for hip young movie stars such as Steve McQueen and Paul Newman who could be found dancing the night away.

During the 1966 Sunset Strip riots (which were immortalized in the Buffalo Springfield song *For What it's Worth*), the efforts of city officials to close The Whisky made it a focal point of the skirmishes between the protestors and the police. Other bands also paid homage to The Whisky in song including: Motley Crue, and Arthur Lee of Love in the album *Forever Changes*.

The Whisky was not only a breeding ground for Los Angeles bands, but a destination for a lot of British bands such as Them, Cream, Led Zeppelin, Jimi Hendrix (The Jimi Hendrix Experience should probably be considered an English band because Hendrix had to go to London before he was discovered by The Animals' Chas Chandler, and he and Hendrix put together The Experience), The Kinks, and The Who.

The Whisky continued to feature bands through the 70's and, as new genres of rock came into being, The Whisky was at the forefront of exploring emerging genres such as New Wave, Punk, and Heavy Metal with bands like The Runaways, X, Quiet Riot, Patti Smith, Elvis Costello, The Germs, The Misfits, Van Halen, Motley Crue, and The Police. During the 80's, The Whisky fell on hard times as the punk bands faded from the scene and The Whisky closed its doors in 1982. In 1986, however, The Whisky reopened. Gone were the go-go dancers, DJ booth, carpeting, and downstairs booths. The Whisky remains open today and still features up and coming bands, looking to find their niche in rock 'n' roll history like The Doors did in the summer of 1965.

Jim Morrison in FSU Promotional Film

It's well known that Jim Morrison went to the UCLA film school to make movies. To many it seems that Jim Morrison becoming famous as the lead singer of The Doors was happenstance, a lucky confluence of events that brought him and The Doors to national attention. But looking at Jim Morrison's actions it seems that Morrison was looking for avenues of artistic outlet that would bring him fame. There hasn't been a lot of information about his pre-UCLA artistic activities. We do know that at Florida State University Jim was in a production of *The Dumbwaiter* because there's a picture of him on stage, and in *No One Here Gets Out Alive* a couple of his fellow actors relate stories of his performance during rehearsals. We also know that he was reading early poems at the Beaux-Arts while still at FSU. Until a few years ago we didn't have any evidence of Jim making or being in films before going to UCLA.

In late February or early March of 2005 a film surfaced of Jim Morrison as an actor in a film. It wasn't any ordinary film, it was a university produced promotional film. The fragment of the film that still exists shows a young, clean-cut Jim Morrison in two scenes. The first scene finds the young actor dressed in a sweater, and his soon to be famous boots, going out to his mail box and receiving a rejection letter from the college - his face reflecting disappointment. The second scene is set in a college administrator's office with both Jim and the administrator clearly giving straightforward readings of the script they were given. It's a fairly standard 60's informational film on college tuition. Jim's acting wasn't going to get him an academy award, although his line reading was smoother than the school administrator who shares the scene with him.

Jim Morrison Sound Man

When you're a student filmmaker your classmates are your cast, crew and collaborators, and so it was true for Jim Morrison and Ray Manzarek at the UCLA film school in 1965. In May, 2011, the Billy Wilder Theater hosted a series: *Celebrating Orphan Films*. The program included films of two former UCLA film students and classmates of Jim Morrison: Alexander Prisadsky and his film *Five Situations for Camera, Recorder and People*, and Ronald Raley's film *Patient 411*. The filmmakers presented their student films, the films that Morrison had worked on as cinematographer and soundman. Both presentations included their recollections of Jim Morrison as part of their crew. Alexander

Prisadsky also included his recollections as part of the UCLA Film and Television Archive.

Alexander Prisadsky's film *Five Situations for Camera, Recorder and People* was filmed after Morrison's famous (or infamous) student film which was (again) famously or infamously illustrated in Oliver Stone's movie *The Doors* and described in Ray Manzarek's *Light My Fire*. The film started with the image of Jim Morrison taking a huge hit off a joint, then cuts to a frat party scene with a bunch of guys sitting around drinking beer and throwing darts at a Playboy centerfold hung upside down. After that the guys started watching a 'stag film' and when the film broke they made finger shadows on the screen while the soundtrack featured an American Indian peyote chant and musique concrete. The next cut was to a blond woman dancing in a black bra, garters and stockings on top of a television then, off-screen, the voice of Jim Morrison is heard yelling "Turn on the TV! Turn on the TV!" The TV shows pictures of a Nazi rally or march with Morrison, again off-screen, saying "Leave it! Leave it! It's perfect!" This is followed by a woman licking an eyeball. The final scene shows the television being turned off with the images fading to a dot then disappearing.

Although Morrison's film was almost universally reviled by classmates, it seems to have affected Prisadsky (and Manzarek, who said that it was "basically… poetry") enough that it made him reevaluate the film he originally wanted to do. One of Prisadsky's ideas for his film was to have his fellow students wearing black suits (in a scene that eerily anticipates the opening sequence of *Reservoir Dogs*). Morrison was the only one who didn't have a black suit, so he acted as the soundman on the film. It seems Jim Morrison, future Doors lead singer, already had a knack for sound, overlaying Bach and the roar of thunder to make another student's film more mysterious. For Prisadsky's film, Morrison suggested a scene where he got in a crowd with a microphone and produced a distorted concussive sound that Prisadsky liked and ended up using. At one point, Morrison told Prisadsky "Maybe I should be in radio instead of film."

Rick and The Ravens: Doors Pre-history

Jim Morrison once said: "There's the known and the unknown and in between are The Doors." A lot of what falls into the unknown is the pre-history of The Doors, and what doesn't get discussed at length is the immediate predecessor group to The Doors: Rick and the Ravens.

Rick and the Ravens consisted of Ray Manzarek with the onstage persona "Screaming Ray Daniels" on keyboards and vocals, Rick Manczarek on guitar, Jim Manczarek on harmonica and piano (both Rick and Jim Manczarek are Ray's brothers, Manczarek being the original Polish spelling), and Vince Thomas on drums. Rick and the Ravens formed around 1961 (Ray may have been playing in more than one band at the time, and a recording of the song *Moanin'* with Ray Daniels and The UCLA Trio is dated circa 1961). Rick and the Ravens frequently played The Turkey Joint West that was also a hangout for UCLA film school students. If the club was empty, Ray would invite his film school friends onstage to sing or bang a tambourine. It was, of course, on one of these occasions that Ray invited fellow UCLA film student Jim Morrison on stage for a raucous version of *Louie, Louie*. An alternate version of the story is that Morrison may have been sitting in the back loudly calling for the band to play *Louie, Louie* and Manzarek invited Jim onstage. Perhaps to keep him quiet? In either rendition of the story it's the first recorded moment that Jim Morrison sang onstage.

Rick and the Ravens hit their apex when they opened for Sonny and Cher. This is another moment when Morrison became involved with Rick and the Ravens. The band was short a guitar player that night and recruited Jim Morrison to appear onstage with an unplugged guitar so they could fulfill their contract. Morrison later quipped "It was the easiest money I ever made." Rick and the Ravens had a recording deal with Aura Records and they recorded several singles including *Soul Train/Geraldine* and *Henrietta/Just For You* that went nowhere in sales or radio play. In lieu of Aura paying for the pressing of another record that wouldn't go anywhere, they offered the band free studio time to finish out the contract. It was during that studio time that they cut the demos of songs written by Jim Morrison that led directly to the creation of The Doors.

Jim Morrison 'bumps' into Ray Manzarek on Venice Beach

July has a lot of memorable events in Doors history and pre-history. Most notably the July 3-4 weekend when Jim Morrison died in Paris in 1971. Early July 1965, however, is when The Doors formed after Jim Morrison reportedly 'bumped' into Ray Manzarek on Venice Beach. But did Jim bump into Ray in the first part of July? Probably not. Throughout the years Ray has enjoyed telling the story of how he bumped into Jim on the beach. I think if it was on, or around, the 4th of July, it's a detail Ray would have found irresistible and therefore included in the story. So it was probably a week or so later. The Doors History website reports the date as July 8th. However, the real question of the story is, did Jim really accidentally 'bump' into Ray on the beach? July is the beginning and end of The Doors story. A beginning and end that are both surrounded in the fog of myth.

Most Doors fans know the story of Ray and Jim's meeting on Venice Beach. It is the origin story of The Doors that has reached mythological proportions (Morrison himself even calling it a 'tale' in his interview with Salli Stevenson), a predestined meeting arranged by the gods. Ray was meditating on Venice Beach in early July 1965. He had graduated from UCLA film school in late May or June of that year, and Morrison had left a little earlier after his student film was vilified by students and teachers alike. Morrison told friends he was going to New York. As Manzarek was meditating, Jim Morrison walked up the beach from the surf. Morrison looked like Adonis after having lost some weight. In the Oliver Stone movie *The Doors*, Stone has Jim approaching Ray out of the sun, a halo of light surrounding him, a very Apollonian image for Jim Morrison. Ray asks what he's been doing and Morrison says he's been living up on Dennis Jakob's (Jim's UCLA roommate) roof, writing songs. Ray encourages him to sing one, and Jim sings *Moonlight Drive*. Ray tells him they should start a rock band and make a million dollars.

But did it happen exactly that way? Was the meeting on the beach chance? I don't think so. I think Jim Morrison had some pretty clear intentions to try to start a rock band and Jim Morrison knew Ray was in a band. He and other film school friends had gone to see Manzarek's band Rick and The Ravens at The Turkey Joint West. Jim had even 'performed' with the band as mentioned previously. Jim also told Dennis Jakob, half-seriously, half-jokingly, that they should start a band called "The Doors: Open and Closed". Clearly, starting a band was on Morrison's mind. When Manzarek filmed his student film *Induction* Morrison appeared in a party scene that was filmed at Manzarek's beach house. Jim Morrison knew not only where Ray lived, but the general area of the beach where Ray might hang out. How many times that July had Jim Morrison walked by and passed that part of the beach, hoping Ray would be there?

July was the beginning.

The Doors Cut a Demo

By the time Ray had 'bumped' into Jim on Venice Beach, John Densmore had joined the band. On September 2, 1965, Rick and the Ravens went into the studio to cut a demo, which included songs that would become the foundation of The Doors: *Hello, I Love You*, *End of the Night*, *Moonlight Drive*, *Summer's Almost Gone*, *My Eyes Have Seen You* and *Go Insane* (later to be incorporated into The Doors' *Celebration of the Lizard*).

The demo doesn't sound as darkly mysterious as The Doors would later become. However, the foundation of what The Doors and what their songs would evolve into were there. Ray was carrying the vocals and playing piano, which at moments, sounded a little tinny. Jim's voice was still weak as he mostly did a lot of screaming. There's a discernible 50's feel or influence of Gene Vincent or Eddie Cochran in the songs. It was also during this session that the nascent Doors had a woman playing bass guitar, although no one seems to be able to remember her name. The recording took two to three hours. In the days afterward each member of the band would take a copy of the demo and visit record companies to get them interested in the band. Ray Manzarek reports in *Light My Fire* that he, Jim and John went to the office of Lou Adler. Adler listened to about ten seconds of each cut on the album *Moonlight Drive*, *End of the Night*, *I Looked at You*, *Go Insane*, and *Hello, I Love You* then pulled the needle off the record and went to the next cut, listened to another couple of seconds until he handed the record back to them saying "There's nothing I can use here". Ray says Jim replied: "That's okay man. We don't want to be used, anyway." That was the reception they received at all the record companies they visited… rejection.

John Densmore Joins The Doors

During the summer of 1965 Ray had taken Jim in and together they worked up arrangements for The Doors' early songs, and presented them to Ray's band Rick and The Ravens. Unfortunately, the Manczarek brothers didn't understand Jim's lyrics, so Ray went on the lookout for musicians who would have more faith in the unproven Morrison.

John Densmore and Ray Manzarek were both members of Maharishi Mahesh Yogi's third street meditation center in Santa Monica. John was there to try to work out a problem he was having with anger, and Ray was seeking an alternative avenue to altered consciousness, instead of drugs, through meditation.

In talking to another student at the center, Ray learned that John was a drummer so Ray approached Densmore to ask if he'd be interested in joining a band. John said he would. Then Ray added something that piqued Denmore's interest, Ray said he'd call in a few months because the time wasn't right yet. John remembers thinking "Gee, that's pretty cosmic, far out."

Some of the exact dates in Doors history are unknown, or various sources give differing dates, but on or around August 20, 1965, fortune's wheel turned a notch and Ray called John leading to John Densmore becoming a member of the nascent Doors. The first thing Ray did was have John meet Jim at the Manhattan Beach garage of Ray's parents. Jim was dressed in brown corduroy and was barefoot. Jim struck John as being shy. During the rehearsal, Jim sang facing the corner of the garage. John was at first hesitant about joining the band, but when he was shown Jim's lyrics he instantly saw the fluidity and rhythm to them and was instantly attracted to them.

John was also in the band The Psychedelic Rangers, whose guitar player was named Robby Krieger. The Doors were almost complete.

The Doors at The London Fog

The Doors decreed 2012 as "The Year of The Doors", but if there was a "Year of The Doors" it was 1966. 1966 took The Doors from obscurity to the edge of fame. It all started at The London Fog where, in late February or early March of 1966 (the exact date is unknown), The Doors auditioned for and became the house band.

By all accounts The London Fog was a non-descript bar. While it was only about half a block down the street from the Whisky a Go-Go, it didn't have the clientele or the reputation for the quality of acts that The Whisky did. The London Fog was a hole in the wall bar with customers that included drunks, prostitutes, and sailors looking for a good time. The nautical décor did nothing to hide the smell of spilled beer and overflowing ashtrays.

When The Doors auditioned, all of Morrison's and Manzarek's film school friends filled the club. Owner Jesse James (he claimed to be the great-grandson of the historical outlaw) probably thought he had found the band to fill his club. However, the club quickly returned to its usual clientele and the bar remained mostly empty giving the band what amounted to paid practice sessions. Morrison was still too shy to face the audience so he performed most of the time with his back to the patrons.

The London Fog is also where The Doors started filling out and expanding the length of their songs, adding solos and jams with Morrison occasionally adding his own poetic improvisations to songs like *When The Music's Over*, *Light My Fire*, and *The End* because the band didn't have a lot of songs in their repertoire. Their songs and sets filled out in length and complexity and Ray Manzarek once said that because of the London Fog - "[The Doors] became this collective entity, this unit of oneness." Although the London Fog gave the band a chance to hone their songs, the group had their eyes on bigger things and hoped word would get out and make its way down to The Whisky. John Densmore said that, in between sets at the Fog, they would run down the street to The Whisky and watch from the back door envious of the bands that played at the more prestigious club. The Doors stayed in residence at the London Fog until late May of 1966 when they were offered the chance to audition at The Whisky.

The Doors Start at The Whisky a Go-Go

On May 16th, 1966, The Doors started a one week appearance at The Whisky a Go-Go that led to them becoming The Whisky's house band. This appearance starts their ascension into the world of the Sunset Strip and eventually catapults them into legendary status and into a recording contract with Elektra Records.

Just a few months before, the future didn't look all that bright for The Doors. When they were playing The London Fog very few people saw or heard the band. They could have languished there but during that time they were able to work up most of the songs that would comprise their first two albums and they finally generated enough of a buzz to catch the ear of The Whisky's talent booker Ronnie Haran. Haran saw them at the Fog, liked what she saw, and recommended them to Whisky owner Elmer Valentine. The Doors were a hard sell to Valentine. He thought Jim Morrison was an amateur who was posing to cover for his lack of talent. Further, he didn't like Morrison's use of foul language. Haran prevailed, or maybe wore Valentine down and on, or about, May 9th, 1966, The Doors auditioned at The Whisky from which they were offered a one week booking before going on to become the house band.

The Whisky represented success to The Doors. Jim Morrison later admitted at one time, while The Doors were at The London Fog, that their goal was to be as big as Love, which was the house band at The Whisky. The Whisky not only gave the band access to a greater audience, and a higher profile on Sunset, but also gave them the chance to play with more established bands such as Them, Buffalo Springfield, Captain Beefheart, and The Animals to name a few.

The Doors tenure at The Whisky would be short, lasting only until July of 1966 when Jim Morrison performed *The End* with the Oedipal section for the first time. It succeeded in getting the band fired.

With The Doors becoming the house band at The Whisky, it ended their journeyman apprenticeship as a band. The higher visibility of the group propelled them from the shadows of their pre-history and closer to fame and fortune. Although that wasn't yet assured, The End was always near.

2
Doors History

When The Doors stepped onto the stage at The Whisky, whether they knew it or not, they were stepping onto a larger stage. A stage where the performances would gain them more and more attention, first from those that frequented the Sunset Strip nightclubs, then attention from record companies, and finally national attention. A stage from which people could witness The Doors' history as it unfolded.

The Doors and Them

The Doors hadn't been at The Whisky a Go-Go very long at all. They had started there in a kind of 'extended audition' from May 16th, 1966, and just a week later they officially became the house band. On June 2nd, 1966, the group Them came to LA, and The Whisky in particular, for a two week residency in which they were the featured act. That residence would end in The Doors joining Them onstage for a couple of songs that turned into extended jams.

Them had taken their name from a 1954 science fiction movie about an invasion of giant ants. The band was from Belfast, Ireland, and with lead singer Van Morrison had cut hits like *Gloria*, *Here Comes the Night*, and *Baby Please Don't Go*, which would soon become rock standards. As the house band, The Doors would open for featured acts like Them (other groups that appeared at The Whisky during Them's residency were Buffalo Springfield, Captain Beefheart, The Association, and Frank Zappa), and although The Doors were the house band, their goal was to blow the other bands off the stage. After their set, The

Doors would watch Them perform. By all accounts, Jim Morrison closely studied Van Morrison's onstage persona and presence from the wings of the jammed club and would later employ some of Van Morrison's stage antics as his own, such as smashing the mic stand into the stage. During their residency at The Whisky, the members of the two bands became friends. On May 18th Them's stay at The Whisky was capped with a two song jam with The Doors!

For this encore exit from The Whisky, both bands' equipment crowded the stage; two drum kits, two keyboards, two guitars, and two Morrisons. They first played Wilson Pickett's *In The Midnight Hour*, then Them's *Gloria. Gloria* was a song The Doors already had in their sets while building their own repertoire of songs. During Them's stay at The Whisky, The Doors had dropped *Gloria* from their set but that night it was back in, and both bands jammed away with a 20 minute version of *Gloria*, and a 25 minute version of *Midnight Hour*. Over the years of their career, The Doors would add and subtract *Gloria* from their playlists with Morrison adding his own lyrical improvisations into the song including the sexually suggestive "she came up to my room" section that would later be included on The Doors' 1990 release *Alive She Cried*. Whether Jim included anything like that in the Them jam is unknown. Although pictures were taken that night, no recordings of the show are known to exist.

This was a first and last US tour for Them as they broke up shortly after completing the tour.

Paul Rothchild Sees The Doors at The Whisky

Jac Holzman, founder of Electra Records, knew he wanted The Doors, finally. Holzman initially didn't like them thinking they were "terrible" but at the insistence of Ronnie Haran, the booker at the Whisky a Go-Go, Holzman returned once more to see The Doors perform. On the word of Love's Arthur Lee and seeing the audience's reaction to The Doors Holzman decided to keep going back to see them. After seeing The Doors three or four times, Holzman finally saw something in the band, thanks to the inclusion of *Alabama Song* from the Kurt Weill-Bertolt Brecht opera *Rise and Fall of City of Mahogany*. The Doors interpretation of that piece suggested to Holzman that the band had some intellectual depth. But before Holzman signed them, he wanted to hear what Elektra's senior producer Paul Rothchild had to say.

Holzman flew Rothchild out to LA on August 15, 1966, to see The Doors. On first viewing Rothchild was unimpressed with the band's performance. The first set was a terrible show. Rothchild stayed for the second set during which the band played songs like *Light My Fire*, *Break on Through*, *Twentieth Century Fox*, and *The End*. At that point, Rothchild said he got "religion" about the band, and he and Holzman were moved to offer The Doors a contract that night. The Doors demurred saying they would have to think it over. The next day the group contacted attorney Max Fink (a friend of Doors' guitarist Robby Krieger's father) and he began negotiations with Elektra. The Doors officially accepted the Elektra contract on August 18th.

Some sources have August 10, 1966, as the date Jac Holzman first saw The Doors at The Whisky, but in both *Follow the Music* and *Becoming Elektra*, Holzman maintains he first saw them in May. So why the discrepancy of dates and the lag time of Holzman getting Rothchild to LA? The sources listing August 10 obviously counted backwards from the date of Rothchild seeing The Doors and then assumed the first time Holzman could have seen The Doors was August 10, 1966. But Holzman could well have seen The Doors in May and not been able to get Rothchild to LA until August because, at the time, Paul Rothchild was on parole for smuggling marijuana! In *Becoming Elektra* Holzman says he had to convince Rothchild's parole officer to let Rothchild leave New Jersey to travel to California. Holzman also had to "guarantee Rothchild's good behavior" before the officer would allow Rothchild to leave his jurisdiction.

Soon after signing their Elektra contract, The Doors were fired from The Whisky and they moved to their next major venue, the recording studio.

The Doors Get Fired

On August 21, 1966, The Doors were fired as the house band at the Whisky a Go-Go. For most bands this might have been the beginning of the end, the highlight of their career and a slide into obscurity, but because of *The End*, it was their launching pad into rock 'n' roll legend and superstardom.

Most rock 'n' roll fans are familiar with the story/legend of how The Doors were fired. During their first set of the night, Jim Morrison was nowhere to be found. Whisky owner Phil Tanzini insisted that he was paying for four band members and that's how many would be there. After the first set, Doors keyboardist Ray Manzarek and drummer John Densmore found Morrison holed up in the Alta-Cineaga motel dressed only in boxer shorts and his boots, blitzed on what he insisted was "ten thousand mics" of LSD. It has been assumed that Jim meant he had taken 10,000 micrograms of acid. Could Jim have been celebrating their recent signing to Elektra and the 10,000 mics was an incoherent reference to singing? Jim (probably rightly so) insisted he couldn't perform that night, but Manzarek convinced Jim by telling him "Let's give Tanzini something to remember." Little did either know that later that night Morrison would indeed give the rock world something to remember. The second set of the night was a disaster. Morrison, still tripping from the full effects of the LSD, was incoherent and stumbled around the stage. After the second set, Morrison started to come down off the acid and wanted to do *The End* in the third set. At that time *The End* was a song about the sadness of love ending which, over time, had become extended with instrumentals and places for Morrison to improvise poetry. This is the night Jim Morrison added the Oedipal section to the song. "Father? Yes, son? I want to kill you. Mother? I want to fuck you!" Morrison screamed and fell to the stage, writhing. The other Doors jammed on their instruments creating dissonant chaos while Morrison twirled around the mic stand. The audience, including the go-go dancers stood staring at the stage either transfixed by the performance or shocked by what they saw and heard. Whisky owner Phil Tanzini was yelling at Morrison and the band that they were fired before the song was even finished.

Should the other Doors have been surprised that Morrison added the Oedipal section? Morrison later said "Something clicked. I realized what the whole song was about, what it had been leading up to." Other friends report that Morrison had been running around LA chanting "Fuck the mother, kill the father" - a slogan that he repeated over and over as some weird Freudian mantra. Morrison said it was a way for him to break through to his subconscious mind.

Regardless of the firing, the fates' die had already been cast for The Doors. Within a couple of weeks they would be in the studio recording their first album.

The Doors Debut

Jac Holzman unleashed The Doors upon the world, in a single week. First, Holzman put up the famous billboard of The Doors on Sunset Boulevard, which was the first billboard for a rock group on Sunset. Next The Doors appeared on the local TV show *She-Bang*, and on January 4th, 1967, Elektra Records released The Doors debut album, a 45 of the first two singles off the album, *Break on Through* and on the flip side, *End of the Night*.

The Doors story is a whirlwind. When The Doors started recording their debut album in August of 1966 it had been thirteen months since Jim Morrison sat up on the roof of Dennis Jakob's apartment building in June/July of 1965 taking acid (LSD) and attending a "fantastic rock concert in my head" writing down the songs he heard. In the course of those thirteen months Morrison had gone from being a homeless kid with a notebook stuffed with songs/poems, finding film school friend Ray Manzarek and enlisting him in creating The Doors, cutting a demo record, getting John Densmore and Robby Krieger to join The Doors, carrying out journeyman work at The London Fog, then becoming house band at The Whisky a Go-Go, getting signed by Columbia records, then dropped by Columbia, and finally getting the attention of Elektra Records' Jac Holzman, and producer Paul Rothchild. The recording of The Doors first album only took a week.

Paul Rothchild played an essential part in the recording process and The Doors found the delicate balance between creating an accurate document of The Doors and experimentation without resorting to faddish or trendy recording techniques or instruments. Rothchild asked the band whether or not they wanted to be remembered in twenty years. That isn't to say Rothchild and The Doors weren't willing to experiment. On the contrary, The Doors were a band on the edge trying not only to capture the music but a poetic and theatrical experience.

Originally, *Break on Through* included the line "she gets high". Elektra feared it wouldn't get airplay because the word "high" could be taken as a drug reference. A more overt drug reference in *The Crystal Ship* was changed from "a thousand pills" to "a thousand thrills" so The Doors edited out "high". In 2007, *The Doors* was released on a remastered CD. It seems like Elektra might have done The Doors a favor editing out the "high" as it breaks up the tension of the song. When Morrison yells "she gets.....high!" it feels intrusive. The Doors may have seen it that way too because they performed the song the way it appeared on the original album.

One of the more famous stories of The Doors recording the first album is the afternoon they recorded *The End*. In the spirit of experimentation, Morrison dropped acid to record the song but after numerous attempts the song wasn't coming out quite right, to the frustration of the band, with Morrison repeating the mantra "kill the father, fuck the mother" (in more slurred tones). Morrison finally shouted into the microphone, "Does anybody understand me?" Rothchild said he did and they sat and talked about *The End* and what it meant, which ended the recording for the night. They decided to try again the next afternoon and the next day's recording went much smoother. Rothchild said it was one of the few moments as a producer that he became purely a spectator and it even seemed "the machines knew what to do." After the previous night's recording session, Morrison, moved by the moment of recording, returned to the studio after everyone had left. He scaled a fence, took off his boots and shirt (they were later found in the studio) and proceeded to douse the studio with a fire extinguisher. The studio staff returned the next morning to find the studio and equipment covered in foam.

The Doors' had finished with recording and overdubs probably after Labor Day of '66. Holzman held the release of *The Doors* because he didn't want the album to get lost in the rush of Christmas releases. He prevailed upon The Doors for patience and promised to release the album in January of '67, plus Elektra wouldn't release any other albums that month giving The Doors an unimpeded window of opportunity to reach fans and critics. Holzman was as good as his word however impatient the band may have been to get the album out.

The Doors' debut album had a cohesiveness that made the album sound thematically unified instead of a collection of songs strung along on an album hoping for a hit. The songs on *The Doors* are now recognized as rock 'n' roll classics and although the album is recognized as one of the seminal albums of rock 'n' roll, the initial release of the single, *Break on Through/End of the Night* didn't burn up the charts. It took *Light My Fire* to do that.

The Doors Play The Matrix

It is an in-between moment for The Doors. Yes, they have attracted the attention of Jac Holzman and Elektra records, their first album has been released, but the single *Break on Through* isn't burning up the charts. The future of The Doors is still in doubt as to whether they will live or die as a band. They still haven't stepped through the door of national stardom and fame that *Light My Fire* as a single will provide. Despite this, The Doors are a congruent and focused group as they play The Matrix Theater in San Francisco.

The Matrix was a renovated pizza shop originally owned by Marty Balin of Jefferson Airplane. Balin opened the club to showcase the Airplane early in their career. The venue was small, only holding about 100 people, and the atmosphere was subdued. On one wall was a mural of the Four Horsemen of the Apocalypse armed with musical instruments. Hunter S. Thompson frequented the nightclub. This was the scene and the atmosphere The Doors played in, at The Matrix, between March 7 and 11, 1967. Balin and partner Peter Abram had installed a reel-to-reel recorder to tape the various bands that played there. Subsequently, a lot of bootleg Matrix tapes of various bands have been released since the original performances.

To some, The Doors recordings at The Matrix seem restrained. Whether that was due to the atmosphere of the club or whether they were trying to get excellent recordings out of the shows is unclear. Because of the extended booking at The Matrix, they played three sets a night and not only did they play their entire repertoire, they fell back on instrumentals and rock 'n' roll and blues standards, such as *Gloria, Who Do You Love?*, *Money*, and *I'm a King Bee*. The band still felt free to take the improvisational forays that had marked their stays at LA clubs such as The London Fog, and The Whisky a Go-Go but listening to The Doors at The Matrix, you hear The Doors at the height of their power as a band. Another benefit to the band was that they were still relatively unknown. *Light My Fire* hadn't yet made them a national act and the audience was willing to go along with the group on the journey they wanted to take - whether into the dark corners of *The End*, or the airiness of *Twentieth Century Fox*. Jim Morrison was now a strong confident lead singer who treated the audience to poetic forays. He was unencumbered by the alcoholism and the disappointment that was to come with success and the twin pressures of recording in a studio and playing for audiences that only wanted to hear the hits.

The Doors released *Live at The Matrix* in November of 2008, but soon rumors were flying that the tapes used for the release weren't from Peter Abram's first generation tapes but second and third generation tapes, and The Doors had circumvented paying Abram for the tapes or even acknowledged him in the liner notes of the release. Doors' manager Jeff Jampol announced that The Doors had reached an agreement with Abram and The Matrix shows would be released in a new limited edition set. This release was originally slated for 2010, but didn't come to fruition, nor did a spring/summer 2012 release date.

Jim Morrison's Missing Time

Missing time, and there's a lot of missing time in Jim Morrison's story, is why novelists and maybe memoirists can create plausible scenarios and events into Morrison's life, adding an air of mystery and legend to Morrison and The Doors. It also created the first major fracturing in The Doors as a group.

On September 20, 1968, The Doors ended their European tour. On the 21st, Jim and Pam Courson (Morrison's "cosmic mate") rented an apartment for a month in London. Ray and Dorothy Manzarek also stayed in London for a while after the

European tour ended. In his memoir, *Light My Fire* Manzarek says of Jim and Pam, "They invited us over for breakfast. It was the most adult thing I ever saw Jim and Pam do. I was so proud of them, they were a couple. A man, and a woman, a unit, making breakfast for their friends... bacon, fried eggs, toast with imported strawberry jam from Poland, and French roast coffee...they seemed quite at home, and quite happy..." Given some room for nostalgic hyperbole and an interjection of some of Manzarek's theory on domesticity, it seemed a calm interlude in Morrison's life. It also firmly placed Jim in London with Manzarek knowing approximately where he was. This would become important later.

It was during this interlude that Jim met beat poet Michael McClure and McClure read Morrison's poems for the first time. McClure was one of the original members of the Beat generation. He read at the Gallery Six the night Allen Ginsberg first read *Howl* and appeared as fictionalized versions of himself in Jack Kerouac's *The Dharma Bums* and *Big Sur*. Morrison and McClure had met before in Los Angeles but Morrison's shyness at meeting one of his childhood heroes caused him to get drunk and the meeting didn't go well. McClure was in London to meet movie producer Elliot Kastner and they wanted Jim for the lead in the film version of McClure's *The Beard.*

It was also in this period that Morrison allegedly met The Beatles at Abbey Road Studios. It's contentious to this day, and it may just be part of the Morrison myth (as well as The Beatles') - people wanting a meeting of Titans. It may also be true! Jac Holzman had met with Lennon and McCartney in 1965 to get their blessing for Elektra to release *The Baroque Beatles Book,* so if Morrison had wanted to meet The Beatles all he had to do was ask Jac Holzman to set up an introduction. The story goes that Jim, in visiting Abbey Road Studios, met The Beatles while they were recording John Lennon's *Happiness is a Warm Gun* for what would be known as *The White Album*. The legend has it that you can hear Morrison singing in the chorus of the song. It has also been rumored that, in late November 1968, George Harrison reciprocated the visit and visited The Doors as they were recording their new album *The Soft Parade*.

It was also during this interlude, not in London but back in LA, that the first serious stress fracture in the relationship between Morrison and the rest of The Doors occurred. While Jim was in London, The Doors were offered $100,000 by Buick to use *Light My Fire* in an ad. Not being able to contact Jim, who may have been recording with The Beatles, talking movie deals with Michael McClure, or just roaming the streets of London visiting all the curious shops on Carnaby Street - Ray, Robby, and John along with Doors' manager Bill Siddons decided to take the offer. It wasn't until Morrison returned from London in October that he objected to the sale of the song to Buick, not liking the commercialization of The Doors and their music. Jim told them to kill the deal or he would smash a Buick to pieces onstage during a show. The deal was killed.

Jim Morrison Meets Patricia Kennealy

It started with a static electric shock. Patricia Kennealy met Jim Morrison for the first time in the Plaza Hotel in New York for an interview for *Jazz & Pop Magazine* on January 25th, 1969. Kennealy, who had seen The Doors perform the night before at Madison Square Garden, didn't know what to expect from Morrison, but from that first meeting started an on-again off-again relationship that lasted for the rest of Morrison's life.

Aside from Pam Courson, Kennealy may be the most well-known of Morrison's courtesans, and the relationship was as 'drama filled' as all of Morrison's others. Kennealy may have fitted Morrison's 'type' of woman as, like Pam Courson, she had red hair and fair skin. Kennealy wrote glowing reviews of Morrison's poetry and even participated in the "Critique" panel discussion on The Doors in May of 1969, which was one of the first positive examinations of The Doors after the 'Miami incident'. Kennealy is most famously known for marrying Morrison in a Celtic pagan handfasting ceremony and she said she became pregnant with Morrison's child after he pulled out her diaphragm during a sexual encounter. Upon telling Morrison she was pregnant (during the Miami trial) they both decided it would be better for both of them if she aborted the pregnancy.

Morrison's relationship with Kennealy was contentious. After the pregnancy was terminated Morrison seems to have backed away from the relationship and tried to avoid her. Kennealy seemed to gain his attention again when she hand-delivered a letter (having come from New York) to Morrison at The Doors' office, impaling it on his desk with a dagger. People who knew Morrison at the time says this ended their relationship, but Kennealy claims she spent time with Morrison in early '71 before he left for Paris, and that he continued to write to her from Paris.

Post Morrison, Kennealy has written a series of sword and sorcery books known as the "Keltiad Series" based on her knowledge of Celtic myth and magic. She was a consultant on Oliver Stone's *The Doors* movie, and wrote her own memoir of her relationship with Morrison in 1992's *Strange Days*. In the 90's Kennealy started publishing her books under the name Patricia Kennealy-Morrison and now publishes under the name Patricia Morrison. Her latest books are mysteries with a rock 'n' roll theme and include *Ungrateful Dead* and *California*

Screamin'. Kennealy has also said that she'd publish Morrison's letters to her under the title *Fireheart* and made public a couple of letters that are widely disputed as being Morrison's. She may have abandoned this project as references to it seem to have disappeared from her online bios and websites.

Rock is Dead

"Finally, we just started playing and we played for about an hour, and we just went through the whole history of rock music - starting with blues, going through rock 'n' roll, surf music, Latin, the whole thing, I call it 'Rock is Dead'. I doubt if anybody will ever hear it." Jim Morrison to Jerry Hopkins in the Rolling Stone interview.

After an afternoon of recording in the ever lengthening *Soft Parade* sessions, The Doors were searching for another song to complete the album but had run into a creative wall. They decided to go to dinner, and along with Paul Rothchild and Bruce Botnick and whomever else was in the studio that day, they went to The Blue Boar, a Mexican restaurant, and indulged in a lavish dinner complete with lots of beer and tequila. When they got back to the studio, the group was feeling much looser and the band started to jam. Jim went into a rap on the history of rock. In the control room Rothchild and Botnick were rolling tape on the jam, but the tape ran out about halfway through and it took them about five minutes before they were able to get a new tape on. While the song never made it onto the album, it became widely bootlegged.

What we know about the *Rock is Dead* session largely comes through interviews. Ray Manzarek said "...it was just a bunch of drunks fooling around and jamming in the studio and then we started getting into something. Unfortunately, the tape ran out halfway through..." Later, Jim Morrison described the session as "I was saying...the initial flash is over. What used to be called rock 'n' roll... got decadent. And then there was a rock revival sparked by the English. That went very far. It was articulate. Then it became self-conscious, which I think is the death of any movement. It became... involuted and kind of incestuous. The energy is gone. There is no longer a belief."

Like *The End* and the Oedipal section, the *Rock is Dead* session also provides a look into Jim's state of mind at the time, and a preview of what was to come in Miami. You can hear Jim include some slogans he would use a few days later in Miami at the Dinner Key Auditorium, including "I'm not talking about no revolution", "I wanna see some fun..."

Jim Morrison Marries Patricia Kennealy

June 21, the summer solstice, the longest day of the year, the crossroads where magic can happen. June 21, 1970, is when Jim Morrison married Patricia Kennealy in a Celtic pagan handfasting ceremony.

As mentioned previously, Morrison had met Kennealy the year before when she interviewed him for *Jazz & Pop Magazine*. She said that upon meeting Morrison she felt an electric shock between them, though she later admitted it could have been static electricity from the rug. They had an on-again, off-again relationship that resumed when Morrison arrived in New York to deliver the *Absolutely Live* tapes to Elektra.

The Celtic handfasting ceremony was realistically dramatized in Oliver Stone's *The Doors* as Kennealy acted as a consultant on the film and also played the part of the high priestess. In the ceremony, a circle is drawn with a consecrated sword, invocations are made to the four quarters (east, west, north and south), and everyone involved in the ceremony is purified by earth, air, fire and water. Morrison and Kennealy then stepped into the circle, took the vows, and cut their palms and dripped the blood into sacramental wine. Their hands were then bound together with a red cord and they drank the wine. As in a traditional wedding they exchanged rings, Irish Claddaghs, of which Kennealy wears both to this day (she said Pam Courson returned Morrison's ring to her after his death). The couple then stepped over fire and a sword and Kennealy blew out a candle to conclude the ceremony, at which point Morrison fainted. Kennealy says it was because Morrison felt the intense energies that are built up during the ceremony, or it may have been a bit of squeamishness on Morrison's part because of the bloodletting, or the onset of pneumonia for which Morrison took to bed for the remainder of the weekend.

Kennealy may have taken the ceremony more seriously than Morrison. She has legally changed her last name to Morrison and maintains to this day she is the only woman that got Jim Morrison into a wedding ceremony of any kind and she is his widow. For Morrison's part, he told friends that the ceremony was a fun thing to do when he was stoned. He later kept his distance and avoided her calls until he left for Paris.

Chapter 2

Were The Doors Trying to Replace Jim Morrison?

A little known secret of The Doors is slowly clawing its way to the surface of consciousness. Were The Doors looking for another singer to replace Jim Morrison?

Contact Music ran an article on March 25, 2011, stating that Ray Manzarek and Robby Krieger liked Paul Rodgers of Free and later of Bad Company, and they went to England with the intention of asking to him to join The Doors as the new lead singer. Rodgers is quoted in *Uncut Magazine* (via *Contact Music*), "I discovered quite recently that I was lined up to join The Doors, which blew my mind. Robby Krieger told me that The Doors were all fans of Free and, after Jim Morrison's death, they came to England looking for me." Rodgers also goes on to say how he doesn't think he would have accepted because "I tend to form bands, that's what I do."

But was Rodgers the only consideration? Ray Manzarek at times has joked that Paul McCartney or Mick Jagger were considered as The Doors' new lead singer, but were there any other real considerations? There seems to be two others who were very real considerations.

The first was Howard Werth of the band Audience. Audience was also with Elektra Records and after the group imploded, Elektra founder Jac Holzman suggested to The Doors that they try out Werth. In the winter of 1973 they went to London to audition and work with Werth. *Melody Maker Magazine* reported on Werth's Doors connection in February 1973, it reads:

"Howard Werth former singer with Audience is virtually certain to become the successor to Jim Morrison as lead singer with The Doors. Audience broke up last September and the job with The Doors has come about due to the friendship between Werth's label boss Tony Stratton-Smith and Jac Holzman head of Elektra in America, The Doors label.

Jac gave the early Audience albums to the Doors and they really liked Howard's singing and writing'... Stratton-Smith told MM this week. 'Then he called me from The States and asked how Howard would feel about working with The Doors. And he is very excited about it.'

The Doors are coming over to England next month to rehearse with Werth and tie up a deal which will put Howard into Jim Morrison's shoes."
Melody Maker 3rd February 1973.

But the association didn't last long and soon The Doors were at loose ends looking for a lead singer. It was probably around the same time they were trying to track down Paul Rodgers.

Former Doors' road manager Bill Siddons throws another name in the ring, Michael Stull, and that the search for a replacement pre-dated Jim Morrison's death! Bill Siddons' quote below infers The Doors may have been auditioning Stull when Jim was still alive and well in Paris.

"We actually auditioned other singers to replace Jim as the lead singer of the Doors. I even ended up managing the guy who was going to replace Jim. His name was Michael Stull. But after Jim died, the other three decided to go on alone."

Michael Stull later was the lead singer in John Densmore's and Robby Krieger's attempt at the second incarnation of The Butts Band.

Jim Morrison Dead in Paris at Age 27

Jim Morrison had come full circle. He went to Paris in March 1971 hoping to reclaim his artistic vision. He had hoped to find in Paris what his literary heroes had, what he had previously found on the Venice Beach rooftop in the initial flash of insight and acid that led to the poems that became the backbone of The Doors. But everything hadn't been going as smoothly as he had wanted. Jim Morrison could escape LA but he couldn't escape himself, and he continued to drink.

The conventional story: After seeing the movie *Pursued* on the evening of July 2nd, 1971, Jim Morrison returned to his and Pam's apartment at 17 Rue Beautreillis and they went to bed. Sometime in the early morning hours of July 3rd, Jim awoke complaining of feeling ill and went into the bathroom to take a warm bath. Pam reported that Jim threw up three times after which he told Pam he felt fine and that she should go back to bed. Pam awoke again about dawn and realized Jim hadn't come back to bed. She went into the bathroom and found Jim still in the tub, his arms on the side, a slight, beatific smile on his face. She immediately thought he was playing a joke on her and she tried to rouse him, but couldn't. She called their Parisian friends Alain Ronay and Agnes Varda to come over and act as an intermediary with the rescue brigade since she couldn't speak any French.

Chapter 2

Over the past 41 years a few other stories have made their way into the collective consciousness of fans. Here are a few of them:

Jim died as described in the conventional story except that Pam was gone that weekend and only discovered Jim upon her return.

Jim snorted some of Pam's heroin thinking it was cocaine, and in combination with the alcohol in his system he OD'd.

Jim and Pam along with Marianne Faithfull and her boyfriend Jean DeBretti, who was a heroin dealer, was sold some heroin, they consumed it and Jim OD'd. It should be noted Marianne Faithful, despite her long history with rock stars, says she never met Jim Morrison.

Jim had taken to heroin shortly before he left for Paris. In Paris he started scoring heroin at the rock 'n' roll Circus. He met a dealer in the washroom there, snorted some heroin and OD'd in a stall. The bouncers, fearing police involvement, hustled Jim out of the club, into a cab, and back to his apartment. Every few years someone comes forward and claims to have been a witness to this. A lot of people, including some who knew Jim claim that, on good authority, this is what actually happened.

Some of the theories of Morrison's death are a little more far out. There are the 'Jim was murdered' theories. Jim was murdered by Pam and either Alain Ronay or Agnes Varda found a bloody knife under the bed before the police arrived and washed it off and put it away. Jim was murdered via witchcraft, ostensibly by Patricia Kennealy. Jim was a CIA spy, and he was recruited as a teenager when his father, a Navy admiral, was posted at Pentagon, and that he had outlived his usefulness to them.

Inevitably there are those that say Jim didn't die, that he staged his death and slipped off into obscurity. Or that he's resurfaced as a cowboy in Oregon, or, as in Ray Manzarek's novel *The Poet in Exile*, Jim slipped off to the Seychelles Islands and is living life in a tropical paradise.

July was the beginning of Jim Morrison's visions that started on a Venice Beach rooftop, that Jim shared with Ray Manzarek, that became The Doors. In Paris six years later, July was the end.

Doors' history not only accompanies the physical actions of The Doors, but also of the physical relics and psychic relics they left behind, namely the music they created. In the 60's bands were expected to pump out albums and singles on a regular basis. The Doors were no exception and that schedule led to five years of hits for the group.

3
Doors Releases

In the 60's people looked forward to the release of their favorite band's new album or a new single on a 45, and record companies were hot to have their top acts pumping out albums and singles to keep the money flowing. The Doors were no exception.

Light My Fire Released as a Single

On April 24, 1967, The Doors' *Light My Fire* was released as a single and quickly pushed The Doors from a struggling L.A. band on a small label to a nationally known band with the song hitting number one on the *Billboard Magazine* charts by July of 1967.

In the spring of 1967, The Doors were an L.A. band with a countercultural buzz around them because of Morrison's mercurial stage persona and songs like *The End.* As it appears on The Doors' debut album, *Light My Fire* is a seven minute song that showcases each of The Doors' talents with a solo section for everyone. While The Doors were getting airplay on the counterculture FM radio stations, the album was getting little airplay on the more conservative AM stations where Jac Holzman wanted to break the band to the larger listening audiences.

Light My Fire started life as a Robby Krieger composition, but as The Doors evolved so did the song. Lacking original material after a rehearsal, Jim Morrison told the other Doors to write a song for the next rehearsal with the admonition that it be about one of the elements: earth, wind or fire. Doors' guitarist Robby

Chapter 3

Krieger was the only one who came back with a song which he reportedly wrote in twenty minutes. Inspired by Buffalo Springfield, *Light My Fire* sounded more like a folk song and Krieger said some of the rough drafts were less than spectacular, like “Come on baby breathe my air”.

Light My Fire is a truly collaborative song. When Krieger brought the song in, he only had the first chorus, “You know it would be untrue / You know that I would be a liar / If I was to say to you / Girl, we couldn’t get much higher” and the guitar chords. Morrison quickly filled in a second verse with “The time to hesitate is through / No time to wallow in the mire”. Drummer John Densmore suggested a latin beat and so they overlaid solos onto the structure, and Ray quickly worked out the now iconic opening to the song. As The Doors played venues like the Whisky a Go-Go they improvised and lengthened the solos.

After *Light My Fire* was finished, it wasn’t guaranteed to go to number one. In fact, it wasn’t even Elektra Records’ first choice to be released as a single. That honor went to *Break On Through* with the flip side being *End of the Night*. Following the stagnation of the *Break on Through/End of the Night* single on the charts at 126, Elektra was planning on releasing *Twentieth Century Fox* as the second single. Elektra Records’ founder Jac Holzman started hearing from DJs that they wanted to play *Light My Fire*, but it was too long for their 2 minute 30 second formats. At first The Doors resisted, they didn’t want to try and record a shorter version, and they thought an edited version would cut the heart out of the solos in the song. The first side of The Doors debut album showcased the lyrics and singing of Jim Morrison while *Light My Fire* was the band’s chance to show the world The Doors were more than Jim Morrison’s lyrics. *Light My Fire* was proof of The Doors’ synergistic melding of words and music.

Holzman decided to release a single of *Light My Fire* and told The Doors’ producer Paul Rothchild to make the edits. Within a half hour Rothchild had an edited version of the song. With some trepidation they approached the band with the three minute version but the edits Rothchild made didn’t compromise the organic integrity of the song and The Doors approved it. *Light My Fire* was released as a single with the “B” side being *The Crystal Ship* and Doors’ keyboardist Ray Manzarek, to this day, claims that when *Light My Fire* comes onto the radio he can’t tell if it’s going to be the edited version or the full length version until it plays out.

Light My Fire hit number one on *Billboard Magazine’s* charts on July 29, 1967, staying at number one for three weeks, and it stayed on the charts for a total of fourteen weeks. *Light My Fire* was also Elektra Records’ first number one hit song after eighteen years as a record label.

The Doors release *Strange Days*

It had been slightly over a year since The Doors had gone into the studio to record their first album, and on September 25th, 1967, they released their second album: *Strange Days.*

Even though the songs on *Strange Days* were recorded almost a full year after the first album, most of the songs on the first two albums were written in the same time period - when Morrison was listening to that rock concert in his head on the Venice rooftop, but the two albums sound drastically different from each other. The debut album, the eponymously named *The Doors* is more like a traditional record of the generation before, a loose assemblage of songs in the hopes that one or two would be a radio hit.

The Doors started recording *Strange Days* in May of 1967 and ended in July, just before or at the same time they hit the big time with *Light My Fire*. *Strange Days* is self-consciously experimental in its approach, from something as simple as moving up to 8 track recording (The Beatles were still using 4 tracks), to the songs themselves, such as *Horse Latitudes* which for rhythm has the band (and visiting members of Jefferson Airplane) yelling and dropping coke bottles into a wastepaper basket. The title track is one of the first examples of a Moog synthesizer on an album, and other songs used a technique of playing instruments or tracks backwards to give the give the listener a sense of unease that demands each song be listened to. The experimentation ran all the way to Morrison's girlfriend Pam Courson giving him oral sex in the vocal booth to try and get the right feel for a song.

Strange Days was a more psychedelically influenced and dangerous sounding album. The best example would be the poetic/theatrical tour de force *When The Music's Over* starting with Morrison's scream, and the psychedelic roar of Robby Krieger's guitar that accompanies Morrison. The LSD influenced lyrics makes other bands' 'acid rock' seem tame and safe by comparison (except for maybe Hendrix). In *Your Lost Little Girl* Robby Krieger shows himself so able to write in Morrison's style that it's usually assumed it's one of Morrison's songs.

Strange Days is arguably one of rock 'n' roll's first concept albums. Listening to the album, one has the sense that it has its own internal logic and coherence, it seems like it is a novel unfolding, each song a new chapter. There is the feeling of the album having a beginning and end point that isn't consistent with the end of a song or the end of a side and this might have been what Jim Morrison had in mind when he said "You might buy a book of our lyrics the same way you might buy a volume of William Blake's poetry."

Recorded at the beginning of the "Summer of Love" and the rise of Flower Power, *Strange Days* is an album that dares to examine the dark side, the alienation we feel in a crowded society, how with more people surrounding us we feel more isolated than ever before. It is also a rare personal look inside an artist who seemed to have all the gifts the gods could offer, a facility for words and poetry at a young age that would make older poets envious, and beauty that all but guaranteed the success of the band by fan and photo magazines of the day, and yet he felt a sense of alienation from the world. The Doors, as conceived by Manzarek and Morrison, was supposed to be a merging of music, poetry and theatre, and while the concept of *Strange Days* isn't explicitly articulated, it comes closest to achieving the artistic vision of Morrison and Manzarek. *Strange Days* reflects on the alienation we feel in a society surrounded by others, we have become islands unto ourselves increasingly isolated by the very things that are supposed to free us: sex, death, and ourselves.

Upon its release *Strange Days* hit the top 20 in albums, and *People Are Strange* made it into the top 10 for singles. *Strange Days* is arguably the most artistically successful album by The Doors.

The Doors Record *Waiting for the Sun*

The Doors started recording their third album *Waiting For The Sun* on February 19, 1968. It wasn't the album The Doors had originally planned on releasing. The album had originally been titled *Celebration of the Lizard* and was closer in tone and concept to The Doors' first two albums. *Celebration of the Lizard* was an extended poem/theatre piece that was supposed to take up most of the second side of the album like its predecessor songs *The End* and *When The Music's Over*. However, the idea was dropped when The Doors couldn't meld the poem into a cohesive song because they didn't have the time to organically develop *Celebration of the Lizard* in clubs like the previous epics. The creative compromise made in the renaming and the re-conceptualizing of the album made visible the first signs of fault lines in the relationship between Jim Morrison and the rest of the group.

Celebration of the Lizard had its beginnings, much as the earlier two albums did, as pieces of Morrison's poetry fashioned together and fused with the Doors' music. Parts of *Celebration of the Lizard* were around from the earliest beginnings of The Doors; *A Little Game* would find its way into *Lizard* as one of the songs The Doors recorded as a demo. But with the success of The Doors, the focus of the group shifted from creation to delivering the hits to larger and larger audiences that didn't want to sit still while the band created onstage. They wanted to hear *Light My Fire*.

The air of creative invention that permeated the first two albums didn't survive into the recording sessions for *Lizard/Sun* either. Morrison's drinking started to take precedence in his life and his interest in recording was starting to wane. Morrison would show up for the *Lizard* sessions drunk or on a combination of alcohol, pills and groupies. At the same time, or perhaps as a reaction to Morrison's lack of interest, Doors' producer Paul Rothchild exerted more of an influence on the recording process and demanded more and more takes of each song.

Joan Didion, who was writing for the *Saturday Evening Post* at the time, was able to sit in on some of the *Lizard* sessions. In what was later included in her book *The White Album*, in the chapter "Waiting for Morrison", Didion describes a dispirited group that was sullenly recording the album with Morrison's interest in the sessions at a minimum.

By early March of 1968, John Densmore was so upset with the recording process and Morrison's drinking that he threw down his drumsticks and quit in disgust. Densmore returned the next day because, as like Richard Gere's character in *An Officer and a Gentleman*, he had nowhere else to go, and recording continued.

Waiting for the Sun ultimately included one portion of *Celebration of the Lizard*, the *Not to Touch the Earth* section which included the line "I am the lizard king, I can do anything". The line, according to Morrison, was meant to be tongue in cheek, but it inadvertently defined Morrison's persona when the press picked it up, and it was used detrimentally.

With the exclusion of *Celebration of the Lizard* leaving both a physical and psychic void to the album, The Doors scrambled for more material to finish *Waiting for the Sun*. They went back to the demos they had cut for Pacific Sound, and Morrison's notebooks. With songs like *Summer's Almost Gone*, *Wintertime Love*, *Love Street* and *Hello, I Love You* next to songs like *Five to One*, *The Unknown Soldier*, and *Not to Touch the Earth*, the result is an album that sounds disjointed and lacks the cohesion of the first two albums.

The inclusion of *Hello, I Love You* proved to be serendipitous. The song turned out to be The Doors' second number one hit single, and it was a song from The Doors' earliest repertoire. Ray Manzarek has said that Jim Morrison wrote it as they sat on a wall on Venice Beach watching a pretty black girl walk by. The Doors recorded the song as one of the demos recorded at Aura Records that was left on the Rick and The Ravens contract, but no one remembered it until Adam Holzman, Jac Holzman's ten-year-old son, recalled the song from the demo and told his father it would be a hit song. Adam Holzman's vision proved to be right. *Hello, I Love You* was released as a single with *Love Street* as the B side on June 4, 1968, and by August of 1968 it hit number one on *Billboard's* charts - a little over a year after *Light My Fire* made The Doors a nationally known band.

There has also been a lot of conjecture or myth over the years that *Hello, I Love You* 'borrowed' (some say stole) a riff from The Kinks *All Day and All of the Night*. Another criticism was that it was too commercial, too 'pop' for a Doors song. Jim Morrison defended the lyrics as being as good as any of his other lyrics, but the appeal of the songs to teenyboppers wasn't shaken. It seemed The Doors couldn't find the dread in the song that might have made it right at home on an album with *Celebration of the Lizard*. That problem was fixed, sort of, when *Stoned Immaculate* came out in 2000, which included a cover of *Hello, I Love You* by the group Oleander, and they found the dread in the song that unusually eluded The Doors.

It was only later on *Absolutely Live* that The Doors were able to finally release a complete version of *Celebration of the Lizard*.

The Unknown Soldier

Light My Fire may have heated up the summer of '67 and become the inadvertent soundtrack for the "Summer of Love" and the fires that accompanied riots in L.A. and Detroit, but there was no way the song could have been construed as political. The only Doors songs that come close to being construed as political are *Five to One* and *The Unknown Soldier.*

The Doors were never an overtly political group, if anything Jim Morrison was interested in existential politics, the interplay between people and not the banal occupation practiced by politicians and governments. Robby Krieger has said that when The Doors went to Europe in 1968 the press would try to get them to say something political or "against America". So, why are The Doors considered to be a 'political' band? Was it just the 60's? None of The Doors at the time seem to have made any overt statements against Vietnam. Was it something in Morrison's lyrics? He certainly advocated revolution, but it was revolution on a personal level. So why do The Doors have a reputation as a political band?

In The Doors' repertoire of songs, and as mentioned above, there are two songs that fans consider 'political' - *Five to One* and *The Unknown Soldier.* With *Five to One* political connotations might be considered purely coincidental but the first stanza includes the lyrics, "They've got the guns/But we got the numbers" but in the second stanza the song is calling for a personal revolution with "Trade in your hours for a handful of dimes", and the ultimate solution in *Five to One* is to "Go up to the mountain with these people and get fucked up."

The Unknown Soldier is probably The Doors most overtly crafted theatre piece with the middle section of the song, where a solo should be, being replaced by the prisoner of war/firing squad passion play, a solo of sorts by Morrison. The martial tone and cadences, and even the ritual of the song were something that Morrison was familiar with – having grown up in and around naval bases.

With the Vietnam War raging and accelerating in society around them, it's natural that as young men who were vulnerable to the draft (although by that time all members of The Doors were ineligible for the draft) the need to comment on what was going on around them was obvious. But The Doors didn't want to write an anti-Vietnam song fearing its timeliness would soon elapse (see how dated Country Joe and the Fish's *I Feel Like I'm Fixin' to Die Rag* sounds). The Doors wanted to write something more universal, they didn't want to end Vietnam - but *all* war. The result is *The Unknown Soldier* which incorporates double entendres and aphorisms, with the meaning of the first stanza repeated in the second but with a different emphasis on the words to make the point. Despite the song's universality, radio stations didn't play it because it was deemed 'too controversial' and it only reached number 39 on the *Billboard* charts by May of 1968 (the B side of the single was *We Could Be So Good Together*), Nonetheless, it satisfied both the audience and the artists looking to make a statement on the war.

Some other *The Unknown Soldier* facts:

- *The Unknown Soldier* was released in early March of 1968 as a single. The Doors also created a film for the song in the same month so it could be shown in venues and areas they couldn't play at. But, due to the scene where the 'shot' Jim Morrison spurts blood out of his mouth - the specter of controversy once again raised its head, so it was mostly shown prior to Doors concerts.
- The recording of the album saw the start of Morrison's growing disinterest in the recording process and producer Paul Rothchild began to become more of a perfectionist in the studio. *The Unknown Soldier* took a monumental 130 takes to finish.

Let us hope the last war, is the last war.

The Soft Parade

The Doors released their fourth studio album *The Soft Parade* on July 18th, 1969, and it was the album which had the longest gestation period of any Doors album - from November 1968 until early July 1969.

The recording of *The Soft Parade* reveals an indecisive moment in the career of The Doors. Their third album, *Waiting for the Sun,* started life as a much more ambitious album but ended up sounding tenuous and lacking the cohesion of their first two albums. Lacking material for the new album, The Doors decided to take a risk in creating *The Soft Parade* - they would create the album in the studio and use string and horn arrangements on the songs.

The string and horn sections would become derisively known as the "La Cienega Symphony" (The Doors' studio was on La Cienega Boulevard). *The Soft Parade* signaled a lot of changes for the band. For the first time songs were given individual writer credits instead of the collective "The Doors". The songs on the album are divided almost equally between Morrison and Krieger, and it is easy to discern who wrote what; the songs written by Krieger have all the string orchestrations, while Morrison's songs adhere to a more rough-hewn rock sound.

It was also the album that producer Paul Rothchild had to practically piece together across different takes because the long recording time left Morrison to his own devices - which was drinking. The end result saw the other Doors become dispirited and their performances adversely affected.

Robby Krieger wrote *Touch Me* - the song that would become the hit single off the album. It was originally titled *Hit Me* and had its origins in Krieger's seemingly tumultuous relationship with his girlfriend Lynn, who would also inspire Krieger to write the line "Don't you love her as she's walkin' out the door" in *Love Her Madly*. The title was changed because Morrison didn't want to be the recipient of what fans would think Morrison was asking of them.

The Soft Parade did mark the return of one Doors tradition, that of the epic poetic/theatre piece at the end of the album, in this case - the title song, *The Soft Parade*. The song was the result of Paul Rothchild and Jim Morrison mining Jim's Venice beach rooftop notebooks' poetic passages - strung together and held together by the music of the song.

The Doors' Tribute to Jim Morrison, *An American Prayer*

It was Robby's idea. Jim had been haunting him for a while. Maybe it wasn't a haunting in the classic sense or definition but Robby had been having dreams of Jim Morrison reciting his poetry. Robby called engineer John Haeny to see if he knew where the tapes were that Jim had recorded on his 27th birthday, on December 8th, 1970. Haeny still had the tapes and the first step was taken in what would be an album of Jim Morrison's poetry that would become *An American Prayer*.

The recordings from December 1970 were originally made with an eye towards Jim Morrison recording a solo album of his poetry. Morrison had secured a contract with Elektra founder Jac Holzman for the album and he wanted to start recording it. He invited Frank and Kathy Lisciandro, Alain Ronay, and Florentine Pabst to the studio for the recording, and John Haeny gave Morrison a bottle of Old Bushmills whiskey (on the *An American Prayer* CD, on the bonus track *Ghost Song*, the tape was still rolling and Morrison says, "One more thing", then you can hear him take a swig off the bottle. You have to turn the volume up to hear it). The session lasted approximately four hours and if the scene sounds familiar, it's because Oliver Stone used it in his movie *The Doors*. Recordings from the March 1969 recording session were also used but by the 1970 "Birthday Sessions" Morrison had revised a lot of the previously recorded poems.

The surviving Doors recorded *An American Prayer* using (besides Morrison's poetry sessions) materials from The Doors' catalog, recordings of live Doors shows, and sound effects. They recorded new music using much of the poetry - editing and splicing Morrison's voice in and around the music.

An American Prayer was released in November of 1978* and roughly outlines the life of Jim Morrison from birth ("Wake up!"), through childhood, teenage years and his coming of age, to being a rock star/sex symbol, and the elegiac epic poem *An American Prayer*. The album was released to generally good reviews. Although it didn't get a lot of radio play because of Morrison's use of expletives, it was the only Doors album nominated for a Grammy and at 250,000 copies sold upon its release makes it the biggest selling spoken-word album.

All the members of The Doors 'family' thought *An American Prayer* a fitting tribute to Morrison and his wish to be regarded as a poet. The lone exception was long time Doors producer Paul Rothchild who called *An American Prayer* "The rape of Jim Morrison" and compared it to "…taking a Picasso and cutting it into postage stamp-sized pieces and spreading it across a supermarket wall." Rothchild also cited Morrison's intentions of producing a poetry album as a solo project separate from The Doors, and without rock music using more classical orchestrations or with avant-garde orchestrations such as with Lalo Schifrin (who did the soundtrack to 60's classics *Cool Hand Luke* and *Mission Impossible*). Part of Morrison's vision for his poetry album was the commissioning of a triptych by artist T.E. Breitenbach; it shows the elements Morrison thought important: a moonlit beach with naked couples running around, a city at noon "insane with activity", and a desert scene at night seen through the windshield of a car.

*Note: The entry in Wikipedia for *An American Prayer* has the release date as Nov 17, 1978. A timeline I received from Doors researchers lists the release date as Nov 30, 1978. I tried to find further information to verify either date but couldn't.

The 40th Anniversary of *L.A. Woman*

April for The Doors fan is not the cruelest month, but the anniversary of the release of *L.A. Woman.*

L.A. Woman is the last album The Doors recorded with Jim Morrison (November 1971, The Doors released *Other Voices*; and *Full Circle* was released in August of 1972). *L.A. Woman* saw the departure of Paul Rothchild as The Doors' producer. During rehearsals for *L.A. Woman*, Rothchild was so bored with the band's playing and Morrison's lethargic delivery he found himself laying his head on the mixing board (the song in question was reportedly *Love Her Madly*). The Doors decided to produce the album themselves along with longtime engineer Bruce Botnick who had previously co-produced Love's *Forever Changes*. *L.A Woman* was virtually recorded live in The Doors' workshop which was refitted for the recording. The studio was downstairs and the mixing and recording equipment were upstairs in The Doors' office.

L.A Woman is the impressionistic autobiography of a rock band in the late '60's and early '70's. The song *L.A. Woman* is Morrison's elegy to Los Angeles, *L'America* is an autobiography of a rock band with "Friendly strangers coming to town and all the women loved their ways." The song was originally written when The Doors were in consideration for providing music for Michelangelo Antonioni's film *Zabriskie Point*. *L.A. Woman* also has some very personal lyrics from Morrison and Doors' guitarist, Robby Krieger. The album starts with *The Changeling* with Morrison practically telling everyone he was splitting. *Love Her Madly* is reportedly based on Krieger's fiery relationship with soon to be wife, Lynn; "Don't you love her as she's walking out the door." *Touch Me*, also written by Krieger, was originally titled Hit Me. *Hyacinth House* was from an earlier demo recorded at Robby Krieger's parents' house. *Riders on the Storm* is a restatement of *The End*, a serial killer murdering a family, this time with maybe a little existential hope in the line "Girl you gotta love your man/Take him by the hand/Make him understand."

After all the months in the forge of creation, the sometimes delicate interplay of personalities and egos, dealing with the record company 'suits' - an artist releases an album, and then it's the critics turn. An album or a book can live or die on the opinion of one person, or a small group of people and those opinions may become the prevailing opinion. In the next chapter we examine the opinions on classic and newer Doors releases.

4
Music Reviews

One of things I've learned in writing *The Doors Examiner* is that The Doors are still relevant today. Not only to fans who never had the opportunity to see or hear The Doors live and who want to hear The Doors' old shows, but also relevant to musicians of all ages who have been influenced by The Doors. The surviving members of The Doors stay relevant not by resting on their laurels, but by playing and producing new music, continuing to push the creative bounds of artistic expression that interests them. As the CDs of The Doors come out I've had the opportunity to review the music and each CD has revealed a new aspect of the band.

Live in New York

After I became a Doors fan, one of the first concerts I started hearing about was the Felt Forum shows. Not only did it sound like a name for a 60's venue, but the shows were said to be great and that you *had* to hear them. I didn't know where to get bootlegs, or even anyone who had a copy, so the anticipation built for 30 years. Rhino Records' release of *The Doors Live In New York* is what fans were waiting for.

The Doors Live In New York was recorded on two nights, January 17th and 18th 1970. The Doors did four shows, and each show is included in its entirety in this box set. Some of the songs have been included on other Doors' live albums. You'll hear *When The Music's Over* that was on *Absolutely Live*, for example, but just when you think you know the song, you realize there's more… *The*

Absolutely Live version was edited. For The Doors fan searching for something new, each CD contains a veritable plethora of previously unreleased versions of songs. It's good to hear the songs in context with all the strengths and shortcomings The Doors had as a band. These recordings give the listener the full sense and feeling of the concert experience - the false starts, the band tuning up, Jim asking the audience what they want to hear, or the silences as the band consults amongst themselves as to what they want to play next. Jim Morrison seems to excise one of his demons, his ongoing struggle with lightmen. His, "Hey, Mr. Lightman!" rap that he did at many shows chiding the lightmen who never seemed to do what he wanted, seems to resolve itself as he compliments the lighting level at the show! The Doors were never a band to play the album version of their songs, and Morrison tinkers with the words of songs as well. This was before concerts became slick clones of each other, where the same thing happens at the same time in the show, each show identical to the other, from concert to concert, city to city. The Doors were stark theatre. A portrayal of reality through their songs, like a novel is a portrayal of reality through words, or a movie through film.

The band opens each show with a couple of songs from *Morrison Hotel*. It's cool to realize that, as you're listening to *Roadhouse Blues* or *Peace Frog*, how the audience is very likely to be hearing those songs for the very first time. It opens you up to that experience. The Doors also experimented with the songs. *Who Do You Love* was played at every show yet no two versions of the song are alike! Curiously, *Peace Frog*, easily one of Morrison's most autobiographical songs, because of the *Dawn's Highway* section where Morrison recounts the mystical experience he had as a child (feeling as if the soul of an Indian had leaped into his) was performed at the Felt Forum. Most versions of *Peace Frog* omit this part. Only in the last show at the Felt Forum does Morrison include that portion of the song.

The boxed set includes a beautiful 40 page booklet with an introduction by Jac Holzman, and Bruce Botnick provides background details about The Doors playing the Felt Forum. James Henke from the Rock 'n' Roll Hall of Fame and author of *The Jim Morrison Scrapbook* has also written an essay for the book which also includes about 15 high gloss photographs from the shows. The sound on the CDs is excellent. Bruce Botnick, in a technical note in the booklet, notes that in parts that were missing from the 8-track master they inserted live 2-tracks and the sound might change in those parts, but I didn't hear it. I listened to the CDs on a car CD player and on my computer. I didn't hear any change of quality. In fact the sound seemed crystal clear. In one section you can clearly hear the maracas Morrison shakes.

This is one of the last full blown tours of The Doors' career. The next year would find the band finishing *L.A. Woman* and Morrison planning his imminent departure to Paris. These shows are The Doors as they wanted be heard, in context and demonstrating the power of what a great rock band can be.

When You're Strange Soundtrack

When You're Strange: Songs From The Motion Picture is a mixture of readings of Jim Morrison's poems and non-sequiturs, interviews from all the members of The Doors, and the music of The Doors. At first a CD which incorporates the poetry of Jim Morrison and the music of The Doors may seem like a sequel to *An American Prayer* but the soundtrack to *When You're Strange* is quite unlike anything The Doors have released before.

This soundtrack doesn't rely on the usual chronological placement of songs or necessarily include all 'the hits', but aims more for giving the listener a sense of what The Doors were about, a fusion and interweaving of poetry with the music. Morrison's poems segue very smoothly into the songs. The poems don't seem to have been picked to add any context to the songs, or complement the songs, or even the reverse (where the songs add context to the poems) but they seem to naturally fit together. They may have been the cement between Morrison and the other Doors. Morrison's poetry and the music of The Doors have always seemed to fit together as if they were meant to be together.

The soundtrack includes the classic album versions of songs such as *Moonlight Drive*, *Hello, I Love You*, and *Soul Kitchen*. The live performances include: *Light My Fire* from The Ed Sullivan show where Morrison famously refused to leave out the word "higher" as requested by the censors, *When The Music's Over* from the Danish television broadcast, and *Break On Through* from the Isle of Wight Festival.

The one misstep on the soundtrack is the inclusion of Johnny Depp reading Jim Morrison's poetry. Depp recorded Morrison's poems on his boat in a darkened, candlelit room and the inclusion of Depp seems a nod to increase the commercial potential of the soundtrack. Even though Depp is one of the biggest contemporary actors with his own hip cache, and was drawn to the project by the allure and legend of The Doors (he's a fan), Jim Morrison will always be cooler than Johnny Depp or any other person that reads his poetry. Despite Depp's strengths as an actor, his readings are understated and don't have the full dramatic weight in the reading that Morrison used when recording his poems. Anyone who has heard Morrison reading his poems finds his voice compelling even without music. Depp's candlelit reading sets the tone, his reading has a sultry almost dusky tone to it, you can almost hear the smoke of those black cigarettes Depp smokes curling around Morrison's words, but it's best to let Morrison be the spokesman for his poems.

This one disc CD includes a booklet with pictures of the band, and quotes from the movie's director Tom DiCillo, Johnny Depp, and producer Dick Wolf. The booklet opens up into a mini-sized print of the movie poster. *When You're Strange: Songs From The Motion Picture* creates an aural documentary of the film that can either complement the viewing of the film, or offer a stand-alone piece that provides some of the documentary elements - giving the listener a feel for the film.

Robby Krieger's *Singularity*

The mark of a good poet is to be able to hold the listener/reader's attention by the power of your words. Likewise, the mark of a great musician is to hold your interest with the power of the music alone, sans words. Jim Morrison, in an interview, was asked what would happen to The Doors if he had to go to jail. He said he hoped they would go on and do instrumentals. In *Singularity* Robby Krieger does just that.

Why am I referencing Jim Morrison and The Doors in a review of Robby Krieger's solo work? Because Krieger references The Doors in *Singularity*, and is able to revisit The Doors without compromising the integrity of the new material. Krieger has mentioned the inspiration for *Singularity* is a painting he did (which is used on the CD cover) of the event horizon of a black hole, the point at which light can't escape and it falls back in on itself. As such, the songs do seem to fall back onto the various influences in Krieger's career. Besides the obvious Doors references, he pays an homage to John Coltrane, and revisits his roots with flamenco and slide guitar explorations.

At its best a Doors song could give the listener the feeling of traveling, or that the music was taking you on a journey. *Let It Slide* is able to incorporate that feeling. *Let It Slide* has little ribbons of *Moonlight Drive* interspersed in it, which are not obvious at first. It seems familiar, but you're not sure why, and then as the song plays out, it slowly occurs to you what's going on in the music.

Krieger also takes a crack at reimagining Doors songs that he was instrumental in developing. In his previous solo CD *Cinematix* Krieger reworked and reimagined *Peace Frog*, which started life as a Doors instrumental (when they played *Peace Frog* live they usually played it as an instrumental), as *War Toad*. On *Singularity* it is *Spanish Caravan* that Krieger has reimagined as *Russian Caravan*. Krieger recreates a solo that was cut from *Spanish Caravan* and uses it as an intro to the new track which has a nice old world feel of Segovia's Spain which was sort of the influence for the original track.

But don't let all the talk of Doors' influences fool you, *Singularity* is also a very traditional cool Jazz exploration piece. Krieger was probably right in naming the CD after something that occurs in outer space. The instrumentals all sound like they're a journey into space, whether it's outer space or just whatever space the music can take you to. Oddly enough, for a CD created by a guitarist, *Singularity* has some heavy keyboard moments. An influence from Doors' keyboardist Ray Manzarek, perhaps?

In *Singularity* Robby Krieger is able to explore his Jazz influences and creativity while simultaneously exploring his Doors roots. *Singularity* is a good vehicle for Doors fans wanting to try something new and explore musical areas they haven't before, but still having the luxury of the comfortable surroundings The Doors' references provide.

Singularity has more reference points for Doors fans than *Cinematix* did without being a reiteration of The Doors, and introduces listeners to Krieger's expanding horizons as a guitarist.

The Doors *Live in Vancouver*

Albert King opened for The Doors in Vancouver on June 6, 1970. The Doors, who were only months away from starting the recording of *L.A. Woman* in the fall of that year, asked him to jam with them for four blues standards. From the versions of the songs The Doors played on *Live in Vancouver* it seems they already had the blues on their minds before King ever stepped onstage.

There was some experimenting going on in Vancouver as well. The Doors seemed to be pushing the limits of rock, or at least stretching those limits between rock and the blues. At first it sounds like the Vancouver show is more sedate (not sedated) than the Felt Forum shows from a few months prior. Upon closer listening you can hear The Doors going for more of a bluesy feel than a hard rock sound. This explains why Morrison, in introducing Albert King, gives a quick tutorial to the audience about the two main indigenous forms of American music - blues and country coming together in rock 'n' roll. He's tipping the audience off as to what they're doing.

The instrumentals in most of the songs highlight the bluesy feeling such as in *Five to One* and *Light My Fire*. While they didn't change the songs substantially, during the instrumental of *Light My Fire* Morrison comes in using *St. James Infirmary* as a starting point and adds his own bucolic, blues tinged lyrics to highlight a bluesier aspect of The Doors by adding lines like: "The fish were jumping, and the cotton is high" from George Gershwin's *Porgy and Bess*. What band today of the same caliber as The Doors would, or could, risk such onstage experimentation?

That's not to say The Doors didn't delve into their psychedelic roots, they played *When The Music's Over* and an interesting rendition of *The End*. Early in their career The Doors were interested in dissonance for their experimental journeys. In Vancouver they show that assonance had taken over their experimental interest. *The End* in Vancouver is a mature rendering of that song. It isn't as frantic as earlier versions and The Doors let it play out like a noir film with Morrison stacking the familiar images upon each other until the dramatic crashing climax, creating a movie for the mind of the audience.

Albert King plays on four songs: *Little Red Rooster*, *Money*, *Rock Me*, and *Who Do You Love*. King's solos on these songs, like the rest of the CD, don't display a lot of unnecessary pyrotechnics but are solid playing all the way through.

I've been to a lot of rock concerts and have listened to a lot of live albums, but none of those seem to have the context or coherence that The Doors were able to imbue into their best shows. This is one of their best.

These "Bright Midnight" (the record label The Doors set up for their live shows) releases are great for fans like me who didn't have the connections to get bootlegs, or weren't collectors but still wanted to hear the shows they've long heard about. The "Bright Midnight" releases are like raiding The Doors archives without having to worry about the quality; the sound is crisp and clear. The liner notes give you some background right from The Doors' own pens, which is more reliable than second generation legend. *The Doors Live in Vancouver* will make a nice addition to your collection.

Ray Manzarek and Roy Rogers at the Crossroads of Rock and The Blues

Jim Morrison used to talk about the crossroads, a place in southern mythology where magic happened. Ray Manzarek's and Roy Rogers' *Translucent Blues* is at the crossroads where the blues meets rock 'n' roll.

Ray Manzarek has always been attracted to literate minded lyrics and *Translucent Blues* is no different, having songs contributed by Jim Carroll, Warren Zevon (both of whom worked with Manzarek before their deaths), Michael C. Ford, and beat poet Michael McClure. It's not only Manzarek at the crossroads, one of the Warren Zevon songs has the music attributed to Rogers.

Manzarek throws in some musical references to The Doors, *New Dodge City Blues* has undercurrents of *Love Her Madly*. Is *Fives and Ones* a reference to The Doors *Five to One*? Maybe. What it is, is a blues song with a traditional subject of having a roll of bills in your pocket. The musical references aren't limited to The Doors. If you're familiar with Manzarek's post Doors' albums from the 70's, you'll hear some musical references to that period of Manzarek's career as well. Some of these blues touch on jazz too. *Kick*, with lyrics by Michael McClure, has a tinge of jazz in it, plus some of the most consciously poetic lyrics on the CD.

Neither Rogers nor Manzarek are going to be noted for their dulcet tones or mellifluous singing. Sometimes Manzarek pushes his vocal abilities a little too far such as on *Game of Skill*. However, both have rough-hewn voices of the old blues men, and that's where Manzarek and Rogers might be. They've become the old blues men they admired in their youth. *Translucent Blues*, despite the somewhat cool title for the CD, is mostly up tempo, goodtime blues in the vein of *Roadhouse Blues*. The songs are divided pretty equally between Manzarek and Rogers, Manzarek having the more rock oriented songs and Rogers the more traditionally blues songs. Rogers' guitar is a strident voice on this album, sometimes pounding it out and at other times laying back and delivering a counterpoint to Manzarek's keyboards. Both Manzarek and Rogers are accomplished musicians who know how to rock the blues. Both play on all the songs throughout the CD. The album has a nice coherent sound and feeling throughout.

You don't have to be a Doors fan, or have prior knowledge of Rogers' work with John Lee Hooker. *Translucent Blues* is something new for each artist, waiting, wanting, and deserving of fans on its own terms. A couple of the criteria I use for reviewing is - will I remember this? And do I want to listen to this again? I can answer "yes" to both for *Translucent Blues.*

Acoustic Tribute to The Doors

The Doors have always been an alternative choice for fans. In their heyday in the 60's The Doors were the alternative to *Incense and Peppermint* and *All You Need is Love*. Today, The Doors are inspiring alternative explorations of their music.

All Wood and Doors are twelve of The Doors best known songs, *Break on Through, Love Me Two Times, Take It As It Comes, Strange Days, Light My Fire, Touch Me, The Crystal Ship, Soul Kitchen, People Are Strange, Moonlight Drive, Riders on the Storm,* and *The End.* Generally speaking, the songs sound as if Jim Morrison had joined The Eagles. I make the comparison not as a shortcut to thinking, but as a reference point, a starting point for fans to climb on board.

James Lee Stanley and Cliff Eberhardt give The Doors songs a rough-hewn, rustic feel, and at moments feel as if they've transcended into acoustic psychedelia. The songs included on *All Wood and Doors* aren't really covers of The Doors' songs as much as they're acoustic interpretations, and explorations that Stanley and Eberhardt allowed themselves to go on. The songs, while sounding familiar, have mysterious and exotic twangings that open a new door into The Doors.

Stanley was inspired by Doors' drummer John Densmore to create *All Wood and Doors*. Densmore had heard Stanley's *All Wood and Stones* and told Stanley that if he was ever going to do a CD on The Doors he'd be glad to play on it. Like any good idea, it sparked Stanley to not only start working out Doors songs for acoustic guitars, but also to ask a variety of musicians, some unexpected, to play on the album. Among them John Densmore, Peter Tork, Timothy B. Schmit, Paul Barrere, and John Batdorf to name but a few. As the project moved along, Doors guitarist Robby Krieger heard about the project and contacted Stanley letting him know he'd be interested in playing if Stanley "wanted him" and Robby joined them in the studio for an afternoon.

I'm not an audiophile so usually sound quality isn't a big issue to me, but when it's outstanding it's worth mentioning. The sound quality on *All Wood and Doors* is so clear, and the clarity is so striking, it impresses the ear as soon as you start to listen.

Ray Manzarek and Michael McClure's Symbiosis and Synergy

I saw Michael McClure and Ray Manzarek at Lounge Ax in Chicago in the 80's and for a moment I was transported by the words and music. It felt like I'd broken through something. In *The Piano Poems*, Manzarek and McClure sit in for a live set in San Francisco and there's always the possibility to be transported by these two and their words and music.

This is Michael McClure's CD, all the 'songs' are McClure's poems with Ray Manzarek accompanying on piano, and flautist Larry Kassin joining in on a few of the tracks. McClure's poems will stand out in your mind. The poems will take you all the way from *Pico Boulevard* in Los Angeles, and back in time to his 'hits' such as *Jean Harlow and the Kid*. The highlight of *The Piano Poems* has got to be *Antechamber of the Night*, which stands out as a celebration of the self and the world we live in much as Whitman's *I Sing the Body Electric*.

Manzarek accompanies not so much as a Jazz accompanist, but shows off his classicist roots. Manzarek's accompaniment never overpowers McClure's poems, but provides dramatic Brahm's like swells when the poem hits climactic moments. Manzarek's aural backdrop animates and illustrates McClure's poems. This is clearly a partnership of words and music that works together. It all sounds natural and unrehearsed, but it is obviously the product of two masters of their respective crafts.

If you're not a huge fan of poetry, don't let that intimidate you. McClure's poems are accessible in language and tone. McClure is one of the last of the original beat poets left, and he uses imagery everyone can identify with. Imagery that is found in nature and on the street.

In *The Piano Poems* there's no guarantee that you'll be transported to some other place in your mind, but you'll never know unless you try.

Would Have Made a Great Live Album in 68!

The Hollywood Bowl was a prestigious booking for any rock band, and maybe more so for The Doors. They were local boys who made it and the Hollywood Bowl was proof of that. It was a hometown crowd and The Doors were out to give the best show they could. They rehearsed for the show (something they didn't ordinarily do, especially after Jim Morrison became more estranged from the band). They also prepared a set-list and they seemed to stick to it. The Doors gave a pretty tight performance at the Hollywood Bowl on July 5, 1968.

The Doors: Live at the Bowl '68 is the companion soundtrack to the DVD/Blu-Ray of the same name that was released on October 22, 2012. While it may not be as good a standalone item as *The Doors: Live at the Bowl '68* DVD/Blu-Ray, it's still a good soundtrack to the Hollywood Bowl shows and would have made a good live album in 1968 if it weren't for technical difficulties.

In the spring of 1968 The Doors had decided to film their shows for a documentary that would later become *Feast of Friends*. The Hollywood Bowl was filmed with an eye to inclusion in the film. But during three songs, *Hello, I Love You*, *The Wasp* (Texas Radio and the Big Beat), and *Spanish Caravan*, Morrison's microphone feed to the recording equipment failed and compromised the show until the technology caught up. Although *The Doors: Live at the Hollywood Bowl* was released in 1989 it was incomplete. There was nothing either The Doors or Bruce Botnick could do to restore the three missing songs, until now. Long time Doors engineer (and co-producer of *L.A. Woman*) Bruce Botnick, through the magic of digital technology, was able to piece together the missing songs and now the Hollywood Bowl show is complete in the release of *The Doors: Live at the Bowl '68*.

The CD sounds great! The sound 'POPS!' out at you, you can hear everything clearly - Morrison shaking maracas near the microphone (which the audience probably never heard), and it sounds like drummer John Densmore is bashing his way to a new drum kit. Morrison's voice is a strong growl, Robby Krieger's guitar tears out into the Hollywood Hills, and Ray Manzarek's keyboards and bass gives the band a full, filled out sound. It must have been something to see and hear the show live!

The strengths of the CD are also some of the strengths of the DVD/Blu-Ray. The deconstruction of *Celebration of the Lizard* that had poetic segues into the more traditional songs such as *Light My Fire* created a jarring theatrical effect.

The CD contains a couple of weaknesses that the DVD/Blu-Ray doesn't. Since this concert was filmed a lot of the crowd reaction you hear on the CD is dependent on seeing what Jim Morrison is doing onstage, without that, it kind of loses its meaning and context within the show. The CD comes in a cardboard CD case and not a jewel case. While the DVD/Blu-Ray contains more than your average bonus features section, the CD contains no bonus tracks or special features.

The CD of *The Doors: Live at the Bowl '68* is great to have in your car to cruise around listening to, playing the movie in your head.

Another aspect of The Doors' music lies not in the physical, but in the psychic, the energy and experience they tried to create in their live shows. The Doors by all accounts were different than other bands and, in fact, could inspire aspiring musicians to pursue the dream of being in a band. That experience was transmitted directly to fans through The Doors live shows.

5
On the Road

The Doors have described themselves as four points in a diamond and, as with any rock band, they have two ways of communicating with their audience. The *physical* through records, CD's and albums, the relics of a band passing our way; and the *psychic* through the energy and experience a band brings to their live shows.

The Doors at the Roundhouse

The Roundhouse in London was aptly named, as it was a former railroad station that was used to turn engines around. It was the start of The Doors' European tour in 1968, and the September 6-7 dates were important not only because they were the start of the tour, but because the pressure was on with such rock notables as Paul McCartney, Mick Jagger and Keith Richards in the audience. Also on the bill was Jefferson Airplane who would alternate with The Doors as the opening act each night.

The Roundhouse was sold out. *Hello, I Love You* had recently hit England making its way up the British charts. On stage Morrison was a contrast in tones, dressed in black leather pants and a white shirt. The Doors pounded out the music at what would be one of their best shows at the height of their performing career. The Doors played their hits such as *Light My Fire*, giving an artistic twist to the performance adding the opening section of *Celebration of the Lizard* as an intro to the song. *When the Music's Over* made you believe The Doors wanted the world and wanted it now. Morrison also interacted with the audience. During the instrumental section of *Light My Fire* he went down into the audience and held out the microphone to let people give out a little Jim Morrison like yelp that he had been doing the entire show. The September 6th show was also filmed for Granada Television and was released as *The Doors are Open.*

The Doors are Open wasn't strictly a concert film, although almost an hour of concert footage is shown. The Doors were the focal point for the producers' political viewpoint and the film featured scenes from the police riot in Chicago at the Democratic Convention, and "The Battle of Grosvenor Square" which had taken place outside the U.S. Embassy in London earlier in the year. The soundtrack for the documentary footage of the riots was some of The Doors more confrontational songs like *Five to One* or *When the Music's Over*. Morrison, a former film student, later said "I thought the film was very exciting…the guys that made the film had a thesis of what it was going to be before we even came over. We were going to be the political rock group…"

Also filmed was an interview with the group in which Jim Morrison dropped some of his more quotable quotes, such as talking about The Doors music as a "heavy, gloomy feeling, like someone not quite at home…" or when asked about comparisons between him and Mick Jagger, "I have always thought comparisons are useless and ugly. It is a shortcut to thinking." When it was over, The Doors had conquered England.

The Doors in Amsterdam

If The Doors had conquered England, then Amsterdam was the first appearance of forces that would later conquer Jim Morrison.

After London, The Doors went on to Germany on September 13, 1968. There, Jim lip-synced *Hello, I Love You* in Romer Square in Frankfurt for the TV show *4-3-2-1 Hot and Sweet*. Then, on September 14th, they played the Kongresshalle in Frankfurt. By September 15th The Doors were in Amsterdam.

The trouble in Amsterdam didn't start in Amsterdam, but at Frankfurt airport. Jim Morrison had some hash on him and to get through customs he swallowed it. On the plane he started drinking. After they arrived in Amsterdam, Morrison continued to drink into the afternoon. Prior to that evening's show at the Concertgebouw, the members of Jefferson Airplane and The Doors were walking down the red light district of Amsterdam, as Paul Kanter and Grace Slick explained in the video *The Doors in Europe 1968*, when fans recognized them:

"People were coming up to them and handing them pot or some hash, and maybe they would take a puff or two or put the drug in their pockets for later." However, Morrison, on the road to William Blake's palace of wisdom, would ingest everything he was given on the spot.

Later that night both bands were playing at the Concertgebouw. Keeping with the precedent started in London of alternating nights as the opening act, The Airplane went on first and when they got to *Fantastic Plastic Lover*, Morrison, moved by the music and/or the drugs he'd taken that day went onstage twirling around in circles, in an almost Sufi-type dance, twisting the microphone cords around the band. The Airplane, piqued at the invasion of their musical territory, started playing faster, encouraging Morrison to spin and dance faster, as the song came to its climax. Airplane singer, Marty Balin remembers how Morrison stopped, looked at him "real funny" and crashed to the floor, passed out. He was rushed to the hospital.

The Doors, angry that Morrison couldn't perform, decided to go on as a trio with Doors keyboardist Ray Manzarek handling the singing, with the phrasing and tone even sounding like Morrison. According to all sources, the show that evening was exceptional and the band won an ovation from the audience.

The next day Morrison was released from the hospital and The Doors continued their European tour.

The Doors in Toronto, 1969

The Toronto Rock 'n' Roll Revival Festival of September 13, 1969, was a prestigious bill with The Doors to headline, and featured The Plastic Ono Band, Bo Diddley, Alice Cooper, Jerry Lee Lewis, Chuck Berry, Gene Vincent, Little Richard, The Chicago Transit Authority (which later changed their name to Chicago), Lord Sutch, and lesser known bands like Cat Mother and the All Night Newsboys, Milkwood, and Whiskey Howl (the only local Toronto band to play the Festival that year). Rolling Stone called it the second most important event in rock 'n' roll history.

The Festival lasted thirteen hours, a ticket cost $6.00. It was also a concert of firsts. It was the first time Bo Diddley, Jerry Lee Lewis, Chuck Berry and Little Richard appeared on the same bill. It was the premiere of The Plastic Ono Band, and it was the occasion of Alice Cooper's famous or infamous (depending on how you look at it) 'chicken incident'.

Chapter 5

Lennon and Ono at first weren't scheduled to appear at the Festival, but ticket sales were lagging. When Kim Fowley, who was to emcee the Festival, heard the promoters were considering cancelling it, he suggested they get Lennon and Ono to emcee the Festival as he was aware of Lennon's love for the music of Chuck Berry, Little Richard, and Gene Vincent. Lennon agreed to do the show with the proviso that he and Ono perform. The promoters agreed and ticket sales went up enough for the Festival to go on.

D.A. Pennebaker filmed the Festival, which would be released as *Sweet Toronto*. Pennebaker had previously filmed Bob Dylan's *Don't Look Back* and would film the Isle of Wight Festival in 1970. Lennon/Ono's performance was supposed to be the centerpiece of Pennebaker's film, but Lennon later had second thoughts because of the audience's reception of Ono, and because his (Lennon's) singing hadn't been up to his standards, so they withdrew their permission for Pennebaker to use their performance in the film. Lennon/Ono would later reconsider their reconsideration and released an album of their performance *Live Peace in Toronto 1969*.

As mentioned above, the 1969 Festival is probably most famously remembered for Alice Cooper's 'chicken incident'. During Cooper's encore the band would tear open pillows and blow feathers out into the audience. When Cooper tore open the pillow someone from the audience threw a live chicken on the stage. Cooper, thinking chickens could fly, threw it back into the audience and the audience tore it apart. Cooper remembers how, on one side of the stage, he saw John Lennon watching him and on the other side of the stage, Jim Morrison egging him on.

The Doors were the headlining act of the Festival and played an abbreviated set (maybe due to the lateness of the hour) but a couple of memorable moments occurred. Doors guitarist Robby Krieger, in an homage to John Lennon, slipped a bit of The Beatles' *Eleanor Rigby* into his instrumental. In turn, Gene Vincent being on the bill in Toronto may have been a nostalgic moment for Morrison as Vincent, who was known in his 50's heyday for wearing leather pants, may have been an early inspiration for Morrison's stage appearance. As The Doors started *The End* in Toronto, Morrison said he was honored to be on the same stage as the "illustrious musical geniuses." Morrison and Vincent became friends for a short period of time and had the shared coincidence of being convicted of public obscenity (although Vincent's may have been manufactured by his manager). Vincent died a little over three months after Morrison in 1971.

It's in dispute whether Pennebaker filmed The Doors or not. Some witnesses say he packed up right before The Doors went on because it was so late, while others say The Doors set was filmed and that perhaps contractual, monetary, or issues similar to Lennon's objections had prevented the release.

The Doors at the Northern California Rock and Folk Festival

The Monterey Pop Festival and Woodstock are usually held up as the apex of 60's rock Festivals and in both cases The Doors famously weren't included. In between those famous Festivals was The Northern California Rock and Folk Festival, and The Doors were there!

The Northern California Rock and Folk Festival was held on May 18-19, 1968, and featured acts like The Grateful Dead, Big Brother and the Holding Company (with Janis Joplin about to go solo), Jefferson Airplane, Country Joe and The Fish, The Animals, The Youngbloods, Taj Mahal, Steve Miller and other lesser known San Francisco area bands. The Doors were the closing act in the late afternoon of May 19th. It was a long day for the audience. Ten groups played before The Doors and as the day progressed the sun grew hotter on the exposed crowd.

There was some Super 8 film shot of the concert on a Bell and Howell "Zoomatic" which is the same type of camera with which Abraham Zapruder filmed the Kennedy assassination. The film briefly shows clips of bands such as The Youngbloods, and Country Joe and The Fish before The Doors, as well as panning shots of the crowd and a skydiver parachuting into the Festival. At the 1:50 minute mark of the film, a man, who may be Harrison Ford, can be seen in a white shirt filming the concert. Ford, before he became famous, did some carpentry work for Jac Holzman and picked up some work as a grip for The Doors, and this show was filmed for *Feast of Friends*. The Doors come on stage about halfway through the film, and the stage was surrounded by banners reminiscent of a Renaissance Faire. The film shows some pretty typical shots of The Doors, mostly Robby playing guitar in close proximity to Morrison and a couple of shots of Ray on the keyboards. John Densmore can't be seen because of the distance from the stage. During the short clip you can also see Jim Morrison in his brown leather pants, white Mexican wedding shirt and beads. He tries to get the audience into the show, he falls a couple of times, once it looks like the band could be playing *The Unknown Soldier* but the audience doesn't seem to be paying much attention to the band. The lack of sound on the film actually helps communicate what The Doors may have been feeling about the performance that day, and outdoor venues for their music. It seems far away and Morrison's theatrics don't translate to an outdoor venue. By all accounts it was a lackluster set by The Doors and it convinced Jim Morrison that outdoor venues diluted the experience The Doors were trying to induce in an audience.

The Doors, riot at the Singer Bowl

Flushing Meadows, NY, August 2, 1968. The security guards and uniformed police officers brought The Doors to the stage of the Singer Bowl through the gauntlet of the crowd. As they made their way to the stage, fans grabbed and pulled at the band members.

Prior to the band going on stage, Jim Morrison wandered around backstage and around the grounds of the concert, followed by the *Feast of Friends* film crew who captured some now iconic scenes of Morrison that were used in the film and which would later be used in *When You're Strange*.

When The Doors took the stage, a phalanx of fans rushed forward and the policemen in charge of security repulsed the audience onslaught, which created a barrier and a challenge for the crowd to breach. In the *Rolling Stone* interview with Jerry Hopkins, Morrison said of rock 'n' riots in general, "The only incentive to charge the stage is because there's a barrier. If there was no barrier there'd be no incentive (to rush the stage)." The stage at the Singer Bowl was supposed to rotate during the show, but during The Doors performance the stage jammed and wouldn't revolve, leaving a portion of the audience unable to see the show.

The Singer Bowl was a concert with The Doors at the height of their career and live performances. Jim Morrison sang the Doors' hits, recited poetry, and previewed new songs (including *Wild Child*). Morrison's performance had him on his knees or writhing on the stage. The audience couldn't see the show and this frustration spurred them on and they tried to get onto the stage while Morrison twirled and danced, consciously or unconsciously enticing them. Then the audience close to the stage started breaking the wooden fold-up chairs and hurled them onstage. Morrison caught one and hurled it back into the audience. The *Feast of Friends* film crew narrowly avoided getting hit, and the cops continued pushing the fans away from the stage. As the band and Morrison reached the Oedipal section of *The End* with Morrison screaming and writhing as the band pounded away, the crowd was spurred on. Morrison and the music climaxed. The crowd pushed, overcoming the police barrier just as The Doors abandoned the stage.

It should be remembered that Jim Morrison, while still at Florida State University, had a theory that crowds could be neurotic just like individuals and like individuals their mass neuroses could be "cured". Morrison came up with a plan where he tried to enlist his friends in a scheme to incite a crowd to riot by placing these friends throughout the crowd - shouting choice slogans to cause the crowd to riot. His friends took a pass on the experiment. Had Morrison found the ultimate position to influence an audience?

It was at the Singer Bowl concert that Who guitarist Pete Townsend, watching The Doors show, witnessed a girl getting hit with a piece of chair and Morrison's indifference to it. Townsend later said this incident inspired the Sally Simpson portion of *Tommy.*

Morrison said that while watching his performance at the Singer Bowl during the editing of *Feast Of Friends* he realized that, "Because being onstage, being one of the central figures, I could only see it from my own viewpoint. But then to see things as they really were…I suddenly realized that I was, to a degree, just a puppet, controlled by a lot of forces I only vaguely understood."

The Doors Show that Created Iggy Pop

Jim Osterberg had dropped out of the University of Michigan but on October 20, 1967, he used his old college identification and attended The Doors concert at the University's Homecoming Dance. That concert changed Osterberg's life.

Osterberg was a smart kid, voted most likely to succeed by his high school graduating class. Although Osterberg already had an interest in rock 'n' roll and had been in a couple of bands - The Iguanas, and the Prime Movers - he hadn't considered it anything more than passing time.

The dance was attended by mostly fraternity brothers and their sorority girlfriends. The Doors came onstage and started to play without Morrison. When Morrison finally came out onstage he was clearly intoxicated and immediately started to antagonize the audience. He refused to sing in anything except a falsetto voice, and made weird sounds with the microphone. He mocked the audience and threw things at them. The audience in turn threw things onstage, booed and left in large numbers. To conclude the show, Doors drummer, John

Densmore threw down his drumsticks and left the stage, followed shortly by Robby Krieger. Ray Manzarek, trying to save the show, grabbed a guitar and sat down while Morrison drunkenly sang an early version of *Maggie M'Gill*, actually more of a drunken ditty than a song. After that Manzarek and Morrison left the stage.

That fifteen or twenty minutes of a show inspired and excited Osterberg who thought: "If this guy can do it, I can do it" (Patti Smith in her book *Just Kids* reports much the same reaction at seeing The Doors). Osterberg went on to form the band The Stooges, taking the name Iggy from his former band: The Iguanas. By 1968 he was Iggy Pop and was in Los Angeles signed with Elektra Records.

The Chicago Coliseum May 10, 1968

May 10, 1968. A riot breaks out at The Doors concert at the Chicago Coliseum, in what may have been the first consciously created riot by Jim Morrison.

While still a student at Florida State University (FSU) Morrison took a class in the psychology of crowds, along with his own independent reading of Norman O. Brown's book *Life Against Death* and came to the conclusion that crowds, just like people could have sexual neuroses, and like people, those neuroses could be diagnosed and treated. As previously mentioned, to try to prove his theory, Morrison tried to suborn his friends into disrupting a speaker by strategically placing them in the crowd and at appropriate moments in the speech shout slogans that could "cure" the crowd, make love to it, or cause it to riot. His friends declined to take him up on the offer. At UCLA Morrison and film school friend Dennis Jakob told people they were going to start a band called "The Doors: Open and Closed". Thwarted in his previous attempts to influence crowd psychology - did Jim Morrison come to the conclusion that through The Doors he had found a way to prove his theories on crowds? Did he find the perfect position to influence crowds, in front of an audience? To cure them? To make love to them? To cause them to riot?

May of 1968 was the beginning of Morrison's dissatisfaction with being a rock star. The Doors wasn't becoming what Morrison had envisioned it as - a mixture of theatre and poetry. Further, The Doors' third album which was to include Morrison's tour-de-force *Celebration of the Lizard* was unraveling. At the Chicago Coliseum, Morrison was escorted to the stage by Chicago police who in August of '68 would be accused of rioting in dispersing the Yippie (Youth International Party) demonstrators at the Democratic National Convention. As

Morrison took to the stage he was greeted by an eruption from the crowd and The Doors played songs most suited for stirring a reaction from the crowd: *Unknown Soldier*, *Break on Through*, *Five to One*, and *When the Music's Over*. Morrison used every trick of stage performance he had learned: writhing, falling and leaping, throwing himself to the ground, sliding the maracas into his pants. When The Doors left the stage, the crowd wanting more rushed the stage and destroyed it.

In The Doors' song *Peace Frog*, Morrison has two very personal references to his past. Venice where, of course, he had the rooftop visions that produced The Doors' first songs. And secondly, New Haven, where Morrison became the first rock star arrested onstage. A third reference in *Peace Frog* is Chicago. Most people assume Chicago is a reference to the police riots of August 1968. But why would Morrison include a more historical reference after two extremely personal references? Could it be that Morrison had his Chicago performance and riot in mind when writing *Peace Frog*?

The Doors Play the Chicago Auditorium

It had been just over a year since The Doors had played Chicago. Since that time Morrison and The Doors had spun out of control and the crash that resulted was the "Miami Incident" in March of 1969. After Miami, The Doors were shunned, suffering a rock 'n' roll exile. All the shows they had lined up for that spring tour cancelled out on them. Doors' manager Bill Siddons said it cost them "a million dollars in gigs." The Doors and Jim Morrison did take advantage of the downtime, however. Ray Manzarek, Robby Krieger and John Densmore went into the studio to work on *The Soft Parade*, and Morrison filmed *HWY*, and had his poetry published. The first signs of a thaw in The Doors performing came with the May '69 airing of the PBS *Critique* show. However, The Doors first concert in front of an audience after Miami was at the Chicago Auditorium, June 14, 1969.

The Chicago show was a slow building of tension. At first a subtle, unconscious anticipation that built expectations. There was a radio ad promising that with the Chicago show "The Doors will begin where they left off in Miami." The tension continued building, the Staple Singers opened for The Doors, and they didn't take the stage until midnight. Jim Morrison shocked the audience by having a full beard, and when the band launched into *When the Music's Over* that's when the conscious creation of tension began. Ray Manzarek's opening riffs were played over and over, while Jim Morrison hung back by the drum riser until, when the audience couldn't take the pressure of anticipation another moment, Morrison jumped at the microphone and screamed over the psychedelic roar of Robby Krieger's guitar. The Doors delivered an excellent show. Despite the late start, it was a full two hours with the band playing new songs off *The Soft Parade*. Everybody liked the show except the media.

A contemporaneous article in the *Chicago Daily News* opened with the line that "Jim Morrison didn't do it", a clear reference to the Miami allegations of indecent exposure. The article goes on to mention how tame the show was including the encore of *Light My Fire*. Talking about The Doors it quotes Morrison as saying "We started with music, then we went into theater but it was so shitty we went back to music." In a backstage interview with the band, Jim Morrison complained about not being able to get a date with a "chick".

The Auditorium Theatre is the one Chicago area venue The Doors played that still exists.

The Doors at the Aquarius Theater

Elektra Records wanted The Doors to record a live album to help offset the production costs of *The Soft Parade* which had run up to $86,000. Also, The Doors wanted to prove to audiences they were still a musical force to be reckoned with, so Elektra rented the Aquarius Theater for two shows during which they would record a live album.

The recording of The Doors live had originally been planned for the Whisky a Go-Go, a return for The Doors to the home where they had started their career a mere three years previously. When the Whisky didn't work out, they moved the recording to the Aquarius theater that Elektra had rented out for concerts on Monday nights which was the night off for *Hair* (previous weeks had included other Elektra acts such as Love, Bread, Lonnie Mack, and A&M's The Flying Burrito Brothers). Elektra parked a van behind the theater, stuffed it with recording equipment with cables snaking into the theater, and that's where producer Paul Rothchild and engineer Bruce Botnick sat and listened to the concerts. The Doors still viewed it as a return to the artistic, not the sensational. When fans starting streaming into the theater they were shocked to see a bearded Jim Morrison sitting onstage wearing a loose fitting white shirt and striped pants. No leathers, no leather clad demon, no lizard king, only The Doors, musicians.

By all accounts the shows were an artistic success. Jim for most of the performances simply sat on a stool and sang while the band played. The shows did have their electric moments though. At the second show during the *Celebration of the Lizard* Morrison climbed the scaffolding of the *Hair* set and delivered the opening lines of the song before grabbing one of the stage ropes and swinging out over the audience, before landing on the stage to continue the song. The one thing the shows weren't was great audio, they didn't sound very good on tape. As The Doors toured, other shows were recorded and Paul Rothchild went into the studio to meticulously edit together an album that Jim Morrison said was "…a fairly true document of what the band sounds like on a fairly good night."

A couple of notes on the Aquarius shows. Before the start of the shows Jim handed out copies of his poem *Ode to L.A. while thinking of Brian Jones, Deceased*, to fans waiting in line to get in. The poem is a tribute to Rolling Stones' founder Brian Jones who had been found dead in his swimming pool earlier in the month. A member of the Los Angeles cast of *Hair* was Marvin Lee Aday, who would later go on to be known and record as Meatloaf.

The Doors Play Madison Square Garden

The Doors played Madison Square Garden on January 24, 1969, becoming one of the first groups to start playing large stadiums while simultaneously hitting the apogee of their career.

In moving to the larger stadiums, just as when they decided that outdoor venues no longer suited their needs as performers, The Doors realized they were losing the intimacy of the smaller venues they had played until then, in favor of larger paydays and reaching a larger audience. Bill Graham warned the band of this previously and even offered them dates at the Fillmore East, but The Doors, at the time, felt they had outgrown the smaller venues, a decision that would later come to haunt them.

At first glance, playing Madison Square Garden would be everything a band could wish for and aspire to, but it was a double edged sword. On the one hand The Doors take home pay for playing "The Garden" was $50,000 making them one of the highest paid bands in the country. The sharper edge of that sword was that the stadiums were built for sporting events and the acoustics and sound systems weren't advantageous for musical acts, even with road manager Vince Treanor's custom built PA system. While the concert was well received by the audience, and the band played well, Morrison was a little bit subdued in his stage show but he demonstrated why he was one of the most exciting performers in rock music. The shows weren't that well received by the rock press, however. Ellen Sandler, a writer for *Hit Parader,* wrote of the concert, "...but it's been over for The Doors for a long time now." Maybe even Morrison was aware of these dichotomies, at one point during the concert he pointed to one side of the arena and said, "You are life," and then pointing to the other side said, "You are death," and then added, "I straddle the fence, and my balls hurt."

Attending the concert that night was the editor of *Jazz & Pop Magazine*, Patricia Kennealy, who Jim would meet the next day for an interview. They would soon start an affair that would have far reaching ramifications into Morrison's life.

The Doors in Mexico City

Jim Morrison came onstage and introduced the band, Ramon Manzarek, Juan Densmore and Roberto Krieger, and he was Fidel Castro! The Doors had gone to Mexico to play between June 28 and July 1, 1969, and were trying to revive their live performance career in light of the Miami show earlier that year. Was Morrison still feeling like an exile with that introduction?

The Mexico City shows had started out with all the best of intentions. The Doors were supposed to play the Plaza Monumental, the city's largest bullring, with ticket prices between forty cents and a dollar. The Doors expected to play shows that even the poorest denizens of Mexico City would be able to attend. But when the mayor and city officials discovered the show was set for the anniversary of the 1968 student revolt in the city, they cancelled The Doors' permit. With promoters scrambling, they were able to save the Mexico City performances by booking El Forum, a nightclub for the city's young and rich, with ticket prices at 200 pesos (about $16.00). Gone was the egalitarian vision of bringing The Doors' music to everyone.

Although the audience was respectful to the band, Morrison didn't garner the reaction that he was trying to evoke or that he was used to. The sole exceptions were when The Doors played *Light My Fire* (*Enciende Mi Fuego*) and *The End.* During the Oedipal section of *The End*, Morrison (as usual) had his eyes closed and as the song approached the climatic passage he heard the audience shushing each other because the song was very popular in Mexico; it was said to have impressed Morrison. The second night's show wasn't much better with the audience being rowdier and calling for the Mexican folk song made popular by

Ritchie Valens, *La Bamba*. The Doors acceded to the request and then quickly left the stage.

The press was less than kind to The Doors labeling them derogatorily as "hippies" and undesirables, and the band was actually denied rooms at a few of Mexico City's more luxurious hotels (The Doors eventually found accommodation in a private hotel). An interesting facet to the visit was when Jim Morrison visited the Aztec Temple of the Sun and was photographed climbing the steps of the pyramid. An interesting choice for the shamanic Lizard King.

The Doors at the Isle of Wight

The Doors had scheduled a European tour for 1970 (Italy, Switzerland, France), in the midst of the Miami trial. The Doors asked for a continuance until October of that year, but Judge Murray Goodman denied the request effectively cancelling the band's second European tour. The only survivor of the tour was the Third Annual Isle of Wight Concert which The Doors played on August 29.

The Isle of Wight is an island off the coast of England, and it's an outdoor event. It wasn't easy to get there. After a day in court The Doors had to fly from Miami to London then take a small shuttle plane over to the concert grounds. By the time they arrived they hadn't slept in 36 hours. The Doors had long since avoided playing outdoor shows because they thought it took away the mystery of their performance, but they took the show to offset legal fees brought about by the trial. The concert was a three day event starring Jimi Hendrix, The Who, The Moody Blues, Sly and the Family Stone, and Emerson, Lake and Palmer.

Like a lot of concerts from the 60's a certain level of chaos existed. The concert had been oversold and fans were turned away, but the crowd rioted and broke down barriers and it became a free concert. That's much the same reason Woodstock became a free concert. Again, like many of the other major concerts of the 60's D.A. Pennebaker was there filming, and his cameras captured a lot of the tone and mood of the audience showing kids running around the grounds with sleeping blankets jostling for prime space to watch the concerts. At one point he captured the walls being breeched by the kids.

The Doors didn't play until about midnight. Once there, Morrison also began drinking which added to his fatigue. Morrison's performance lacked not only histrionics but energy. The Pennebaker film shows Morrison holding onto the microphone, a cigarette tucked between two fingers while the band played mostly songs from the first two albums. After the show John Densmore, in a pique of anger threw his drumsticks down and said he was he never playing with "that asshole (Morrison) again."

The day after they performed Morrison took a tour of the Festival grounds and bumped into John Tobler of *Zig Zag Magazine*. Morrison gave him an interview, and a few things that Morrison talked about in the interview were the nature of revolution, wanting to start a small literary magazine or newspaper, and the future of Elektra Records. Tobler also asked Morrison if the reason they had played songs off the first two albums was because the audience would know them better. Morrison replied "No, we knew them better."

The Doors Live in NY, January 1970

January 17, 1970, The Doors start a two night stand at the Felt Forum that was to be a tour in support of the forthcoming release *Morrison Hotel*. It was also the start of the final year of The Doors as a live touring band with Jim Morrison.

The previous year had been a bad one for The Doors. In the aftermath of the March 1969 concert in Miami, Jim Morrison was charged with indecent exposure and the rest of their tour was cancelled. The Doors took advantage of this enforced hiatus from touring by going back into the studio and going back to the basics of rock and the blues. *Morrison Hotel* was recorded quickly, starting in November of 1969 with the album released in February 1970.

The Felt Forum was a small intimate venue for The Doors to start their touring schedule for 1970. Doors' keyboardist Ray Manzarek likened it to the Whisky a Go-Go. Although it was only two nights, The Doors played two shows each evening. The shows were recorded for *Absolutely Live* and in The Doors' 1997 box set release, a disc included *Live in New York*. However, it wouldn't be until 2009 that the concerts would show up in their entirety in *The Doors: Live in New York, The Felt Forum.*

Although *Morrison Hotel* was not yet released, fans greeted the album's songs enthusiastically and The Doors played a lot of songs including *Roadhouse Blues, Ship of Fools, Peace Frog*, as well as The Doors' standards. They also threw in songs like *Crawling King Snake, Little Red Rooster*, and *Love Hides*. The Felt Forum shows took their toll on Morrison's voice and by the fourth show his voice sounded hoarse. Nonetheless, it didn't stop Morrison and the rest of the band from putting on great shows which included having John Sebastian sit in, and in a Doors rarity, also having Dallas Taylor sit in with John Densmore on drums.

After the Felt Forum shows, Elektra Records' president threw an after party for the band, both in celebration of The Doors fulfilling their contract with Elektra and in part to woo them to sign a new contract. As Jim Morrison and Pam Courson were leaving the lavish party, arms draped around each other, Pam said to Holzman, "Well, in case we're on Atlantic next year, thanks for the swell party." As Holzman's jaw dropped, Morrison had a smirk on his face and Holzman knew he had been the target of one of Morrison's jokes to elicit a reaction.

Dallas 1970, The Doors Second from Last Show with Jim Morrison

By the early 80's Ray Manzarek had learned to forget. He was quoted as saying he wished Jim Morrison had lived past Paris so they could have played the *L.A. Woman* songs live in concert. Fans lamented that too but The Doors had played two shows while recording *L.A. Woman* and previewed the songs. These shows were the last two shows The Doors played with Jim Morrison and the sold out events were played at the State Fair Music Hall in Dallas, Texas, on December 11, 1970. A soundboard recording exists of one of those shows.

Not much had been known about the Dallas 1970 show. Although the show sounds a little dark and murky, maybe given to its soundboard origin, it opened with *Love Her Madly* and there is a bluesy medley of songs, including *The Changeling* and *Ship of Fools* (from that year's *Morrison Hotel*). Some of the solos delve a little into jazzy sections, and in the middle of *L.A. Woman* it seems The Doors were consciously trying to go back to their roots at The Whisky to create a song that had extended solos and room for Morrison's poetry, just like earlier songs *The End* and *When the Music's Over*.

The Dallas show seems like it was well received by the audience and is a lot more coherent than the Miami show was, but the reaction from the press was different to the audience's reaction, and probably different to fans listening to the concert. The Dallas press described the show as subdued and sedate, with *Dallas News* critic Pat Pope writing, "Their performance was casual, informal. No encore was played, but the set was a satisfying one that rounded out their music, giving it an electronic, blues dimension that doesn't come through as strongly on record."

Chapter 5

The Doors Come to the End in New Orleans

It has been described as the most mythical of Doors shows, The Doors' final live appearance with Jim Morrison as lead singer. On December 12, 1970, The Doors appeared at The Warehouse, a night club in New Orleans.

The Warehouse was formerly a warehouse for cotton, built in the 1850s. It was a fairly new venue having opened in January of 1970. In its tenure it became one of New Orleans' and even the South's premiere music venues. Groups like the Grateful Dead, Fleetwood Mac, the Allman Brothers, The Who, The Police, Bob Marley, David Bowie, The Clash, Pink Floyd, and hundreds of other bands played there. The Doors' performances in Dallas the night before had been subdued but successful, but New Orleans would be the end for The Doors as a touring band with Jim Morrison.

The band again was premiering songs from *L.A. Woman* which they had started working on in L.A. That night something went terribly wrong. Midway through The Doors' set Morrison began to forget the lyrics to the songs, so he tried telling a long rambling joke that fell flat. Morrison then began to hang listlessly on the microphone stand for support. When the band started to play *Light My Fire* Morrison got through the first verse of the song and when the solos came Morrison sat down on John Densmore's drum riser. When they came to the end of the solos and Morrison had to sing the last verse he didn't get up. The band went through the cue two or three more times while Morrison sat there, until Densmore pushed Morrison with his foot urging him towards the microphone. Morrison finally got up to sing, but it seemed everything had left him. Ray Manzarek describes seeing all of Morrison's "psychic energy go out the top of his head." In frustration, Morrison starting pounding the microphone stand into the wooden floor of the stage, splintering it. Then he threw down the microphone stand and walked off the stage. The band agreed to indefinitely suspend live touring and went back to L.A. to finish recording *L.A. Woman*. The Doors with Jim Morrison as lead singer was over.

The Warehouse, realizing the historical significance of the smashed stage, didn't repair it for several years afterwards. It closed its doors in 1982 and was torn down seven years later, but filmmaker Jessy Williamson has been working on a documentary on The Warehouse titled *A Warehouse on Tchoupitoulas*.

The Doors affected people. But in any social intercourse there are many people that come into contact with us on a daily basis; they help us, hinder us, or influence us in one way or another. They're part of our lives. The next chapter will take a look at those extra-curricular persons who were in The Doors' lives.

6

People in the Doors' World

None of us is truly an island 'separate and apart from the main'. The same is true with The Doors and the world of The Doors. The Doors stood in the river of life. They formed alliances and were helped by people. They influenced others, they were friends, lovers, and the children of others. Here are a few of those people that populated The Doors' world.

The Work of Paul Rothchild

If anyone qualifies as being 'the fifth Door', it's Paul Rothchild. As a producer for Elektra Records he was there from the beginning of The Doors' professional career until almost the end.

Born April 18, 1935, Paul Rothchild grew up in New Jersey with music a part of his life from the beginning as his mother was an opera singer. Rothchild met Elektra Records' founder Jac Holzman when he worked at a record shop and Holzman delivered Elektra records from the back of his Vespa scooter. Rothchild and Holzman kept in contact. Rothchild went to work for a Boston record company that distributed Elektra records in the area but it was when Rothchild became the head of Prestige Records' folk division that Holzman started thinking of stealing him away to Elektra because of Rothchild's knowledge of music. Rothchild was perceived by musicians as the 'real deal' while Holzman was seen as a stuffy business type.

Chapter 6

Rothchild arrived at Elektra Records in 1963 at a critical period in its history. Elektra was expanding into folk and was already eyeing the growing folk-rock scene in Los Angeles. Rothchild was a key player in Holzman's and Elektra's expansion and in the first two years of Rothchild's tenure as a producer, Holzman kept him busy in the studio until Rothchild was arrested in 1965 for possession of marijuana. Rothchild had to serve eight months of prison time but Holzman kept him on the payroll. When Rothchild was released from prison, Holzman was moving Elektra towards rock 'n' roll and had him work on The Butterfield Blues Bands' second album *East-West* which has been hailed as an early example of 'acid rock'.

When Holzman started scouting L.A. bands he was hindered because of the conditions of Rothchild's parole, but by August of 1966 he was able to bring Rothchild to L.A. to see The Doors. The Doors had come to the attention of Holzman from Arthur Lee of *Love*. At first Rothchild wasn't impressed with The Doors, but upon seeing a second show he saw the literary influences and the dark theatre the band possessed. Rothchild went into the studio with The Doors and by all accounts worked with the band as an equal (in an age when the producer was the final authority in the studio), listening to what the band wanted to accomplish as well as making suggestions. Rothchild was willing to experiment along with the band suggesting a section of Robby Krieger's guitar be played backwards on a song, or putting a microphone in an empty garbage can while everyone shouted into it. He was also a perfectionist in the studio. As Jim Morrison's alcoholism and behavior in the studio grew more erratic, he clashed with Rothchild's perfectionism which resulted in longer and longer periods of time to create an album's worth of songs. The clash of wills came to a head in *The Soft Parade* sessions during which Rothchild said he practically had to piece together songs from the many takes. Rothchild produced all The Doors' albums except *L.A. Woman*. During rehearsals for *L.A. Woman* he said the music reminded him of "cocktail lounge music". Rothchild's leaving The Doors allowed them to regroup and find themselves as a band again, thus enabling them to make one of the classic albums of rock 'n' roll.

As a producer for Elektra Records Rothchild worked on everything from folk albums to rock 'n' roll. He produced either albums or singles for groups such as The Lovin' Spoonful, Neil Young, Bonnie Raitt, Tim Buckley, and Love. Holzman also gave Rothchild the leeway (and money) to experiment as a producer. A band that Rothchild was closely aligned with was Clear Light whom he produced immediately after The Doors' first album. Clear Light was notable because it had two drummers. One of those drummers, Dallas Taylor, would join The Doors onstage at the Felt Forum in January of 1970. Doug Lubahn was also a member of Clear Light and at one point was offered the opportunity to join The Doors as the bass player which he turned down to remain in Clear Light.

Another band Rothchild was deeply involved with was Rhinoceros. Rhinoceros was an idea for a "super group" that Paul would build from scratch. His idea was to audition L.A. musicians and pick the very best for the group. Jac Holzman said "Paul believed super groups were a big deal." Rhinoceros produced one self-titled album which included *Apricot Brandy*, a song that that was licensed for a Bob Hope special. Holzman thought Rhinoceros was "contrived" and a "paint by the numbers" group.

After The Doors, Paul Rothchild is probably most famous for producing Janis Joplin's *Pearl* album, which brought Joplin her only number one hit single with *Me and Bobby McGee*, achieved posthumously. Rothchild also produced the soundtrack for the movie *The Rose* which was based loosely on Joplin's life.

Paul Rothchild died of lung cancer on April 30, 1995 at the age of 59, and will be remembered for the body of work he produced and the artists for whom he helped bring out the best in their recordings.

Pam Courson

Pam Courson was Jim Morrison's "cosmic mate" and common-law wife. She was also his muse, and he wrote songs, such as *Love Street*, for and about her. She also appears in *Celebration of the Lizard* in the lines "Her dark red hair/The white soft skin." The lines: "Keep your eyes on the road/Your hands upon the wheel" in *Roadhouse Blues* were reportedly driving instructions Morrison gave Courson. Morrison's final ode to Courson was in the song *Orange County Suite*. On April 25, 1974, Courson died of a reported heroin overdose.

Courson was born in Weed, California, on December 22, 1946, and lived the rock 'n' roll lifestyle much as Morrison did. Before she met Morrison she was rebelling on her own, cutting classes in school, smoking cigarettes and hitchhiking to L.A. It isn't known when she met Morrison. Oliver Stone's Doors movie has Jim and Pam meeting on Venice Beach, Ray Manzarek says it was at The London Fog. Even before she met Morrison, Courson was interested in design and fashion and with Morrison's money she opened a boutique on Santa Monica Boulevard called *Themis*. Morrison invested heavily to decorate the shop, it had feathers on the ceiling, and soon Pam was buying the hippest clothes from around the world.

Pam was also Morrison's equal in daring and adventure, including driving without headlights on Mulholland Drive (a winding road). She was also well read. Their relationship was volatile and they frequently had arguments with Pam throwing plates and cups at Morrison (Morrison told people "That chick has one hell of an arm."). Both Courson and Morrison were involved with others but always came back to each other. Pam was also involved in drugs, and her drug of choice seemed to be heroin. Pam was with Jim in Paris in the spring of 1971 when he died mysteriously in the bathtub.

Pam is also supposed to have inspired other 60's Sunset Strip era singer/songwriters. Neil Young's *Cinnamon Girl* is rumored to have been written about Pam. There's also supposition that The Eagles based the song *Hotel California* on Pam and Morrison's relationship.

After Morrison died, Pam took it badly and blamed herself for his death. Many think that Morrison may have gotten into Pam's heroin, and in combination with the alcohol in his system - it arrested his heart. Ray Manzarek recalls seeing her once after Jim's death and all she could do was cry while Manzarek held her.

Courson's life after Morrison spiraled out of control. She sued The Doors for Morrison's share of the royalties while some people allege she took to prostitution. Such claims are unverified, and seem to come from those with an animus towards Courson. Danny Sugerman, in *Wonderland Avenue*, reports that Pam had taken up with a UCLA film student who had started a band, trying to relive the early years with Morrison. Shortly before her death, Pam won her lawsuit with The Doors and was recognized as his heir. One thing that is undeniable is that she became more involved in drugs until, in an almost self-fulfilling prophecy, she died on April 25, 1974, like Jim Morrison at the age of 27.

The Doors enthrall Danny Sugerman

On October 6, 1967, The Doors played the Cal State Gymnasium. The summer of '67 had been a big one for the band: *Light My Fire* hit number one on the *Billboard Magazine* charts, they had appeared on the *Ed Sullivan show*, shot publicity photos with Joel Brodsky (which included Morrison's 'young lion' photographs), played Steve Paul's The Scene to rave reviews, appeared on the *Murray the K* TV show, and their second album *Strange Days* had been released. But none of these milestones is what sets the date at Cal State apart. What sets October 6th apart is that it is the concert where future Doors' manager Danny

Sugerman first saw The Doors in concert, encountered Jim Morrison, and became enthralled with the band.

In 1967 Sugerman was a twelve year old Los Angeles wild child (Indeed Doors' keyboardist Ray Manzarek claims Jim Morrison wrote the song *Wild Child* about Sugerman) who was having problems with his step-father and needed to escape the house. Evan Parker was Sugerman's little league umpire and a friend of The Doors' roadie Bill Siddons (Siddons would later become The Doors' manager) and during a little league game, Sugerman was at bat. In his best Babe Ruth bravado he decided to call his shot and said he was going to hit a home run. Parker said that if he did that, he'd take him to see The Doors that night. Sugerman hit a home run.

Good to his word Parker took him to the concert. Parker helped Siddons as a roadie, and enlisted Sugerman to help with the equipment. As Siddons and Parker started taking equipment into the gymnasium they left Sugerman to unload the van. It was then that Sugerman encountered a lean shadowy figure with long brown hair who accused him of stealing the equipment. It was, of course, Jim Morrison. Parker later told Sugerman, "That was Jim Morrison, you two oughta really get along. He's crazier than you are." After Sugerman had helped setup the stage for the band, it was past the start time for The Doors to go on. Sugerman who was just loitering around backstage was suddenly charged by Siddons to run downstairs to the band's dressing room and tell them it was time to start the show or they'd be in default of their contract. Sugerman ran the message down to the waiting band and was told to tell Siddons that waiting is good for the audience. Sugerman ran this circuit three more times until The Doors consented to start the show.

After the band came upstairs Sugerman found a seat in a front row close to the stage. The band started to play but Sugerman didn't see the shadowy figure from the parking lot, and then there was a scream and Morrison lurched onto the stage screaming with the sound of a "thousand curtains torn" and he crumpled to the stage while the band played on. Then he jumped straight up, approached the microphone and opened his mouth as if he were about to sing (some members of Andy Warhol's factory saw Morrison do this in New York and thought it a cheap way to draw an audience in), then backed away from the microphone. As the music continued to build, Morrison started singing *When the Music's Over*. Sugerman later wrote in his autobiography, *Wonderland Avenue*, "It was the end. It was the end of the world as I had known it. Nothing would ever be the same for me again."

Chapter 6

Sugerman went on to hang out at The Doors' office so much that Morrison gave him a job answering fan mail. He also gave Sugerman an interview, typing out a list of questions and told Sugerman to read them and add more if he thought of any other questions to ask them. They taped the interview and Morrison got the tape transcribed and later published in a rock magazine under Sugerman's byline.

Jim Morrison died when Danny was just 16 years old. He took Jim's death hard, grieved for him deeply, and in an effort to keep him close, started to emulate the wild, excessive, self-destructive side of his hero. Danny knew better than most that Jim also had another side and once said that Jim was "a better teacher than a role model." In the haze of not knowing which direction to take at this sudden fork in the road, he chose the path he thought would hurt the least. Being numb to reality sure seemed less painful than having to stare it in the eye and deal with it. "The road of excess leads to the palace of wisdom," William Blake once wrote, and Danny had watched Jim Morrison go down that road. If it was good enough for Jim, he figured, it was good enough for him. Except, of course, that Jim Morrison never reached that palace of wisdom. Jim Morrison simply died.

Sugerman's passion for The Doors didn't lessen with Jim's death. It intensified. With unending energy and persistence, he spent the better part of the next thirty years keeping the music of The Doors and the memory of Jim Morrison alive. He became The Doors' manager, a title he wore with pride, second only to the first title he had worn and would always wear: that of their number one fan.

When Sugerman found out Jerry Hopkins had written a biography of Jim Morrison, he shopped it around until he found a publisher that sparked The Doors' resurrection of the early 80's (it's been rumored that Sugerman along with Ray Manzarek added to the more sensational elements of the book). Danny himself authored two books about The Doors, *The Illustrated History* and *The Complete Lyrics*, as well as his own stunning, often funny and chilling, autobiography *Wonderland Avenue*. It told the story of his childhood - his time with The Doors before and after Jim Morrison's death - and his battle with drug addiction and subsequent recovery. He has been credited by fans all over the world for helping them beat their own drug addictions. Sugerman also wrote the book *Appetite for Destruction* about the band Guns 'n' Roses.

Danny Sugerman died at the age of 50 on January 5, 2005 after a long battle with cancer. He was survived by his wife Fawn Hall of Iran-Contra/Oliver North infamy. Doors' drummer, John Densmore, who visited Danny shortly before his death was quoted by Reuters news service as saying: "Danny was the number one Doors fan of the world. I told him no one loved Jim as much as he did." And Densmore was right. In one of Danny's last e-mails to a friend, he talked about

Jim Morrison leaving for Paris in March 1971. He said they talked for a few minutes, and Danny asked Jim if he'd ever see him again. "Count on it Danny," was the reply that he got. "I've been counting on it my whole fucking life," Danny wrote to his friend. Here's hoping it happened for him.

Robert Gover

Robert Gover has a story to tell. Well, a few actually. He's a critically acclaimed author for his novel *The $100 Misunderstanding*, about a college boy who meets up with a teenage prostitute and events push them together for twenty-four hours. Published in 1961 it was hailed as a novel that challenged racial stereotypes. Other novels include *The Manic Responsible* which examines the 'why' of a rape-murder case and which was hailed by *Newsweek* as "a work of art". Gover also has many stories about the people he has met and befriended over the lifetime of an author. He corresponded with his literary hero Henry Miller, James Baldwin tried to talk him into moving to Paris, he had a few drinks with Norman Mailer, Gore Vidal served him cheese, he was kicked out of a restaurant with Bob Dylan, and he was arrested in Las Vegas with Jim Morrison.

You may remember the tale of his arrest with Jim Morrison from the essay, *A Hell of a Way to Peddle Poems* which he wrote for Frank Lisciandro's *An Hour for Magic*. In 1967 Gover got a call from the editor of *The New York Times Magazine* asking him if he'd like to write an article about an up and coming rock band called The Doors, and their lead singer Jim Morrison. Gover agreed and met with Morrison. However, he disagreed with the editor's angle that Morrison was a creation of the Hollywood hype machine and he was taken off the assignment. He and Morrison became friends. Morrison dropped by Gover's house on the beach at all hours of the day or night, crashing on a couch, reading over Gover's shoulder as he wrote a novel, and engaging in philosophical conversations. Morrison suggested that he write a screenplay of Gover's *The Maniac Responsible* that Morrison would also star in and direct. At the time the novel was already optioned to a producer and nothing more came of it. On one of his visits Morrison said he'd never been to Las Vegas, so Gover volunteered to give Jim the tour of Vegas, including dinner and a show. Little did Gover know Morrison was going to be the show.

Gover took his girlfriend Beverly along and Morrison was supposed to bring Pam Courson, but prior to leaving Morrison and Courson got into an argument and the trio went to Vegas sans Courson. Dinner in Vegas was uneventful and afterward their party headed to a club called The Pussycat. Upon arrival Morrison lit a cigarette smoking it like a joint. One of the bouncers, seeing a racially mixed group with a couple of 'longhairs' pulled a billyclub out and hit Morrison over the head and he started bleeding. After that, chaos ensued. The club's security people called the police and upon their arrival they saw the bleeding Morrison and assumed he was the source of the trouble and arrested him. They also arrested Gover on the general principle that since he also had long hair he should be arrested. During the ride to the police station Morrison's demons kicked in and he started baiting the police. He wouldn't stop even after they threatened "a date" after their shift was over, a not so subtle euphemism for being worked over. After booking, Morrison's behavior didn't abate and perhaps got worse. Luckily, Gover's girlfriend bailed them out before the end of the cops' shift.

Gover lost touch with Morrison after Morrison asked him to accompany The Doors on their European tour in '68 to document it for a book. With his novel to finish, Gover took a pass and a disappointed Morrison sent his copy of *The Maniac Responsible* back to Gover without a note. He never heard from Morrison again.

More recently, Gover has been writing non-fiction books on 'Astrological Economics' and has returned to fiction. His most recent is *Two Brothers* which, like *The $100 Misunderstanding*, tells a story from two different points of view. *Two Brothers* can best be described as an economic thriller, perhaps a genre he has invented. It's about two brothers, Robert and John, whose fortunes in life have drastically changed. The dashing, athletic Robert ends up destitute in a mental hospital. John the awkward, introverted brother makes a literal fortune. As Robert and John struggle to reconnect with each other after decades of separation, they're hounded by a murderous private security guard trying to blackmail John, and who succeeds in kidnapping his girlfriend. Like its author's life, it's a novel that will keep you guessing as to what happens next.

Jim Morrison's Father Dies

On November 17, 2008, Rear Admiral George Stephen "Steve" Morrison died at age 89. Steve Morrison was Jim Morrison's father.

Steve Morrison was born in Rome, Georgia, on January 7, 1919. Morrison entered the U.S. Naval Academy in 1938, graduating in the spring of 1941. He was assigned to the minelayer Pruitt, at Pearl Harbor, and witnessed the Japanese attack on Pearl Harbor on December 7, 1941.

Morrison met Clara Clarke in Hawaii in 1941 on a blind date. They were married in April of 1942. After the attack on Pearl Harbor, Morrison applied for flight training and was transferred to Pensacola, Florida, where on December 8, 1943, his and Clara's first son, James Douglas Morrison, was born. The Morrisons had two other children Anne and Andy Morrison. After graduating from flight school in 1944 Morrison was stationed in the South Pacific for the duration of the war, while Clara and son Jim lived with Morrison's parents in Florida.

After the war Morrison was assigned to secret nuclear weapons projects in Albuquerque, New Mexico. It was while the Morrison family was moving to New Mexico that they witnessed the aftermath of a car crash in which a truckload of Indian workers were hurt. This incident greatly affected the young Jim Morrison (approximately four years old) and he later related that he had the sensation of the souls of one or two of the Indians jumping into his own soul. He became distraught and his mother calmed him by telling him it was all a dream, probably cementing the incident in young Jim's mind. After Jim's death the family was asked about the incident and they didn't give it much credence, chalking it up to Jim's active imagination. In the *Indian and the Coyote* Jim mentioned the incident stuck with him because he realized his parents didn't know what was happening any more than he did, and it was the first time "I tasted fear."

The Morrison family moved frequently as Steve Morrison's career advanced. During the Korean War, Morrison was assigned to Seoul, Korea, and took part in actions against the North Korean and Chinese earning him a Bronze Star. In 1958 Morrison was promoted to Captain and assigned to the Pentagon. It was in Alexandria that the young Jim Morrison's reading intensified and he would often steal away to the Library of Congress to find and read arcane books, as well as sneaking off to the blues bars outside of town. In 1963 Morrison was given command of the aircraft carrier Bon Homme Richard. During this command a teenaged Jim Morrison visited his father on the ship and was struck by how his father had absolute command, giving the order for the ship to leave the harbor with a barely perceptible nod. In stark contrast at home his mother was in charge and the Captain took orders from her.

After Jim attended the UCLA film school and graduated he, along with fellow student Ray Manzarek, started The Doors. Jim wrote home to his parents and told them of his plans to be a singer. His father replied that he thought it was a "crock" and that Jim was wasting his time. Jim never spoke to his parents again. After The Doors' first album was released, Jim's brother, Andy brought home a copy and he and his parents listened to it while Steve Morrison read the evening paper. When it came to the Oedipal section of *The End*, the newspaper began to shake in sublimated fury. Steve Morrison never publically commented on Jim or The Doors until he was interviewed for the book *The Doors* by The Doors in 2005.

As Jim Morrison was graduating from UCLA and living on a rooftop, writing the first songs/poems that would become the basis of The Doors, Steve Morrison was at the Gulf of Tonkin Incident that escalated the Vietnam War. In 1966 Morrison was promoted to Rear Admiral at the age of 46. In his later career Morrison was named Commander Naval Forces Marianas and was in charge of relief efforts for Vietnamese refugees after the fall of Saigon. Morrison retired from active service in 1975.

Admiral Morrison was the keynote speaker at the decommissioning ceremony of the Bon Homme Richard on July 3, 1971, the same day his son, Jim Morrison, died in Paris.

An Actor Out On Loan: Tom Baker

Tom Baker is a rarely examined character from Jim Morrison's life even though he was there at pivotal points. Although he is mentioned in most, if not all, of the Morrison biographies, he is only seen in Morrison's shadow (except for possibly the Phoenix flight incident). New Doors fans mistake him for the British actor Tom Baker, who played Dr. Who. Even though he wrote an autobiography, it is hard to find information about him (except for an excerpt that appeared in *High Times*) so most material is sifted out and gleaned from the Morrison biographies.

Tom Baker was born August 23, 1940, and he had a lot in common with Jim Morrison. Baker's father was also a military man, Baker shared Morrison's propensity for drinking and finding trouble (or if you prefer 'adventure seeking'), they shared Pam Courson for a while and, almost as intimately, they shared jail time.

In 1966 Baker had been living in New York working as a bartender, and acting in off-Broadway plays, and had been instrumental in the stage adaptation of Norman Mailer's *Deer Park*. In November of 1966 he was offered a seven year contract with Universal Studios, and moved to Los Angeles. Baker met Pam Courson when he moved into an apartment in Laurel Canyon. Morrison and Courson were his neighbors, and he met Courson within minutes of moving in and quickly began a relationship with her (ironically Morrison was in New York with The Doors at the time). When Morrison returned to L.A. he and Baker talked about art and Norman Mailer and developed a friendship. Baker's relationship with Courson ended when he asked her to move in with him and not see Morrison anymore, Courson stuck with Morrison.

Baker's seven year contract with Universal quickly went nowhere and Baker returned to New York where, unable to find work, he appeared in Andy Warhol's film *I, A Man* (it has been rumored that Baker only got the part because Jim Morrison, in turning down Warhol, recommended Baker). In 1970 Baker directed his own movie *Bongo Wolf's Revenge* which included music by The Doors and Mike Bloomfield, and he recruited Morrison's UCLA film school friends Paul Ferrara, Frank Lisciandro and Babe Hill to work on the crew.

Baker is most widely known from his and Morrison's 1970 arrest aboard an airplane heading for Phoenix - for interfering with the operations of a flight crew. Baker had been the main instigator of the incident but Morrison felt that since he was famous and the well-known face he had unfairly taken the rap for Baker. Morrison paid for their bail and defense. After they were acquitted from the Phoenix charges Baker didn't see Morrison until eight months later, shortly before Morrison left for Paris.

After Morrison's death Baker saw Pam Courson a few times and she seemed to be delving deeper into drugs and alcohol each time. Baker also claims that Courson called him the night before she died making tentative plans to see him the next day but when he called the phone was answered by her mother and she told Baker that Pam had died.

For his own part Baker also followed the road to dissipation and an OD. He was found dead on September 2, 1982, on the lower east side of New York in a house known as a heroin shooting gallery.

Although Baker will probably be remembered as a friend of Jim Morrison he was also a part of the jet-set working in New York with Andy Warhol and Norman Mailer, as well as Los Angeles. Other projects took him to London and Paris to work. His life and his death also influenced other writers and artists - his death is the starting point of the Kinky Freeman novel *Elvis, Jesus & Coca-Cola*, and the documentary filmmaker Jana Bokova includes a scene in her film *Hollywood* of two actors sitting in Schwab's Drugstore talking about Baker's death.

Chapter 6

Harrison Ford and The Doors

Harrison Ford, born on July 10, 1942, in Chicago, Illinois, is best known for his roles as Han Solo and Indiana Jones. Ford kicked around Hollywood for a long time before making it big as Solo in George Lucas' *Star Wars*. In fact, Ford arrived in Hollywood in 1964 and was hired by Columbia Pictures and placed in their 'New Talent' program where he got a little work in uncredited parts or as an extra. With a wife and children to support he worked as a carpenter relying on his talents as an actor to convince people that he knew what he was doing as a carpenter (when he didn't have vast experience in that profession). In one anecdote he recalls telling George Lucas that he knew how to build a roof when in fact he didn't. When he was hired to build the roof he learned how to do so by taking a book on carpentry to the job with him.

Other carpentry jobs led him into contact with The Doors' world. He worked for Elektra Records' founder Jac Holzman. In his book, *Follow The Music*, Holzman tells a story of Ford building the in-house studio for him. This contact may have led him to work as a grip on The Doors' *Feast of Friends*, or it is possible that Ford met Paul Ferrara through film channels. Ferrara worked in the film industry for many years after UCLA film school. Dennis Jakob, Jim Morrison's UCLA roommate, also had ties to Francis Ford Coppola (Ford appeared in a cameo in *Apocalypse Now*). Ford could have met Ferrara through any or all of these contacts. In the *Feast of Friends* footage, Ford is visible in a few scenes, most notably the 'Fred L. Stagmeyer minister at large' scene that was included in *The Soft Parade*. Ford is briefly visible as Jim Morrison turns to talk with the traveling minister (the Stagmeyer scene is fairly hilarious and should be watched on its own).

In another sort of Doors connection, Ford had an uncredited role in Michelangelo Antonioni's film *Zabriskie Point*, a movie The Doors were asked to write a song for. The result was *L'America*, but Antonioni rejected the song for the film.

Harrison Ford may rejoin The Doors, this time in a starring capacity. Ford has been mentioned as a possibility to star in the feature film version of Ray Manzarek's novel, *A Poet in Exile*.

Patti Smith Meets Jim Morrison

Patti Smith has always been an admirer of Jim Morrison, the poet. Indeed, one of the first things that brought Smith to the public's attention was her poetic review of *An American Prayer*. In her 2010 memoir, *Just Kids*, Smith briefly mentions Morrison's influence on her. The CBS television show *Sunday Morning* had Smith on as a guest for an hour long feature on April 1, 2012, during which she elaborated on Jim Morrison.

In that hour, Smith, interviewed by Anthony Mason, was asked about Morrison's influence on her. She saw The Doors live in 1967 and upon seeing Morrison's performance thought, "I could do that!" (Jim Osterberg upon seeing The Doors had the same epiphany). Smith went on to explain that it wasn't because the show was bad or anything, but she felt a kinship with Morrison, and that maybe rock 'n' roll was something she could do. She also recalled her salad days when she and Robert Mapplethorpe couldn't afford food and she would crash rock bands' press parties and put food from the buffet tables into a plastic bag. She described meeting Jim Morrison at the press party after the Felt Forum show in January 1970. She was going through the buffet table when she heard a voice say: "The hamburgers are good too," and she looked up to see Morrison sitting by himself. She was too stunned to say anything, and the only thing she thought to do was take a hamburger.

Happy Birthday Jac Holzman

Jac Holzman started Elektra Records in his college dorm room and at the start his equipment was World War II surplus. He recorded albums in his apartment and artists' living rooms then delivered the albums to record stores on the back of his Vespa scooter. In the 1950's he recorded folk singers and sound effect records. In the 1960's he signed The Doors to Elektra, a move that would make The Doors an internationally known group and make Elektra both artistically and monetarily successful.

Jac Holzman was born on September 15, 1931, and grew up in New York City. His father was an emotionally distant but domineering force in his life. In order to escape, young Holzman discovered movies seeing "eight out of ten Hollywood movies made every year…" For Holzman the movies provided the emotional stability he sought. Another escape was an early graduation from high school at the age of 16. He attended St. John's in Annapolis, Maryland, a college chosen by Holzman's father, which was far enough away for Holzman's freedom and close enough for his Father to think it would keep young Jac in check from his "mischief".

Holzman was introduced to folk music by his college roommate and soon discovered Woody Guthrie, Burl Ives, Leadbelly and a host of others with folk music taking the place of movies in Holzman's life. Holzman was a diffident student at the same time, caught up in the intellectual opportunities that being away from home offered. Barely passing the yearly entrance exams the school required, the headmaster 'suggested' Holzman take a year off to discover where his particular genius lay. By then Holzman had already taken the initial steps of creating Elektra Records and with new freedom plunged headlong into making a success of the enterprise.

Elektra wasn't only a product of Holzman's ambition or the rise of interest in folk music, but also and probably most importantly a change of technology. Because of the war, equipment was made to be portable and that included recording equipment, which after the war flooded into Army surplus stores. Besides intellectual pursuits, Holzman had a technical interest and was able to tinker with the equipment treated badly through war use, and was able to cobble together pieces to make what he called "some quite sophisticated equipment". It was a time of an explosion in technology that the average person would not see again until home computers became available, both bringing a democratization and freedom with them. This is the period when many of the record companies that would become big record companies in the 60's due to rock 'n' roll were created.

Holzman named the record company after of the Greek demi-goddess, Elektra, who avenged her father's death and presided over the muses. It is also the feminine mirror story to Oedipus, a story Jim Morrison was remarkably familiar with.

Holzman's parents bought him a portable disc recorder after attending a recital of literary readings by Georgiana Bannister in which she was accompanied on piano by John Gruen. He convinced Bannister and Gruen to record with his still formative record company, they agreed, and Holzman recorded them. He took the tapes to RCA for mastering and pressing, paying a $40 fee. On the album cover Jac Holzman was listed as producer. Elektra Records had begun.

During the 50's Holzman became a well-known figure on the Greenwich Village and New York folk scene, and it was there that he met Paul Rothchild. Both Holzman and Rothchild were impressed by one another. Over the years the two kept in touch with Holzman thinking Rothchild had more street savvy then he did, at least as far as the folk scene was concerned. The artists trusted Rothchild who they saw as one of them while Holzman was seen as more of a businessman. In 1963 Holzman was able to bring Rothchild over to Elektra and the stage was set for rock 'n' roll and The Doors.

By the mid-60's Holzman, who kept his ear to the ground regarding music, started to hear rumblings about the growing rock 'n' roll scene in Los Angeles. Holzman had already put his toe in the rock 'n' roll waters when in 1965 he released *The Baroque Beatles Book,* an album of Lennon-McCartney songs interpreted in a Baroque style by Josh Rifkin (Holzman met with Lennon and McCartney to secure their blessings for the project). Holzman started to frequent the L.A. clubs and was soon courting the band Love for Elektra. He had started hearing about a band called The Doors and when they became the house band at the Whisky a Go-Go in May of 1966, Holzman went to see the band a few times. He finally began to see the potential in them when they played the *Alabama Song* from the Kurt Weill Bertolt Brecht play, *Rise and Fall of the City of Mahoganny*. Holzman saw the literary and intellectual component of the band. Shortly thereafter he brought Paul Rothchild from New York to Los Angeles to see the band, which was good timing because, only a few days later, The Doors were fired by The Whisky for Jim Morrison's Oedipal section addition to *The End.*

The Doors brought Elektra their first number one single with *Light My Fire* and thereafter Elektra became a force to be reckoned with in the music industry signing acts such as the MC5, Iggy Pop, Queen, and Tim Buckley. Holzman merged Elektra with Warner Communications in 1970 and The Doors remained on Elektra Records until 1974 when Holzman gave them their freedom by giving them the rights to their catalog; a move which has secured the band members financially for the rest of their lives.

In the intervening years Holzman has by no means retired. He's been active in the music, TV and film industry in some capacity. In the 1970's his Pioneer Electronics adopted the compact disc (CD) and laserdisc, in 1979 he worked with former Monkee Mike Nesmith to develop an idea of Nesmith's called PopClips which was the first iteration of what would later become MTV.

A complete telling of Jac Holzman's story and his accomplishments would take up a whole book, as a matter of fact, a couple of books. If you would like to read a good history of Holzman and Elektra Records check out the books: *Follow the Music*, and/or *Becoming Elektra*. Holzman is still very much a part of The Doors world. He frequently appears with band members at movie premieres and award ceremonies. John Densmore gave the speech for Holzman's induction into the

Rock Hall of Fame in March of 2011. The Doors are very much the legacy of Holzman and they're both moving that legacy forward into the future.

Influence is a two way street. The Doors influenced those around them and were also influenced by those around them. Before they became The Doors, they were young artists absorbing the culture around them. It affected not only how they perceived the world but affected *who* and *what* The Doors would become.

7

The Doors' Influences

The Doors were a band heavily influenced by literature. Some of the literary influences are well documented, such as the band's name coming from Aldous Huxley, alongside quotations from William Blake, Celine, Rimbaud, and Kerouac. But there are also some obscure influences on The Doors. In this chapter we'll take a look at some of those influences: known and unknown, the obscure and the obvious.

Weldon Kees, the Lost Literary Influence of Jim Morrison

Most Doors fans know that Jim Morrison's ambition in life was to be taken seriously as a poet. Even his going to the Venice Beach rooftop to write what would more or less become the lyrics for The Doors' first two albums was more the act of the poet seeking a garret than someone planning to start a rock band.

The Doors were a very literary band and when they became famous they practically released a reading list for fans, mentioning the beats such as Jack Kerouac, Arthur Rimbaud, Baudelaire, and Hart Crane to name only a few. Morrison himself befriended beat poets Allen Ginsburg (whose influence you see in Morrison's poems) and Michael McClure. As a teenager, Morrison visited Lawrence Ferlinghetti's City Lights Bookstore in San Francisco when his family lived there. He was also surely aware of Kenneth Rexroth who was well known in the bay area for hosting a 'salon' in his house where poets, local and visiting, stopped by for wine, reading and commiseration. A poet we have never heard in connection with Jim Morrison is Weldon Kees, a man who was as restless as Morrison in finding new avenues of artistic expression, and whose death/disappearance is more mysterious than Morrison's own in Paris.

Weldon Kees was born in Beatrice, Nebraska, on February 24, 1914. On the heels of the successful release of his first book of poems, *The Last Man*, he moved to New York in 1943 and began making the social scene there, attending the parties of Edmund Wilson and Lionel Trilling. His writings, mostly fiction, started to appear in magazines like the *New York Times*, *The New Republic*, *Partisan Review*, *Poetry*, and *Furioso*. Despite his success Kees never felt comfortable in the literary scene and started to paint. Influenced by abstract expressionists like Willem de Kooning, his paintings hung in galleries next to Picasso. Ever restless in 1947 he published another book of poems, *The Fall of the Magician*.

Dissatisfied with life in New York, Kees moved to San Francisco where he started playing New Orleans style jazz and was good enough to play professionally. He also developed an interest in experimental filmmaking and provided soundtracks for others' films. He still maintained an interest in poetry, reading at places such as Kenneth Rexroth's house. The story of his disappearance was recently the subject of the New Yorker article *The Disappearing Poet*. The agreed upon facts are these: on July 19, 1955, his car was found on the north side of the Golden Gate Bridge, keys still in the ignition, suicide presumed. Prior to his disappearance, however, he told friends that, like Hart Crane, he wanted to disappear into Mexico and that "sometimes a person needs to change his life completely." Upon searching his apartment all that was found was his cat (named Lonesome) and a pair of red socks in the sink. His bank account was emptied and his sleeping bag was missing.

Besides these biographical details and similarities that would have attracted Morrison, what else is there to lead us to believe Kees was an influence on Jim Morrison? Two poems, one of Kees' and one of Morrison's.

"Subtitle"

We present for you this evening

A movie of death: observe

These scenes chipped celluloid

reveals unsponsored and tax-free

We request these things only

All gum must be placed beneath the seats

or swallowed quickly, all popcorn sacks

must be left in the foyer. The doors

Will remain closed throughout

The performance. Kindly consult

Your programs: observe that

there are no exits. This is

A necessary precaution

Look for no dialogue, or for the

Sound of any human voice: we have seen fit

To synchronize this play with

Squealing of pigs, slow sounds of guns

The sharp dead click

Chapter 7

Of empty chocolatebar machines.

We say again: there are

no exits here, no guards to bribe,

No washroom windows.

No finis to the film unless

the ending is your own

Turn off the lights, remind

The operator of his union card:

Sit forward, let the screen reveal

Your heritage, the logic of your destiny.

Weldon Kees, 1935

And Jim Morrison's *The Movie* which was first on *An American Prayer*:

> The Movie will begin in five moments,
>
> The mindless voice announced,
>
> All those unseated will await the next show.
>
> We filed slowly, languidly into the hall.
>
> The auditorium was vast and silent.
>
> As we seated and were darkened, the voice continued:
>
> The program for this evening is not new,
>
> You've seen this entertainment through and through.
>
> You've seen your birth, your life and death,
>
> You might recall all the rest.
>
> Did you have a good world when you died?
>
> Enough to base a movie on?

As you can see the subject is an identical theme, sitting in a movie theater and seeing your life projected on the screen for you and others to watch. The ideas of no exiting, locked doors, and the end are all things that would have attracted Morrison, and ideas he used time and again in his lyrics and poetry. The structure is similar with Morrison's having a more musical quality to it. I think it's safe to assume that we can add Weldon Kees to the list of influences on Jim Morrison, if not biographically then poetically. I don't know about you but I think this is a very exciting find and I've already ordered my copy of Kees' biography, *The Vanished Act: The Life and Art of Weldon Kees* by James Reidel.

Chapter 7

Jim Morrison and Jack Kerouac Part 1

"I suppose if Jack Kerouac had never written 'On The Road', The Doors never would have existed." Ray Manzarek

Manzarek might have added that if Jack Kerouac hadn't written *On The Road*, none of the late 60's might have happened the way they did, with kids hitting the road in search of themselves and the transcendental experiences that Kerouac had described in his novels.

On The Road came out at a very formative period for the baby boomer generation, 1957, and depending on what year you consider the start of the baby boom, they were in their early to late teens. The draw to Kerouac was almost irresistible. The romantic descriptions of Dean Moriarty and Sal Paradise's travels across the country, meeting people and adventures head on as they traveled a road seeking some sort of enlightenment; they weren't sure of what it was, but would recognize it when it happened. Kerouac's visceral descriptions of music coincided with Elvis and the birth of rock 'n' roll. Even though Kerouac was describing jazz instruments and playing, Kerouac saw the correlation between his writing and rock 'n' roll, urging his publisher to get *On The Road* published before the rock 'n' roll "fad" had passed.

On The Road opened up the possibilities of the world to a generation when they came of age, they sought the enlightenment and destinations Kerouac had described. For Jim Morrison *On The Road* may have opened a world of thought for him. All of Kerouac's characters talk about Rimbaud, Nietzsche, William Blake, Kafka and Baudelaire, all writers that would become stated favorites of Morrison's. Reading *On The Road* makes one wonder if a young Jim Morrison may have adopted Dean Moriarty as the model for his persona.

All the biographies of Jim Morrison acknowledge that he started hitchhiking when he was at St. Petersburg Junior College. He would hitch to FSU every weekend to visit Mary Werebelow, or he hitchhiked west to visit his family for Thanksgiving. Morrison had adventures like meeting a cousin of LBJ's and going to a barbecue, or with a friend hitching a ride with a woman who seemed to be willing to have sex with one or both of them. This was more than transportation for Morrison, it was a way to seek adventure and experience; he was known to turn down rides from people that didn't look "interesting".

Kerouac's descriptions of Moriarty could have well applied as much to Jim Morrison as to Kerouac's character. "My first impression of Dean was of a young Gene Autry - trim, thin hipped, blue eyed with a real Oklahoma accent - a side burned hero of the snowy west." Or the often quoted, "The only people for me are the mad ones, the ones who are mad to live, mad to talk, mad to be saved, desirous of everything at the same time, the ones who never yawn or say a commonplace thing, but burn, burn, burn, like fabulous yellow roman candles exploding like spiders across the stars and in the middle you see the blue center light pop and everybody goes 'Awww!'" Morrison paraphrased this to describe himself, "I see myself as a huge fiery comet, a shooting star. Everyone stops, points up and gasps, "Oh look at that!" then - whoosh, and I'm gone... and they'll never see anything like it ever again... and they won't be able to forget me - ever."

Jim Morrison and Jack Kerouac Part 2

We want to meet our heroes, and we want our heroes to meet. We engage in this kind of intellectual game all the time. What if Jesus and Gandhi got together for a chat? Or Karl Marx and Thomas Jefferson? Or da Vinci and Van Gogh? Or Einstein and Marilyn Monroe? Or even Alien vs. Predator!

Did Jim Morrison meet Jack Kerouac? There is some anecdotal evidence to suggest he may have. The first instance may be pure happenstance as Kerouac and Morrison lived in the Clearwater, Florida, area at the same time 1961-1962, and Morrison is said to have haunted some of the same coffee houses Kerouac did, namely the House of Seven Sorrows Café and the Beaux Arts. Both are known to have frequented the establishments, so both Morrison and Kerouac being there at the same time is not entirely inconceivable. Kerouac is known at times to have had teen fans hanging out with him. It's tempting to imagine a teenaged Morrison sharing a beer with Kerouac and listening to him talk literature. Or would Morrison have reacted like he did when he lived in San Francisco and saw Lawrence Ferlinghetti outside the City Lights Bookstore? Morrison became shy and couldn't introduce himself.

One Kerouac biography (*Subterranean Kerouac* by Ellis Amburn) has Morrison trying to visit Kerouac at his Lowell, Massachusetts, house in 1968. In the anecdote, a leather clad and long haired Morrison is left standing on Kerouac's front porch by Kerouac's mother who didn't like hippies and wouldn't let him in because his hair was too long (shades of his father!). By that time, Kerouac had become insular and insulated and didn't approve of hippies or what he thought was their disrespectful attitude towards America. Did this incident happen? Amburn's biography may not be the most factually definitive Kerouac biography. Amburn did know Kerouac, and was his last editor, but the book offers no documentation of the incident. Although, in his defense, all the people in the anecdote act within their known character traits and personalities.

If Jim Morrison and Jack Kerouac ever did meet accidentally in Clearwater it was never recorded, and if Morrison did seek Kerouac after he achieved fame he may not have gotten past Kerouac's mother who may have been a more irresistible force than even Morrison's parents. We may never know if they met but we can always wonder, what if?

Did Jim Morrison Name Alice Cooper?

I'll be the first to admit this falls into the realm of supposition. It can't be proved and I don't think it can be disproved (which is the beauty of it). But I think I can make a case for Jim Morrison telling fledgling rocker Vincent Furnier the story of Alice Cooper.

Vincent Furnier, who later named his band and himself Alice Cooper, was from Phoenix, Arizona, where he had been a member of high school and garage bands. The first band was the Earwigs which, despite having the name of an annoying insect, was an homage to The Beatles. The group dressed like The Beatles and because the band didn't know how to play their instruments they mimed. After making the jump of learning how to actually play instruments the group renamed themselves The Spiders and frequently played with a spider web backdrop behind them. It seems as if Furnier and the band always had a bent towards the dark side. They recorded a song that became a local hit, moved to Los Angeles, and changed their name to The Nazz.

Upon arriving in L.A. they fell in with some well-established L.A. bands. Frank Zappa wanted to produce The Nazz, and the group met The Doors. They also discovered that Todd Rundgren already had a band called The Nazz - so Furnier's group needed a new name. There are a lot of suggestions as to how the band came up with the name Alice Cooper. Cooper (Furnier adopted the name Alice Cooper as his own in the 70's) himself has offered several versions of where the name came from.

I've been reading Alice Cooper biographies to see where Furnier might have run across the name Alice Cooper, but none offers a good explanation. Some theories over the years are that Furnier and the band got the name when they were messing around with a Ouija board, another is that Furnier is the reincarnation of a 17th century witch burned at the stake (the most common explanation), the name came from newspapers of a murdered girl, or even that the band picked it because they thought it sounded like the name of a nice innocent girl who had an axe behind her back.

At the very least the name just appeared and was adopted. Listening to a radio interview with Alice a few years ago the DJ took questions from callers and one caller asked if Alice knew Jim Morrison. The most Alice would say is that he "had a few beers with the man." That got me to thinking. I could easily imagine Furnier and Morrison sitting in a bar talking about Furnier's need for a band name and Morrison mentions Alice Cooper (the witch). It is known that Jim Morrison, in his high school years in Alexandria, Virginia, went to the Library of Congress and read up on arcane subjects like the occult and demonology. So it is more than likely that Jim Morrison would have known of a witch burned at the stake named Alice Cooper.

The Doors and Elvis

"Elvis had sex-wise/mature voice at 19."
Jim Morrison, *As I Look Back*, from *The American Night*.

Jim Morrison and Elvis Presley, each an icon of the type of rock music they represent. Elvis, the "King" of rock 'n' roll, the first successful rock 'n' roll star to make it to the national market. And Jim Morrison, the Lizard King of acid rock.

Elvis is a near unanimous influence for the baby boom generation. Bob Dylan described hearing Elvis for the first time as, "like busting out of jail." The Beatles were so nervous upon meeting Elvis they got high and tripped over their own words in his presence. For the boomers Elvis was a clarion call against the conformity of the 50's. Elvis was a bellwether for the baby boomers, his obvious sexually charged performances communicated in his hip gyrating movements and stage shows. Elvis crossed the color line in choosing his influences, everything from gospel to country. He was pushing on the barriers that the baby boom generation later advocated, free-love and equality of the races, and would batter down those barriers.

Members of The Doors weren't immune from Elvis' influence. Ray Manzarek frequently mentions in interviews hearing Elvis for the first time and calling it a life changing event. Friends of Jim Morrison would attest to his Elvis impersonation, a homage you can hear in *When the Music's Over*, during the line "I hear a very gentle sound."

The Doors are known as a band that didn't have a bass player, but in the studio that frequently wasn't the case. The Doors hired session musicians or brought in musicians they wanted to work with. For the first Doors' album, Larry Knechtel played bass on the album. Knechtel a member of the famous 'Wrecking Crew' (Los Angeles session musicians who worked with a lot of high profile bands and singers) had worked with Elvis on sessions. A more conscious attempt on The Doors part to connect with Elvis was in the hiring of Jerry Scheff for the *L.A. Woman* sessions. Scheff had played on Elvis' *Double Trouble* soundtrack and later played with Elvis on his first Las Vegas shows. Having Scheff playing on *L.A. Woman* stood out enough in Morrison's mind to mention it in his impromptu interview with *Rolling Stone* reporter Ben Fong-Torres.

The doors of influence swings both ways. Jim Morrison was of course well known for his leather suits and in Elvis' 1968 Comeback Special, in the live portion of the show, Elvis wore a suit of leathers. Did Elvis do that in some sort of recognition of the rockers he influenced?

In the book *Elvis My Brother* by Billy Stanley, Stanley reports a conversation with Elvis about Morrison and The Doors in which Elvis said: "But Jim Morrison had special abilities.... He was the new poet laureate... But he died before he could understand his power and what he could do with it. That's a tragedy. So much unspoken. Just like James Dean."

JFK's Assassination and Jim Morrison

The assassination of President John F. Kennedy deeply affected people. When the news became public, people remembered exactly where they were when they heard the news. It was also an awakening of sorts for the baby boom generation that Morrison was part of. Almost instantaneously conspiracy theories manifested and many to this day can't be convinced otherwise that the assassination wasn't part of a grand conspiracy.

Jim Morrison himself seemed to have been obsessed by the assassination, or at least deeply affected by it. Morrison's poetry doesn't lend itself easily to autobiographical interpretation but Kennedy's assassination seems to be a different matter and references can be found throughout Morrison's poetry and thoughts.

The Lords and The New Creatures was Morrison's first volume of poetry that he wrote, while still in college, as a paper on the cinema. A lot of the poems concern assassins, and snipers. In passages such as: "The sniper's rifle is an extension of his eye. He kills with an injurious vision" Oswald himself is mentioned:

> Modern circles of Hell: Oswald (?) kills President.
> Oswald enters taxi. Oswald stops at rooming house.
> Oswald leaves taxi. Oswald kills Officer Tippit.
> Oswald sheds jacket. Oswald is captured.
> He escaped into a movie house.

This obsession stayed with Morrison after forming The Doors. When The Doors went to England in 1968 Morrison was quoted as saying, "...especially in the States you have to be a politician or an assassin to really be a superstar." The most famous usage of the Kennedy assassination imagery was in the song *Not to Touch the Earth* with the lines "Dead President's corpse in the driver's car/The engine runs on glue and tar." *Not to Touch the Earth* was a section from the larger *Celebration of the Lizard* which was a poetic journey across a desolate frontier. In an introduction to *Celebration*, during a Doors concert, Morrison told the audience to imagine this as a group of people coming together at night and telling their tales around a campfire. Did Morrison think assassination would become an important theme in America, or did he see it as something that would become a recurring event in American politics?

William Blake in Doors History

"If the doors of perception were cleansed everything would appear to man as it is. Infinite." William Blake, from *The Marriage of Heaven and Hell.*

Doors fans know this is the poetic epigram that English poet and mystic William Blake wrote that inspired The Doors name, but few know the man or his art that has inspired for almost 200 years. Since Blake was so influential in the naming of The Doors and Jim Morrison's thinking, and information about Blake isn't widely known, we'll take a look at this influence on The Doors.

Born November 28, 1757, William Blake claimed to have religious visions from an early age, the iconology of which he may have picked up from his parents' belief and his reading of the Bible. One day while walking in the countryside, at age eight, he saw a tree filled with angels. When he told his parents, he was almost beaten by his father for lying, but fortunately his mother intervened. The visions proved to be a lifelong accompaniment and in later years he claimed to talk with deceased relatives and archangels.

Blake found an early affinity for drawing and poetry, drawing pictures of Greek antiquities from illustrations his father bought him. In turn, early examples of Blake's poetry demonstrate a knowledge of Ben Jonson and Edmund Spenser. Instead of sending the boy to school, his parents enrolled him in drawing classes and he was allowed to read whatever and wherever his curiosity led. As was the practice of the day, he was apprenticed at age fourteen to an engraver where he learned the trade that would sustain him through life and provide a vehicle for the realization of his visions.

Blake was not much in step with his times. Because of his opinions and artistic aesthetic, he found himself opposite his contemporaries and the public at large, and was never successful or well-known during his lifetime for his poetry. Blake published his first volume of poetry in 1783 and during his lifetime found several patrons that supported him and his work, as well as commissioning others. At age thirty-one Blake started using relief etching which he placed alongside his poems, a technique that is known as illuminated manuscripts. This is the medium Blake is best known for and his most striking work comes to us from that period in which he produced *The Marriage of Heaven and Hell*, *Songs of Innocence and Experience*, and *Jerusalem.*

Blake also had a close marriage to his wife Catherine, who was illiterate when they married but Blake taught her to read and write and even how to engrave and she was known to help Blake in his later years. Blake died as mystically as he had lived his life. After working all day he drew a picture of his wife, told her he would be with her always, and died singing hymns of visions he was seeing.

Blake's influence on Jim Morrison is obvious; besides taking the Doors name from Blake's quote, he also liked the Blake quote: "The road of excess leads to the palace of wisdom," and lived his life adhering to that philosophy. Blake has also been an influence on our culture and writers of the last fifty years. Blake is credited with inspiring Allen Ginsberg (who claimed his own Blakean visions), Bob Dylan, and writers like Philip Jose Farmer in his *World of Tiers trilogy.* Blake's drawings also come to us in popular culture, his drawing the *Ancient of Days* is frequently referenced on TV and in films.

William Blake died August 12, 1827, at the age of 69 with his wife at his side.

Gene Vincent

Early rocker Gene Vincent was born February 11, 1935. Vincent was not only an early player in the nascent rock 'n' roll world with hits like *Be-Bop-A-Lula* but was also an influence on The Doors and Jim Morrison. Vincent was the first rock star to wear full leather suits onstage.

Vincent was born Vincent Eugene Craddock in Norfolk, Virginia, and counts many of the same influences as Elvis did, namely rhythm and blues, gospel, and country music. He received his first guitar when he was twelve years old. The young Vincent also had some things in common with Jim Morrison, the first being the Navy. Vincent dropped out of high school and joined the Navy at age seventeen, where he proved to be a good sailor, and while he never saw action he is credited with a deployment during the American involvement in the Korean War. He was also known as being a troublemaker when on liberty. Vincent was planning on making a career outside the Navy and with a $612 re-enlistment bonus bought a Triumph motorcycle. In July 1955 he was involved in a severe motorcycle accident that almost caused the amputation of his left leg. He refused to allow his leg to be amputated and the leg was saved, but due to the extent of his injuries Vincent was discharged from the Navy.

Following his discharge Vincent became involved in the Norfolk music scene, changed his name to Gene Vincent, and formed the rockabilly group: Gene Vincent and the Blue Caps. The band proved quickly to be successful. Vincent and the Blue Caps played local Norfolk country bars and won a talent contest that gained the band a manager. In 1956 Vincent wrote *Be-Bop-A-Lula*, and was signed by Capitol Records which released the song, and it gained national airplay and attention - peaking at number seven on *Billboard's* pop charts. Vincent was unable to follow up *Be-Bop-A-Lula* with another hit although he had critically acclaimed songs such as *Race with the Devil*, and *Bluejean Bop*. In another parallel to Morrison's career, Vincent was convicted of public obscenity and fined $10,000 for an erotic performance of the song *Woman Love*.

In 1959, Vincent, after a dispute with the IRS, left for England where he started appearing in leather suits, and where he became a well-known popular act. Could Vincent have influenced the early Beatles' leather look as well as Jim Morrison's later style? In April 1960, Vincent was in the same car that killed rock star and early guitar hero Eddie Cochran. Vincent survived the crash, but reinjured his leg.

As the 60's rolled around and music changed in a post-Beatles world Vincent found his efforts to reestablish his career were unsuccessful although he did tour throughout the 60's and played at the 1969 Toronto Rock 'n' Roll Revival along with The Doors (see related articles) where he and Morrison met and Morrison hung out with Vincent for a while afterwards. In a final coincidence between Vincent and Morrison, Vincent outlived Morrison by three months dying in October of 1971 from a ruptured stomach ulcer. Vincent was later inducted into the Rockabilly Hall of Fame, as well as the Rock 'n' Roll Hall of Fame.

The Story of Bo Diddley

In 2008, the world lost one of the innovators, if not one of the creators of rock 'n' roll. Bo Diddley. Diddley influenced everyone from Buddy Holly, to the Rolling Stones, The Animals, Jimi Hendrix, and The Doors.

Born December 30, 1928, as Ellas Otha Bates, he later recorded and wrote songs as Ellas McDaniel. Like many of the famous bluesmen he was born in Mississippi and moved to Chicago as a child where, as a member of the Ebenezer Baptist Church, he learned to play the trombone and the violin. It wasn't until he attended a local Pentecostal church that he learned to play the guitar and heard the throbbing beat that would become his trademark. After he saw John Lee Hooker playing, he was inspired to take up playing and by the time he was fifteen he had carved out a niche for himself playing on Maxwell Street in Chicago. By the time he was twenty-three he had a regular spot at the 708 Club, and by the time he was twenty-five had started recording for Chess Records.

At Chess he took the name Bo Diddley. The name wasn't meaningless, it could have been derived from a 'Diddley bow' which was a stringed instrument of African origin, or more likely it came from the American slang 'bo diddley' meaning "absolutely nothing". Could music and Bo Diddley have been an early example of Jim Morrison's "activities that seem to have no meaning?"

In 1955, Diddley appeared on the Ed Sullivan show and instead of singing the Sullivan requested song *Sixteen Tons*, sang the song *Bo Diddley* drawing Sullivan's ire. He was never asked to appear on the show again. Despite that, Diddley continued to record for Chess records, producing eleven albums between 1958 and 1963. As rock 'n' roll started to grow, Diddley was able to 'crossover' to white audiences and appeared in Alan Freed's rock shows and started touring in England where the young Rolling Stones opened for him. He also encountered The Animals and they were moved to record *The Story of Bo Diddley*.

After rock 'n' roll became the dominant musical entertainment, Diddley appeared with the Grateful Dead, The Doors, The Rolling Stones, The Clash, Sheryl Crow, and Robert Cray. He also appeared in the *Blues Brothers* movie as well as *Trading Places*.

The Doors covered many of their idols, including Willie Dixon, John Lee Hooker and Diddley's *Who Do You Love?* In fact, *Who Do You Love?* may be the first rock 'n' roll horror song with lyrics like "I walked forty-seven miles of barbed wire," "Used a cobra snake for a neck tie," "Got a brand new house on the roadside/Made out of rattlesnake hide/I got a brand new chimney made on top/Made of human skulls," and a couple of lyrics that may have appealed to Jim Morrison: "I got a tombstone hand and a graveyard mind/I'm twenty-two and I don't mind dying."

The Doors changed *Who Do You Love?* from the rollicking rocker that Diddley had made and turned it into a languid waltz through love. Diddley covered *Love Her Madly* for The Doors' 2000 release *Stoned Immaculate* but it would have been more interesting if Diddley had covered The Doors' cover of *Who Do You Love?*

Bo Diddley died of heart failure on June 2, 2008.

Another heavy influence on Jim Morrison and Ray Manzarek's lives was movies, and film. After Morrison and Manzarek met at the UCLA film school their interest in film didn't abate, it extended into their career with The Doors, and past. The Doors music has been included in movies and their career has inspired feature films.

8

The Doors at The Movies

Ray Manzarek and Jim Morrison were film students at UCLA when they met. They both had an abiding interest in film and the past masters as well as creating a new cinema. Through The Doors they did create cinema. At first, one strictly of The Doors, but as their influence and legend spread through culture they, in turn, inspired those that were creating movies.

The Doors Film *Feast of Friends*

Late in March 1968 (the exact date is unknown) The Doors decided to film a documentary of their forthcoming tour. The idea may have come about because Bobby Neuwirth, who was hired to hang out with Jim and try to direct his energies to more productive pursuits than drinking, produced a film *Not to Touch the Earth* that utilized behind the scenes film of The Doors.

The band set up an initial budget of $20,000 for the project. Former UCLA film students Jim Morrison and Ray Manzarek hired film school friends Paul Ferrara as director of photography, Frank Lisciandro as editor, and Morrison friend Babe Hill as the sound recorder. The first show shot, for what would be later named *Feast of Friends,* was the April 13th performance at the Santa Rosa Fairgrounds. Overall shooting of the film lasted for five months between March and September, and captured the riots in Cleveland and the Singer Bowl. Filming culminated in Saratoga Springs, New York, where backstage Morrison goofed around on a warm up piano and improvised a hilarious ode to Frederick Nietzsche.

After filming started, the concept grew and *Feast of Friends* was to incorporate fictional scenes (some version of *HWY*?). But problems started to arise. The live sound, in parts, was unusable so the decision was made to use the album cuts of Doors songs. The budget grew by another $10,000 and the film still wasn't finished. A decision was made by Ray, Robby and John to pull the plug on the film, but Paul Ferrara appealed to Jim and a compromise was worked out. The fictional scenes would be dropped and another $4,000 was added to the budget to complete the editing.

The completed film runs to about thirty-eight minutes and is mostly images taken from different shows, or the band prior to a show. It has some footage of the Singer Bowl riot, which shows the riot in full flower, the stage crowded with policemen and fans. Occasionally, Morrison comes out of nowhere to encourage it all. The centerpiece of the film is *The End* from the Hollywood Bowl show. The film suffers a bit from not using live sound, the superimposition of album cuts of songs (except the Hollywood Bowl footage) removes the viewer from the immediacy and impact of The Doors.

Feast of Friends was later accepted at five major film festivals, including the Atlanta International Film Festival that Frank Lisciandro describes in *An Hour For Magic*.

In later years *Feast of Friends* was shelved, missing the late 70's midnight movie circuit showing rock films. In the 80's with the advent of MTV, Ray Manzarek started producing videos of Doors songs for showing on MTV and they relied heavily on the *Feast of Friends* footage. Chances are that even if you haven't seen *Feast of Friends* you've seen a lot of the footage.

Jim Morrison Films *HWY*

The Doors had laid low for just over a month. On March 1, 1969, the 'Miami Incident' had occurred, at first with no reaction more than any other Doors show, and the band went off on a prearranged Jamaican vacation in anticipation of the national tour that faced them. But word of the concert, and Morrison's alleged exposure, started getting out. By March 3rd, WTVJ in Miami ran an editorial decrying the show and asked what authorities were going to do about it. By March 5th, The Doors heard the first echoes of the concert when the Dade County Sheriff's Department issued a warrant for Jim Morrison's arrest. Concerts were cancelled, radio stations pulled Doors songs, and magazines and newspapers ran stories vilifying Morrison and The Doors.

But Jim Morrison was determined not to lie fallow. In mid-March of '69 he went into the Elektra studios and recorded poems that would later be used on The Doors album *An American Prayer*. On, or about, April 4th Jim started filming *HWY* with UCLA film school friends Frank Lisciandro, Paul Ferrara, and Babe Hill as his production team. They went into the Palm Springs desert and over the course of the next few days filmed *HWY.*

HWY was based on a screenplay written by Jim called *The Hitchhiker: An American Pastoral* (which was later published in *The American Night*). *The Hitchhiker* starts with a prelude of the character named Billy in a barroom talking about going to L.A. to earn some money. He starts hitching to L.A., he's picked up by a businessman who makes a sexual advance towards him. Billy pulls a gun on the man and kills him in the desert. As Billy continues on his journey he goes on a killing spree until he gets to L.A. where he meets up with friends that can only be described as archetypes and they move to a transcendental ending to the film.

HWY doesn't follow the screenplay exactly, it's more like they were filming the desert scenes of *The Hitchhiker* and were allowing for a lot of freedom in the filming. When they ran across something interesting, they filmed it, like Jim dancing with some Indian kids. The *HWY* that comes to us today runs just over forty minutes in length and was meant by Morrison to be used to generate financing to make a feature length version of the film, one that would be closer presumably to the screenplay Morrison had written.

Also during the filming they came across a coyote pup that was hit by a car and lay dying on the highway and they filmed it and incorporated it into *HWY.* After filming was done Jim was sitting around with Lisciandro, Ferrara, and Hill having a beer and one of them was running a tape recorder as Jim, moved by the death of the coyote, related the story of the Indians bleeding on dawn's highway incident he experienced when he was a child. The excerpt of Jim talking about the accident with the truck of Indian workers was later incorporated into *An American Prayer*, and Morrison very vividly describes the over-turned truck and how it affected him and, more importantly, how it still seemed to affect him and his world view.

Chapter 8

Feast of Friends Wins at Atlanta International Film Festival

June 20, 1969, Jim Morrison accepts the Golden Phoenix Award for *Feast of Friends* at the 2nd Annual Atlanta International Film Festival.

The Doors had entered *Feast of Friends* in film festivals across the country and won a number of awards and honors which Morrison took as vindication for the investment in shooting the film. The Atlanta International Film Festival ran from June 16-21 with the award ceremony being held on the evening of the 20th. Both Jim Morrison and Frank Lisciandro attended the event.

The screening of *Feast of Friends* not only sold out but saw the organizers having to add another screening to accommodate all the fans who wanted to see it. Lisciandro describes the day in Atlanta in his book *An Hour for Magic*. Some of the highlights of the day included meeting with the organizer of the film festival who had a rare (for the time) mobile phone in his briefcase which Morrison wanted to try out by calling a local DJ. Then the festival organizer took them out to lunch with Ted Turner, after which they went to a rent party in the 'hippie' section of Atlanta, and then to the award ceremony itself. Morrison and Lisciandro were seated with the producers of Atlanta TV commercials who didn't like the fact that they were seated with hippies who made "X-perri-mental films". Morrison magnanimously ordered bottles of Pouilly Fuissé for the table and proceeded to drink water tumblers full of the wine. Upon receiving the award, a tipsy Morrison traded his room key with the voluptuous girl presenting the award.

Other films screened at the Atlanta International Film Festival that also received awards were George Lucas' USC student film *THX-1138* and Steven Speilberg's film *Amblin'* which seems a distant cousin to Morrison's *HWY*, in that *Amblin'* is also a story of a hitchhiker in the desert.

The Jim Morrison Film Festival

Poppin' magazine hosted the "Jim Morrison Film Festival" which showed Morrison's newly finished film *Hiway* (later be retitled *HWY* and which had, of course, started life as *The Hitchhiker*). The festival was held on March 27, 1970. Despite a rash of logistical problems, all The Doors' films were shown including: *Feast of Friends*, the films The Doors made for the songs *Break on Through*, and

Unknown Soldier, as well as the Granada Television documentary *The Doors are Open.*

Poppin' magazine was a rock magazine out of Vancouver, British Columbia, Canada that was trying to expand into the U.S. but which had run into cash flow problems. One of the owners of the magazine, Hank Zevallos, knew Jim Morrison because of an article Zevallos wrote praising Morrison, the artist, instead of the sex symbol, and Morrison contacted him. Zevallos mentioned his problem to Morrison who suggested having a benefit for the magazine that would include a poetry reading and a showing of *Hiway*.

Zevallos quickly hired a theater in Vancouver and flew down to Los Angeles to work out the details of the benefit. The first problem he encountered was the length of the film itself. When they originally discussed the film it was assumed that *Hiway* was going to be a feature length movie, i.e. at least ninety minutes long, but when he was talking with Morrison in L.A., he discovered that the movie would only be an hour in length (the version we have now is only about fifteen minutes long). Therefore they came up with the "Jim Morrison Film Festival" idea that would include Morrison's and Manzarek's UCLA films. In the end, the UCLA films fell through, leaving only The Doors' films of the songs and documentaries, but those were enough to fill out a program.

As the date of the festival approached it turned out Morrison wouldn't be able to attend because of Doors' commitments. Then a larger problem presented itself, the print of *Hiway* was a 35mm film, but the equipment at the movie theater they rented out was only for 16mm films. They hit upon the rather unique solution of hiring a nearby theater that had the proper equipment to use after the theater's last show. Then the audience at the Jim Morrison Film Festival would leave the first theater after seeing the other films and walk the couple of blocks to the second theater where *Hiway* was to be screened. The audience was told this was a stipulation of Morrison in loaning the film to the Festival; Morrison had wanted the audience to participate in the film in some way.

Hiway was received with silence at its conclusion. The benefit of the "Jim Morrison Film Festival wasn't enough to save *Poppin'* and the magazine later folded.

Chapter 8

The Doors and *Apocalypse Now*

We're supposed to have six degrees of separation from any other person on the planet (or from Kevin Bacon), but in Los Angeles proximity makes it a lot less than six degrees. The fact that Jim Morrison and Ray Manzarek were UCLA film students gave them ties and connections to the Hollywood film industry that came of age in the early 70's.

It's fairly well known by Doors fans that Harrison Ford, before he became famous as Han Solo in *Star Wars*, worked on The Doors' film *Feast of Friends* (see chapter 6) as a gaffer (Ford also worked for Jac Holzman as a carpenter and built him a cabinet, as well as building a studio for Elektra recording artist Cyrus Faryar). Ford also had a cameo in Francis Ford Coppola's *Apocalypse Now*.

The writer/director John Milius said he wrote *Apocalypse Now* listening to Richard Wagner and The Doors. Another connection to The Doors and Francis Ford Coppola and *Apocalypse Now* is a lot closer - Dennis Jakob. Jakob was Jim Morrison's roommate at UCLA for a time, and Morrison first proposed starting a rock band to Jakob called *The Doors: Open and Closed*. It was also Dennis Jakob who gave Morrison access to the rooftop of the building on Venice Beach where Morrison took LSD and wrote the songs that became the backbone of The Doors.

Jakob later went to work for Francis Ford Coppola and was a close associate. It has long been rumored that it was Jakob who suggested to Coppola that he use *The End* in *Apocalypse Now*. Jakob, a character unto himself, apparently took exception to how *Apocalypse Now* was being edited and at night would sneak in and reedit the film. After Coppola told him to stop it, Jakob stole part of the work print, burned it, and sent Coppola the ashes each day for a week.

A rock 'n' roll note: George Lucas was a cameraman for the Rolling Stones' film *Gimme Shelter* and at Altamont. According to John Milius' it was Lucas who filmed the Hell's Angels beating and killing Meredith Hunter. For his part, Lucas has said he doesn't remember.

Oliver Stone's *The Doors* Reconsidered

With the release of *When You're Strange* on April 9, 2010, I thought it might be interesting to take a look back at the first Doors movie, Oliver Stone's *The Doors*.

Over the years *The Doors* has been a much maligned film. Sometimes fairly, and sometimes unfairly. The reasons for this vary as well.

One of the main reasons for antipathy towards this movie is that The Doors themselves, especially Ray Manzarek, have railed against it. John Densmore and Robby Krieger may have been disappointed with the film, but Manzarek has much more personal reasons for his dislike of the movie. Like Densmore and Krieger, Manzarek was an advisor to the film (and may have even had a cameo in it like they did), but his approach to 'advising' brought him into conflict with Oliver Stone. Manzarek has said that he thought The Doors movie would be a good idea and that Stone would be open to ideas from Manzarek. When Stone rebuffed further input, Manzarek tried to lobby Stone, but Stone soon asked him to leave the set for good. Since then Manzarek has pointed out the shortcomings and deficiencies of the film stating that Stone missed Morrison altogether, that the Jim Morrison of the film was a Jim Morrison of Stone's own creation and fantasies, which may be true. But isn't that how we all see Jim Morrison, the reflection we want to see?

All of Stone's movies have been accused of gross inaccuracies in fact. Perhaps they're being looked at incorrectly. They should be considered allegorical. Certainly, *Platoon* is a symbolic battle for the good and evil of an average soldier's soul. Maybe *The Doors* is supposed to be the same thing, how the intentions of hippies and those ideals started naively, innocently, but they became lost in their own excesses much as Jim Morrison did. This isn't meant to say the movie is successful at that. I think, ultimately, Stone missed the mark and *The Doors* is something less than he intended.

There is a shooting script of *The Doors* movie posted online. It's an early draft of the script, and there are some interesting differences compared to the movie that was released. The first is that more of Jim Morrison's poetry was included in the draft. A poet was how Morrison wanted to be remembered and it appears that's how they wanted to present Morrison: The Poet. But somewhere along the line most of the poetry was taken out of the movie. Also, it seems that the Coursons (Pam Courson's parents who own the rights to Morrison's poetry) had a disagreement with Stone over how their daughter would be portrayed and reneged on their approval to use more of Morrison's poetry. The personal conflicts between the members of The Doors is included in the early draft but not the movie. The original screenwriter of *The Doors* was Randall Jahnson (credited in the movie as J. Randall Jahanson). He was commissioned in the mid-80's to write the screenplay but his screenplay was shelved. When Oliver Stone came into the picture he decided to use Jahnson's screenplay as his starting point, but as time and events went on during the shooting of the movie, the storyline evolved.

It is fair to say *The Doors* has its share of shortcomings. One of those is the interjection of Doors lyrics as dialogue, and the movie drags in the middle. But the movie has been unfairly criticized as sensationalizing Jim Morrison and portraying him as a drunken buffoon. Jim Morrison was acutely aware of his persona and the manipulation of it, and he may have done his fair share to help propagate the myth. He's reported by Elektra publicists as asking them if they thought he had accumulated enough of a mythic reputation to carry the band into the future. Later, he may have regretted that approach, and he told Salli Stevenson in their *Circus Magazine* interview that if he could have done it over he would have chosen: "…the quiet, undemonstrative artist, plodding away in his own garden." The fact is that *The Doors* movie uses the same outline as *No One Here Gets Out Alive* did and for that matter *When You're Strange* does. It's a narrative that has been used almost since The Doors' inception.

Another problem may just be one of perception; that we may be looking at *The Doors* in the wrong context. *The Doors* might not strictly be meant to be a biography of The Doors or Jim Morrison, but might serve as an archetype or allegorical story of the times. It can be argued that Oliver Stone had put together a trilogy of movies that were meant to reflect the overall experiences of the 60's. *Platoon* is the experience of Vietnam, *JFK* is the loss of faith in government that started with the Kennedy assassination, and *The Doors* is supposed to represent the hedonistic side of the 60's, LSD, and the hippie experience. All three movies provide a view of the 60's from beginning to end and cover the gamut of the '60's experience. During the 80's, Doors' guitarist Robby Krieger was saying any movie about Jim Morrison should be surrealistic. You can kind of see that in the story of Morrison, how a person gets wrapped in the swirl of fame and celebrity and the very real place they started seems a distant shore. I think *The Doors* tries to present the surreal/impressionistic feel of The Doors in the use of montages to illustrate how Jim Morrison's, "This is the strangest life I've ever known", felt to him.

Amongst the other members of the 60's rock 'n' roll trinity of Jim Morrison, Jimi Hendrix and Janis Joplin, there still hasn't been a credible bio-pic of Hendrix, and every few years a Janis Joplin movie is announced starring whomever the hot new actress is (in the years before *The Doors* was filmed just about every big name male star was said to be interested in, or attached to, the movie). Whatever the intentions of *The Doors* movie were, or how it was brought to fruition, it did bring a new generation of fans to The Doors' music.

The Doors in the Movies

The Doors' music was informed by film. The Doors' music can be seen as a dark, noir-esque soundtrack for the times, and filmmakers have agreed. The Doors' music sets the tone and atmosphere of the 60's.

After The Doors became one of the biggest bands in America with *Light My Fire* in the summer of '67 - offers came in from all sides. Jim Morrison was approached by stars such as Paul Newman and Steve McQueen but the projects were never followed up on. Until, that is, they were approached by Michael Antonioni for his film *Zabriskie Point*. The Doors wrote the song *L'America* with the film in mind and auditioned it for Antonioni, but he didn't like it and passed on it. The Doors later used the song on the album *L.A. Woman.*

Hollywood of the 70's didn't offer The Doors much opportunity for their music in major mainstream movies. Legend has it that Francis Ford Coppola met Jim Morrison at UCLA, which is more than possible because Coppola was leaving the film school right about the same time Morrison was entering it. As mentioned above, Coppola used The Doors' *The End* over the introductory scenes of *Apocalypse Now* in what is probably one of the best usages of a soundtrack melded to the images on the screen. Coppola set the tone of the movie with surrealistic images, and Morrison's haunting voice intoning "The End" hang over those scenes like the smoke billowing from the napalmed jungle.

Light My Fire is probably The Doors' most recognizable song and Coppola filmed a scene for *Apocalypse Now* that had the native followers of Kurtz singing the song although the scene was edited out of the finished film. A film that did use *Light My Fire* is the 1980 movie *Altered States. Altered States* is about a college professor who is chasing existential experience down to its primal origins through the use of hallucinogens. Anyone remotely familiar with Morrison's biography would recognize Morrison might have had some interest in a film such as this (had he lived to fulfill his dream of making films) because Morrison was interested in the nature of reality and how we perceive it. In the party scene where William Hurt meets his love interest, Blair Brown, the instrumental solos section of *Light My Fire* is playing in the background. If you don't know it's there, you could miss it.

Forrest Gump is virtually a rock 'n' roll movie. It has Forrest bumping into not only Elvis and John Lennon, but the movie is stuffed with Doors songs from *Soul Kitchen* as Forrest marches through Vietnam, to *Hello, I Love You* and *Love Her Madly* summing up the 70's.

The Lost Boys were enamored of Jim Morrison. They had the 'Jim Morrison, American Poet' poster on their cave wall, and had the Echo and Bunnymen cover of *People Are Strange* on the soundtrack.

And 'Jim Morrison' has shown up in such movies as *Death Becomes Her*, and *Wayne's World 2.*

Every year new movies come out that use The Doors on the soundtrack. Not only do the songs set the tone or mood for a movie, but The Doors carry a hip cachet that a lot of people and movies want to benefit from. Here are some movies that have used Doors' songs, in no particular order: *Neighbors, Strange Days, The Banger Sisters, The School of Rock, Jarhead, Roadhouse, The Basketball Diaries,* and *Taking Woodstock.* That's only a partial list and the list grows every year.

When You're Strange

Man, there's been a lot said about this movie, then there's the word, and the word is, get *When You're Strange.*

When You're Strange isn't a true documentary in the sense of a Ken Burns style of documentary, an intensive, exhaustive look into a subject. *When You're Strange* starts with scenes of Jim Morrison's *HWY* and uses the conceit of Morrison hearing the announcement of his own death in Paris. The movie tells The Doors' story from UCLA on, and touches quickly on each member's childhood, moving chronologically through The Doors' career. This is The Doors through The Doors' own lens, almost literally. All the footage derives from *HWY* and the concert film *Feast of Friends.* We also see footage from Ray Manzarek's student films, 60's period footage for context, and there's some previously unseen footage, except for maybe the hardcore collectors.

For years Doors fans have been asking when, where, and if Jim Morrison's *HWY* and *Feast of Friends* will be released. *When You're Strange* is the movie Doors fans have been asking for. Writer/Director Tom DiCillo (*Johnny Suede, Delirious*) intricately weaves together *HWY* and *Feast of Friends* and provides a narrative the footage has lacked before. Perhaps if Jim Morrison had lived, combining the two might have been a solution he would have chosen. DiCillo also makes choices that are a little riskier in presentation. As an example, he doesn't use the songs and the footage as obviously as before. Usually, *Riders On The Storm* is presented with images of thunderclouds and storms but DiCillo chooses images of Vietnamese jungles flowering in explosion.

The footage from *HWY* and *Feast* has been restored and it looks as good as it did, if not better than, when it was shot forty years ago. Not only has the film been restored, so has the sound and it seems as though things have been pulled from the background. You can hear things that were previously only muttered or obscured by crowd noises. The complete effect of the film is a much more immediate, impressionistic, visceral view of The Doors than before.

Narration for *When You're Strange* is provided by Johnny Depp. Although it is a little basic and simplistic, and at times intrusive, it has to be because there isn't enough expository footage to move the narrative along without adding the intrusion of contemporary or even period interviews. Depp's narration is subtle and understated. Depp's phrasing, while not overly dramatic, has the timing of the poetic.

While a lot of fans and The Doors themselves were critical of Oliver Stone's movie, this movie has been 'Doors approved' (they've given their seal of approval) so it won't suffer the backlash Stone's movie has. Regardless, I think the fans are going to like it too, and may consider it the definitive version/vision of the band.

Bonus Features: Filmed interviews of Jim Morrison's family were made and were going to be used in the movie before DiCillo came onboard and employed a different narrative tack. These interviews are the bonus features. One missed opportunity is that the unedited versions of *HWY* and *Feast of Friends* aren't included as bonus features. It would've been cool for fans to have these and see them in context as they were intended.

Role Cast in Fictional Jim Morrison Film

December 15, 2010, Director Robert Saitzyk has announced he has cast actress Virginie Ledoyen for his forthcoming film *The Last Beat*.

The Last Beat is a fictional look at the last days of an American rock star, Jay Douglas, and his girlfriend, and is based on Jim Morrison and girlfriend Pam Courson.

Ledoyen is known for her role in *The Beach*, which starred Leonardo DiCaprio, but in *The Last Beat* Ledoyen will play a French countess named Clemence who forms one corner of a love triangle. Taking the role of Jay Douglas is Shawn Andrews. Andrews has appeared in the films *Dazed and Confused*, *City of Ghosts* (starring Matt Dillon), and Saitzyk's *After the Flood*. No one has been cast in the Courson role as of yet. Filming of *The Last Beat* is expected to start in the late spring of 2011 and is to be shot on location in Paris with a release date of 2013.

Saitzyk is best known for directing thrillers such as *Godspeed*, *After the Flood*, and *White of Winter*. *The Last Beat* may be a departure for him with the film promising to be more like Gus Van Sant's *Last Days*, a fictional look at the last days of Kurt Cobain.

Casting *The Last Beat* Nears Completion

April 26, 2011, Director Robert Saitzyk has finished casting the major roles for his film *The Last Beat*.

Yesterday Saitzyk announced the casting of the remaining major roles. The newly cast Cameron Richardson will be taking the role of Valerie Eason, which is based loosely on Jim Morrison's 'cosmic mate' Pam Courson. Saitzyk described Richardson as having: "true depth and soul." Richardson has previously appeared in the movies *Open Water 2: Adrift*, *Rise: Blood Hunter*, and *Alvin and The Chipmunks*.

Also joining the cast are Kevin Corrigan (*The Departed*) whose character Saitzyk intriguingly describes as: "A blend of Ken Kesey and John the Baptist." Seymour Cassel will have a cameo in the movie. Cassel is best known for his work in John Cassavetes' film *Faces* for which he was nominated for an Oscar for Best Supporting Actor. Cassel has said he once had the opportunity to appear with Jim Morrison at the Cinematheque poetry reading which was a benefit to raise funds for Norman Mailer's 1969 New York mayoral campaign.

Cyndi Lauper Cast in *The Last Beat*

June 10, 2011, Director Robert Saitzyk has announced that Cyndi Lauper has joined the cast of his film *The Last Beat*.

Lauper will play a character named Bebe Markham; who and how this character fits into the film is still unknown. The two main women in the film, "Valerie Eason" who is Jay Douglas' girlfriend and soul mate will be played by Cameron

Richardson. The role of "Clemence" has been filled by French actress Virginie Ledoyen.

Lauper is best known for her 80's hit *Girls Just Wanna' Have Fun*, and having wrestler Captain Lou Albano in her videos. Her videos played more like small movies and not the usual fare for MTV. Lauper's singing talents also went deeper than pop songs and she recorded songs like *Time After Time*, and *True Colors. The Last Beat* isn't her first movie, she has appeared in films such as *Off and Running, Mrs. Parker and The Vicious Circle*, *Life with Mikey*, and *Vibes*. In a note for Doors fans, she appeared as Jenny in the *Threepenny Opera* from which The Doors covered *Alabama Song*.

As of this writing *The Last Beat* has moved the shooting to Buenos Aires, which has a French flavor to the architecture and locales.

Ray Manzarek's *The Poet in Exile* to be Made into Movie

Ray Manzarek's 2002 novel, *The Poet in Exile* is being turned into a feature film with shooting to start in 2012 and a probable release date in 2013.

The Poet in Exile tells the story of Roy, a keyboardist in a legendary rock band of the 60's whose lead singer 'died' under mysterious circumstances. Roy starts receiving postcards from the Seychelles Islands enigmatically signed J and Roy starts his journey to the Seychelles to track down Jody, the "snake man" of rock 'n' roll. It is best described as a "clumsy rock novel" (*Publishers Weekly*), and considering it was written by a man who had a unique insight into the 60's music scene, the book was a novel of missed opportunities.

Manzarek is producing *The Poet in Exile* film alongside Tim Sullivan who is also writing, directing and producing the film. Sullivan will share co-writing credits with editor Gavin Heffernon and poet Liz Sullivan. Sullivan has worked with Manzarek on a documentary: *The Doors of the 21st Century* which was shelved due to legal problems concerning usage of The Doors' name. Manzarek will also be scoring the film.

Tim Sullivan's directing credits so far have included horror movies *Driftwood*, *Chillerama*, and *2001 Maniacs*. This isn't Manzarek's first foray into a feature film. Manzarek is famously a graduate of UCLA's film school and his credits include 2000's *Love Her Madly*, a story of obsessive love between a beautiful college student, a professor and an art student. Manzarek said it was based on a story he discussed with Jim Morrison before his death.

Manzarek has long been seeking what he considers an antidote to Oliver Stone's 1991 movie *The Doors*, which Manzarek maintains is Stone's "white powder" vision of Jim Morrison.

Mr. Mojo Risin'

For the second time in two years The Doors released a documentary on film about the band. In spring of 2010 it was *When You're Strange* with footage taken mostly from Jim Morrison's film *HWY*. In 2012, to kick off the self-described "The Year of The Doors" is the film *The Doors Mr. Mojo Risin': The Making of L.A. Woman.*

The Doors Mr. Mojo Risin': The Making of L.A. Woman tells the story of the making of The Doors' seminal album *L.A. Woman*. Relying mostly on footage taken from The Doors documentary *Feast of Friends* and new interviews with the surviving members of The Doors, including Bruce Botnick, and Paul Rothchild explaining why he decided not to produce *L.A. Woman* (every previous Doors' album was produced by Rothchild) and exactly which song he considered "cocktail music". Other interviews include Morrison's film school friend, Frank Lisciandro, early Doors advocate DJ, Jim Ladd, and music journalists, Ben Fong-Torres and David Fricke.

Mr. Mojo Risin' is a good mixture of discussions about the songs and puts *L.A. Woman* in the cultural context of the times when it was recorded and released, without getting bogged down in the technicalities of either.

All the songs on *L.A. Woman* are discussed in the film with the lone exception of *L'America*, but interesting facts and stories surrounding the genesis and recording are included with demonstrations by The Doors on their instrumental contributions. Ray Manzarek tells how Jerry Scheff, who played bass for Elvis Presley, got involved in the recording and of the contortions he went through to play the bass lines Manzarek showed him.

The DVD also features more than the usual amount of bonus features found on The Doors' DVDs. There's the raw footage of John Densmore's and Ray Manzarek's interviews, a tour of 'The Doors' L.A.' set to the song *L.A. Woman* and a video of *She Smells so Nice/Rock Me* that includes a lot of pictures of the early Doors.

The Doors at the Hollywood Bowl Classic Restored!

When The Doors were planning the Hollywood Bowl show in 1968 Ray Manzarek floated out the idea of coming out in Kabuki masks and Japanese robes. Alternatively, Jim Morrison, who was already showing the disillusionment of being a rock star, said: "Just give me my microphone, and do whatever you want to do." Maybe if Morrison had been more receptive to the idea, and they had gone through with it, the costumes would have distracted them from giving one of the best concerts of their career. A concert that was filmed.

Live at the Bowl '68 shows The Doors at the height of their musical prowess and their career. The summer before, *Light My Fire* had made The Doors a nationally known act when it hit number one on *Billboard's* charts. Later, in July of 1968, *Hello, I Love You* would do the same, and in September of 1968 the band flew to Europe on what would become their one European tour. The Hollywood Bowl show was to be a celebration of The Doors and it was a hometown audience for the band, as well as an extremely prestigious venue. Before the show The Doors met and had dinner with Mick Jagger and Keith Richards, both of whom attended the Hollywood Bowl show with Pam Courson reportedly sitting on Jagger's lap during the show. That spring The Doors had started filming the shows that would become *Feast of Friends* so they decided to film the Hollywood Bowl show. If all that wasn't enough pressure, Morrison took a hit of acid before going on.

Live at the Bowl '68 reveals the stark theatre of The Doors; Morrison prowling the stage, the rat-a-tat-tat of John Densmore's drums, Manzarek's apparent joy as he played, and Doors' guitarist Robby Krieger wandering the stage like a lost troubadour. The Hollywood Bowl was an atypical Doors show in a couple of ways, one that they rehearsed prior to the show, and the second was that they had a set list and stuck to it! Something they rarely did. The deconstruction of *Celebration of the Lizard* had poetic segues into the more traditional songs such as *Light My Fire* creating a jarring, disconcerting and theatrical effect. Morrison demonstrates his command of an audience, highlighted during *The End*, his "Have you seen the accident outside" section creates the feel and mood of a house party with a rumor running through it, and when Morrison saw a grasshopper onstage he created the impromptu Ode to a Grasshopper. When he realized it was a moth, said "Uh-oh, I blew it, it's a moth," and gets a laugh. Then he pulls everyone back into the tension and drama of the song.

Then there's the reason for the release of this DVD, the restored three songs *Hello, I Love You*, *The Wasp* (Texas Radio and the Big Beat), and *Spanish Caravan*, finally make this show complete. The show was remastered and digitally transferred. The color has also been restored. You can see the green of the carpeting The Doors were playing on and Jim Morrison's face doesn't turn purple or look fuzzy as it does on *The Doors Live at the Hollywood Bowl*. The restoration lives up to the claims on the promotional materials that it: "feels like you're on stage with the band."

Something else that is unusual for The Doors is how the DVD contains many bonus features, including 'Echoes From the Bowl', a brief history of the Hollywood Bowl, and which also includes The Doors history that led to the show at the Bowl. 'You Had to Be There' provides The Doors members' reminiscences of the show, and 'Reworking The Doors' sees Bruce Botnick tell how he remastered the film and audio to give as close to a pristine Doors performance as possible. Also included is the 1984 music video of The Doors cover of *Gloria*, and their TV show appearances on the Smothers Brothers Show and Jonathon Winters show.

If you already have *The Doors Live at the Hollywood Bowl* and you're wondering if you need *Live at the Bowl '68*, consider the improved quality of the sound and the film, the restoration of the previously missing songs, and the inclusion of many bonus features. It's a package that you will find you need for your collection.

Jim Morrison's reputation is that of the rebel and rebellion will bring you into contact with authority; it did in Jim Morrison's case. Morrison was arrested several times before The Doors and afterwards. The aura of the outlaw so permeated Jim Morrison that upon meeting Robby Krieger's father, he suggested they get a good criminal lawyer. We'll take a look at Jim Morrison's arrests, including a couple that are rarely touched upon and which might give us a look into Morrison's psyche at that moment.

9
Jim Morrison's Arrests

"I fought the law and the law won" is a little rock 'n' roll aphorism from Sonny Curtis (in the post Buddy Holly Crickets, he would later go on to write the theme song to the Mary Tyler Moore Show Love is All Around), and no one fought the law harder than Jim Morrison. In the end the law won. What Jim Morrison probably didn't realize, until it was too late, was that it was a stacked deck. Authority doesn't assert itself unless it's sure it will win. Jim Morrison's run-ins with the law took their toll on him.

Jim Morrison's First Arrest

Jim Morrison's first arrest, or at least his first documented arrest, led to the first of many mug shots that would fill Jim Morrison's life.

It started, as a lot of junior college escapades do, without any anticipation or intention that anything was going to happen, just a good time. However, it turned out to be an adventure worth telling your children about. Morrison and some friends were on their way to a Saturday afternoon football game with the seasons changing. It was a cool fall afternoon, a little bit of rain in the air. Morrison and his friends got drunk on wine, and on the way to the game Jim engaged one of his friends in a mock sword fight with the umbrellas they were carrying. Morrison saw a cop's helmet sitting in an unattended patrol car and took it which not unsurprisingly drew the attention of the police. Morrison was arrested, put in handcuffs and in the ensuing confusion caused by his friends trying to intercede, he attempted an escape. He was re-apprehended and charged with petty larceny, public drunkenness, disturbing the peace, and resisting arrest.

The arrest and its consequences must have scared Morrison to some degree because the next day he went to a teacher he trusted and asked for his help. The teacher accompanied Morrison to a barber shop, went with him to buy a suit, went to court with him, and later called the dean of students on Morrison's behalf. As a result Morrison only received probation from the university.

This of course would not be Morrison's first arrest and it does show some patterns developing in his behavior. In a later L.A. arrest Morrison would be charged with stealing another policeman's hat, and in concerts Morrison would take a cop's hat off and sail it into the audience. A willingness to confront authority, perhaps.

It's hard to read a mug shot. What is the person thinking? Is he mad? Is there a rebellious smirk on his face? Are they embarrassed? Morrison, in his September 28, 1963, mug shot has short hair, and isn't the lithe rock star of the photos that would be taken in December 1967 with a hint of smile on his face, or the bearded Jim Morrison that will come from his Miami 1969 booking. All that is still in Morrison's future.

The 'Murder of Phil O'Leno'

One of Jim Morrison's arrests that is shrouded in mystery (because Morrison may never have been formally booked) was when he was brought in for questioning for the murder of Phil O'Leno.

Felix Venable, Phil O'Leno, and Jim Morrison were film school friends. Venable was the oldest in his 30's and Ray Manzarek credits Venable with leading Morrison down the road of drugs and alcohol abuse. In truth, there are plenty of stories of Morrison raiding his father's liquor cabinet even before he got to UCLA. Phil O'Leno was more of a dark, brooding type who was reputed to have read the complete works of Carl Jung. The three film school friends set out into the desert to find some peyote or mescaline and it turned out to be a far greater adventure than they first thought. In fact it changed the nature of their friendship.

The adventure started out with a four a.m. phone call from Jim Morrison to sometime girlfriend Carol Winters. He had jumped a fence to a golf course with Venable and O'Leno and they needed a ride. Winters took them to O'Leno's parent's house where the trio appropriated a car and headed for the desert or Mexico (the destination was never clear). On the way out of the city, at a stoplight, Morrison jumped out of the car and kissed a cute girl on the street corner before jumping back into the vehicle. None of their friends heard anything from them until a couple of days later when Morrison and Venable reappeared in Los Angeles looking like they had been in fight. They were battered and bruised, but O'Leno was missing. When asked by their friends where O'Leno was, Morrison and Venable started telling a story in which they murdered O'Leno and buried him in a riverbed. No one believed the story because Morrison and Venable seemed to enjoy telling it so much.

When the story started to get around, O'Leno's father, an attorney, got wind of it. Since Phil still hadn't returned from the road trip he started to get worried about his son's whereabouts. He found the girl Morrison had kissed (she must have been part of the story) and convinced her to press charges against Morrison for assault. On January 23, 1966, Jim Morrison was arrested for assault, so he could be questioned with regard to the O'Leno disappearance. Luckily, at about the same time Morrison was arrested - Phil had made his way back to Los Angeles.

To this day no one knows what really happened on that road trip. Did the trio run into a gang that beat them up for having long hair? Was there a fight over a girl? Or did they in fact find the peyote and/or the mescaline they were looking for and have the mystical experience they wanted? No one seems to know, but one of the ramifications was that it ended the friendship of Jim Morrison and Phil O'Leno. O'Leno, who was more serious about mystical experiences, thought Morrison a dilettante who was just interested in adventure and having a good time.

Whatever did happen in the desert turned into a bad joke that was pushed too far, and it was a bad joke that Morrison continued throughout the rest of his life. In his film *HWY* there's a scene of 'the hitchhiker/killer' in a phone booth. On the audio he confesses to killing a guy because he gave him "trouble" but he shouldn't worry about it because he didn't think anybody would find out. This was no exercise in acting, Morrison actually called the poet Michael McClure from the phone booth and made the admission leaving a bewildered McClure on the other end. McClure chalked up the call to Morrison's bizarre sense of humor.

Chapter 9

Jim Morrison vs. New Haven

Concatenation. A series of events that leads from one to another, the cosmic clicking of kinetic balls that, in retrospect, seem inexorable and inevitable. That's arguably what led up to the events in New Haven, Connecticut, on December 9, 1967.

The first ball was set in motion the night before the New Haven show, in Troy, New York. December 8, 1967, was Jim Morrison's 24th birthday. By all accounts, the Troy show was terrible. First, Morrison missed a plane and ended up taking a limo to the show. The audience was unresponsive, Morrison couldn't get them interested in the songs and at one point he said, "If this is Troy then I'm with the Greeks," (probably one of the most erudite things a rock star has said from the stage). After The Doors set there were no calls for an encore. Depressed that the show had bombed, and instead of taking a plane to New Haven for the next night's show, Morrison insisted on being driven down in the hired car.

The next ball to click was backstage at the New Haven Arena. Morrison had picked up a coed from Connecticut State University, and had found a shower for privacy for them to "talk". While they were in there, a cop who had been assigned to the security detail discovered Morrison and the girl and ordered them out of the stall. In the face of authority Morrison grabbed his crotch and told the cop to "Eat it!" The cop then pulled a can of mace from his belt and told Morrison it was his last chance, whereupon Morrison said: "Last chance to eat it!" The cop maced Morrison. After Morrison's eyes were flushed out and he had recovered, the cop still wanted to arrest him, but the entreaties of The Doors' manager Bill Siddons prevailed, and the cop and Morrison apologized to each other. The incident was forgiven and forgotten, seemingly.

The Doors went on and the show seemed a typical Doors gig with a set that included *Five to One*, *Unhappy Girl*, *People Are Strange*, and *Break on Through*. Then came *When the Music's Over* which, like *The End*, was one of The Doors' "theatre pieces" that included long instrumental sections where Morrison could and usually did improvise or throw in fragments of his poetry. Then in perfect time to the music Morrison started relating the night's events starting with "I want to tell you about something that happened just two minutes ago right here in New Haven… this is New Haven, Connecticut, United States of America?" and then he told how the cop maced him and how he was blinded for about thirty minutes (one picture of the night shows Morrison coming from backstage, his eyes red and irritated), then he yelled: "The whole fucking world hates me!" and the band and Morrison pounded back into the song.

It was about thirty seconds before the lights in the auditorium went on and Morrison asked why the lights were on and asked the audience if they wanted more. The answer was a resounding "YES!" at which point Morrison demanded the lights be turned off. It was then that Ray Manzarek got up and went over to Morrison and told him the cops were getting upset, but Morrison kept up the chant of "Turn off the lights!" At that point the police decided to arrest Morrison for breaching the peace. A certain Lieutenant Kelly of the New Haven Police Department approached Morrison on stage and in one of the most iconic moments and images of rock 'n' roll history Morrison thrust the microphone into the face of Kelly and said, "Say your thing, man!" The policeman then grabbed the microphone and Morrison, dragged him offstage, and arrested him. On the way to the police station Morrison was roughed up, and the cops beat him for 'resisting arrest'. The police also arrested a photographer from *Life Magazine* (for taking a picture of a cop roughing up a teenager), and a reporter from the *Village Voice*. When the arrest was reported the account was sympathetic to Morrison and The Doors.

The New Haven incident made Jim Morrison the first rock star arrested onstage, but the arrest of Jim Morrison wasn't the first time the New Haven Police Department faced charges of using excessive force. Two weeks before Jim's arrest they were accused of using excessive force during an anti-war demonstration. In the irony department (or maybe not), the site of the New Haven Coliseum is now the headquarters of the New Haven division of the FBI. All charges stemming from Jim Morrison's arrest in New Haven were later dropped.

Flight to Phoenix

It had started as a lark and ended in arrest. Jim Morrison had been toeing the theoretical line after Miami. But on November 11, 1969, with a fistful of Rolling Stones tickets in hand, Morrison, along with drinking buddy and provocateur Tom Baker, Frank Lisciandro and Leon Barnard, decided to catch a plane to Phoenix to see the Stones' show. It was a decision that would have repercussions far more serious than the harmless adventure they had planned.

The Stones had been in attendance at The Doors' 1968 Hollywood Bowl show and afterwards had said it wasn't all that exciting. So, Morrison, as a kind of practical joke, was going to stand outside the stadium handing out The Stones tickets to kids who didn't have any saying: "This is courtesy of your old friend Jim Morrison. Enjoy the show."

Chapter 9

For Morrison and Baker the drinking started before they left for the airport and by the time they boarded flight 172 they were in a boisterous mood. Morrison was seated a row in front and across from Baker who had an aisle seat. The flight was delayed and as the plane sat on the tarmac Baker became restless and started trying to grab the stewardess and started walking around the cabin of the plane, while Morrison lit up a cigar despite the no smoking sign. After takeoff the pair started telling obscene jokes, grabbing at the stewardess again as she tried to serve drinks. When the other passengers started to complain the stewardess threatened to report their behavior to the captain. The threat only deterred them for a short while and when they returned to their high jinks she reported them to the captain. Undeterred, Baker kept misbehaving. After going to the lavatory, he came back with bars of airline soap and started throwing them around the cabin. One landed in Morrison's drink and when Morrison complained the stewardess went back to the plane's captain who came out and reprimanded them. He noticed that it seemed to be Baker causing most of the trouble and directed most of his remarks at him. Baker and Morrison both tried to "back talk" the captain who threatened to either turn the plane around, or land at the nearest airport where they would be arrested. After the lecture by the captain Morrison and Baker started passing back and forth a bottle of Cognac. Baker got up to go to the lavatory again and saw the stewardess close to the door, so he threw the door open and it struck her. A little later Baker tried to trip her as she went up the aisle and also tried to kick a drink out of Morrison's hand. The captain hearing the commotion in the cockpit radioed ahead to have the police meet them at the gate.

As the plane taxied to the terminal, Morrison and Baker rushed to gather their things and waited by the door to make a hasty exit. But not only were the police at the gate to meet the flight, so were the FBI because the Phoenix police didn't know if they had jurisdiction or not. The police found Baker to be carrying a big knife and both Morrison and Baker were arrested for interfering with the operations of a flight crew, a federal charge under a recently passed law to battle hijackings.

The arrest on a federal charge couldn't come at a worse time and meant big trouble for Morrison and possible jail time for Jim who, only two days before, had been in Miami to officially enter a not guilty plea to the charges stemming from the 'Miami Incident'. Newspaper reports picked up quickly on the incident saying Morrison "was nabbed" in Phoenix as if he were a fugitive. Morrison and Baker made bail the following day after Bill Siddons, who was the promoter of the Stones concert, paid the bond out of his share of the receipts from the show.

The duo went on trial on March 26, 1970, and at first the stewardess identified Morrison as the main instigator of the trouble, but after Morrison's attorneys asked her to identify the men by the seat number they were in, she realized Baker had been the main instigator of the ruckus. That confusion won Morrison an acquittal and he later said: "They were just trying to hang me because I was the only one that had a well-known face."

Thirty years later Axl Rose, perhaps trying to cement his own rock 'n' roll myth and legend, and seeking to tie himself as the rock 'n' roll inheritor of Jim Morrison's mantle, provoked an incident at Phoenix airport and was also arrested.

Jim Arrested in Clearwater, Florida

It may have seemed to Jim Morrison that it had all started in Clearwater, Florida, and possibly he thought it had all ended in Florida. Morrison had been a student at Florida State University, and had started his studies in acting and set design with an eye towards going to the UCLA film school. Clearwater was where he met his first serious girlfriend, Mary Werblow. It is also where he haunted the coffee shops and read his first poems, where he may or may not have run into Jack Kerouac, and where he was first arrested for essentially a college prank. So, after being officially convicted and booked for the 'Miami Incident' Morrison may have been feeling nostalgic. After being released on a $50,000 bail, and instead of heading back to L.A., he headed to Clearwater where he was arrested on September 23, 1970.

Little is known about the incident and most biographies skip over it, either not knowing about it or deeming it a not very important arrest. Morrison was drinking at a bar on Pier 60, a fishing strand, with 'Babe' Hill (Darryl Arthur Hill) when the two became disruptive and the owner asked them to leave. They refused and the owner called the police. When the police arrived, Morrison and Hill were taken into custody for being drunk. After they were arrested some of the other patrons (who may have known who Morrison was) threatened the owner. Again the police were called, but by the time they had arrived the crowd had dispersed.

The arrest itself may have been insignificant, but maybe the reason for Morrison staying in Florida wasn't. After paying the bond for the 'Miami Incident' why didn't he just go back to L.A.? As already noted, Morrison had a lot of history in the area. Was he taking a sentimental trip through his past? Showing Babe his early haunts? Perhaps trying to figure out where it had all gone wrong? Certainly, he did this same sort of nostalgic visitation to his L.A. haunts before leaving for Paris in the spring of 1971 some six months later. We may never know the reason why Jim Morrison decided to visit his old stomping grounds. Morrison and Hill were later bailed out, got on a plane and returned to Los Angeles without any further incident.

The only arrest missing from this chapter is from March 1, 1969. It's from The Doors concert at the Dinner Key Auditorium in Miami, Florida, and it would forever be known by The Doors and fans as "The Miami Incident". Its causes and effects are worthy of their own chapter.

10

Miami: From Incident to Pardon

Jim Morrison's arrest for the 'Miami Incident' was only the surface event seen by the public but there were precipitating events that led to the controversial concert. From beginning to end, there are many reasons why it happened and some were set in motion months before that night. When the story of Jim Morrison's pardon for the 'Miami Incident' came to light, it afforded the opportunity to see Doors history move in almost real time.

The Living Theatre Opens in L.A.

February 24, 1969. The Living Theatre opened at USC's Bovard Auditorium in Los Angeles. Former theater student, and adherent of Antonin Artaud who brought theories of the theater to the rock stage, Jim Morrison was at every performance of the week long engagement which would lead directly to the events at the Dinner Key Auditorium in Miami on March 1, 1969.

The Living Theatre was founded in 1947 by Julian Beck (who is probably known to audiences today as the Reverend Kane in *Poltergeist II: The Other Side*) and Judith Malina. From the very beginning it produced the unconventional poetic plays of Gertrude Stein, Bertolt Brecht, and Jean Cocteau. Also from the beginning, The Living Theatre was targeted by authorities. In New York, for example, they were closed down because of zoning violations, an action which led to The Living Theatre's departure from the city.

When The Living Theatre got to L.A. they were to perform a different production each night from their repertoire of plays, including *Frankenstein* which, as performed, was more the 'theme' of *Frankenstein* than the traditional story. The next night was *Antigone* which was a more conventional performance of the play and the most conventional of the plays presented that week. On the last night was *Paradise Now!* which would affect Morrison very profoundly.

Paradise Now! had actors walking the aisles of the theater shouting slogans to, and at, the audience. "I'm not allowed to smoke marijuana!", "I'm not allowed to take my clothes off!" This was an effort to confront and engage audience members, and challenge their preconceived ideas. The actors then took off their clothes and exhorted the audience to do the same. Soon the line between audience and actors began to blur as the audience was encouraged to participate and join the actors on stage and in the aisles and to encourage those who remained seated to join them. Morrison was excited by this. Reportedly Tom Baker (who attended the play with Morrison) said: "He had a madder than usual look in his eyes." Jim Morrison was a true believer in what The Living Theatre was trying to do. Morrison fully participated in the *Paradise Now!* spectacle, joining the actors in the aisles and on stage. After the Living Theatre was asked to leave Los Angeles, Morrison met with Beck and Malina to contribute money to the theatre. *Paradise Now!* gave Morrison a methodology and an outline that he would present to his audience at the Dinner Key Auditorium on March 1, 1969.

The Living Theatre still lives on today bringing their theatre experience to contemporary audiences.

The Miami Incident

March 1st is the anniversary of The Doors' 'Miami Incident' at the Dinner Key Auditorium where Jim Morrison was accused of indecent exposure. The subsequent trial, and Morrison's conviction, affected the rest of his life and the career of The Doors - even down to the fall of 2010 when the Florida Board of Clemency pardoned Jim Morrison.

Miami didn't exist in a vacuum. Morrison didn't just get drunk on that night and start shouting slogans and berating his audience. There was a method and a reason, it just got lost in the alcoholic haze Morrison drank himself into.

Six months prior to playing in Florida, Jim Morrison told Doors' members Ray Manzarek, John Densmore, and Robby Krieger that he wanted to quit the band because "…at one time it's what he wanted to do, but not any longer." The other members were, of course, alarmed because the band had gold records in *Light My Fire*, *Hello, I Love You* and the debut album as a whole. The band was also one of the biggest groups touring in America at the time, the premier group on Elektra Records, making a lot of money and a lot of people depended on them as their source of income. Manzarek, in his role as the voice of reason within the band, was the person who smoothed things out and persuaded Morrison to give The Doors six more months. The group went to Miami almost exactly six months later.

As mentioned above, the week before the Miami shows, The Living Theatre had come to L.A. for a week of performances. Jim Morrison attended every performance and was greatly impressed with their presentation of *Paradise Now!* It provided him with a blueprint for change that he wanted to effect in Miami. That change was to change the nature of the band for the rest of their career.

En route to Miami, Morrison started drinking and missing flights. By the time he arrived in the city not only was he drunk, he was several hours late.

The Dinner Key Auditorium was an old airplane hangar converted into a concert hall. The Doors had sold out the show, and the Miami promoter had torn out the seats to sell more tickets. The Doors didn't discover this until after they had arrived. By the time Morrison got there in the humid evening, the audience was surly and in a raucous and confrontational mood. When The Doors went on stage Jim Morrison attempted to do a Doors' version of *Paradise Now!*

The Doors recorded the Miami show as they had started taping performances for a live album. In those recordings you can hear Jim Morrison exhorting and hectoring the audience members, telling them: "There are no rules, it's your concert," and that they could do whatever they wanted. He challenged them saying: "You're all a bunch of fucking idiots!" In a nod to the conditions in the auditorium, Morrison asked them how long they were going to take it. He called them slaves and asked what they were going to do about it. Then he encouraged the audience to take off their clothes and leading by example, took off his shirt. Then he started to ask the audience what they were there for? Did they want to see a good band play or were they there for something else? At this point Morrison started fiddling with his pants to feign exposing himself. Ray, seeing what Morrison was trying to do, got The Doors' road manager Vince Treanor to stop him. Treanor came up behind Morrison and hitched up Morrison's leather pants so that he couldn't unbutton the front of them. After that - the scene got chaotic with fans rushing the stage.

Security tried to clear the stage by throwing kids off. Finally, under the weight of all the people on the stage, it collapsed and the band had to abandon it. All the while Jim Morrison was in the audience singing and leading a conga line, before disappearing into the rafters of The Dinner Key Auditorium.

Despite all that happened during the show, none of the police present tried to arrest Morrison. In fact, during the trial that was to come, it was noted how the police had a beer with the band members after the show, and no one had arrested Jim Morrison at the time. It was only in the week afterwards that stories of Jim Morrison exposing himself circulated around Miami. Newspapers and TV editorials expressed outrage over the "lewd behavior" and soon the political mood demanded a scapegoat.

Five days after the show, charges were filed against Morrison for lewd and lascivious behavior (a felony), and misdemeanor charges of indecent exposure (despite the fact that no pictures of Morrison exposing himself have ever been produced), public profanity, and public drunkenness.

Jim Morrison's Obscenity Trial

August 12, 1970. Jim Morrison went on trial for the obscenity charges stemming from the 'Miami incident' of a year and a half before. Morrison and his defense attorneys hoped the trial would be a first amendment case on the issues of a performer being free to use profanities and nudity in a theatrical performance, but Judge Murray Goodman ruled that the first amendment arguments weren't relevant thereby gutting the defense plan.

Morrison did a couple of interviews on what he hoped the trial would be, stating that artists should be free to use nudity in a performance if they feel it is necessary. When the defense wanted to bring in expert witnesses as to prevailing community standards or the introduction of works of art that were already playing in the Miami area such as *Hair* or *Woodstock*, Judge Goodman ruled the defense could only present issues consistent with the charges against Morrison.

To outside spectators it was obvious, if not stated outright, that the outcome of the trial was predetermined. Jim Morrison wasn't going to be allowed an affirmative defense. It was an election year for Judge Goodman and finding Morrison guilty could only help his election in a case that the public and the 'silent majority' were watching closely. At one point the prosecution's attempt to railroad Morrison was so blatant that they tried to slip a misleading photo negative into evidence. When Morrison's lawyers objected, Judge Goodman laughed and commented: "They made a nice try and it didn't work," which in itself would probably have been enough for an appeal.

The Doors also hoped that the counterculture press would cover the trial sympathetically for Morrison. At first, interest was there from both the mainstream and the counterculture press, but Judge Goodman soon ruled that the trial would be held every other day (because of his trial schedule). At times Goodman rescheduled his calendar, and Jim Morrison and The Doors never knew when they would be in court. Soon afterwards media interest waned.

Morrison himself took the stand, although later he said in an interview with Salli Stevenson that: "I didn't have to testify, but we decided that it might be a good thing for the jury to see what I was like because all they could do is look at me for six weeks or as long as it went. So, I testified for a couple of days. I don't think it meant anything one way or another." Morrison's testimony at the trial has been released because of the Freedom of Information Act and in it you can see how Morrison, at times, has a bit of fun with the prosecutors parrying questions and answers on his pants and why he got down on his knees to study Robby Krieger's finger work on the solo of *Light My Fire* because: "He gets better all the time."

In the end Morrison was found guilty of indecent exposure and profanity, both misdemeanors, and not guilty on the felony counts of lewd and lascivious behavior, and not guilty of public drunkenness, another misdemeanor. The sentence for the guilty verdict was six months in jail and a $500 fine for indecent exposure, and two months in jail and $25 for the profanity, with the jail terms being served concurrently. Morrison's attorneys asked for and got Morrison out on a $50,000 bond while appealing the decision.

Did Jim Morrison receive a fair trial in Miami? Probably not. There were several appealable incidents that occurred during the trial: Morrison not being able to mount the defense he wanted to, prosecutors trying to slip in misleading evidence, and Judge Goodman 'forgetting' to give the jury an instruction that there wasn't enough evidence to prove exposure. What about having the trial on alternating days? That isn't usual procedure during a trial. When the trial started, public attention was at full interest. The press was attending and covering the story as well as Morrison's supporters. Were alternating days an overt attempt to prolong the trial until public and press interest waned? Was it an attempt to deny The Doors the ability to earn money because they couldn't schedule concerts due to the ever changing court schedule? Only Judge Goodman could answer those questions. Within a few months of sentencing Jim Morrison, Judge Goodman himself was found guilty of taking a bribe to influence the outcome of a trial. He died a few years later.

In the weeks prior to Morrison's sentencing, Jimi Hendrix and Janis Joplin had died, and Pam Courson had left for Paris. When Jim Morrison left for Paris in March of 1971 he was still awaiting his appeal.

Crist to Pardon Jim Morrison?

November 9, 2010. Florida Governor Charlie Crist is once again floating the rumor he may pardon Jim Morrison before his term of office expires. If Governor Crist had brought this up BEFORE the election he might have discovered a heretofore unknown voting bloc, Doors fans, and he might be a Senator-Elect today!

Online petitions to pardon Morrison have circulated previously and were delivered to Crist and his predecessor Jeb Bush. While the Governors have addressed the issue before, none has seriously pursued the matter, and it looks like Crist might be following the same course, saying in Washington, D.C.'s *The Hill*: "Candidly, it's something that I haven't given a lot of thought to, but it's something I'm willing to look into in the time I have left. Anything is possible."

Among Doors fans it's a pretty common opinion that Morrison should be granted a pardon on the back of irregularities in the trial that would have granted Morrison a new trial, and probable exoneration.

I would like to offer an alternate idea. Jim Morrison once said: "If you make your peace with authority, you become an authority." Morrison is now known as a rebel who flouted authority and that image attracts young people of every new generation. If Morrison is granted that pardon (as justified as it may be), aren't we making Morrison's peace with authority? Aren't we saying that Jim Morrison has now become a safe commodity? No longer the rebel, no longer a threat to the establishment? And wouldn't young people stop seeing Morrison and his message as an outlet of their angst and outrage at the prevailing wisdoms of society? And in the end would it finally make Jim Morrison a safe, sanitized idol? His voice muted by absorption into the establishment he struggled against.

Florida Governor to Submit Doors Lead Singer for Pardon

November 16, 2010. In an afternoon announcement, Florida Governor Charlie Crist announced he would submit Jim Morrison, as a candidate for a pardon, to the state's clemency board for charges stemming from his March 1969 performance at the Dinner Key Auditorium.

Mr. Crist was quoted in the *New York Times* as saying: "I've decided to do it, for the pure and simple reason that I just think it's the right thing to do. In some ways it seems like a tragic conclusion to a young man's life to have maybe this be a lasting legacy, where we're not even sure that it actually occurred. The more that I've read about the case and the more I get briefed on it, the more convinced I am that maybe an injustice has been done here."

Morrison's possible pardon had come to Florida's governors in the past, including Crist, but no real consideration seemed to have been given to Morrison's case. Morrison's conviction in September of 1970 was immediately appealed by Morrison's attorney Max Fink, on the grounds referenced above, such as the judge 'forgetting' to give a jury instruction that there wasn't enough evidence to prove exposure, and the failure to allow testimony that Morrison was within his first amendment rights and was within the Supreme Court's definition of community standards.

Morrison's pardon still needed to run the gauntlet of the full Board of Executive Clemency, which included Governor Crist. The Board was set to meet on December 9th, the day after what would have been Morrison's 67th birthday.

Jim Morrison Still Provoking the Establishment?

November 17, 2010. It seems Jim Morrison may still know how to provoke the establishment. Or is it writers' pens? In a *New York Times* article *Pardon Bid for Jim Morrison Relights Old Fires* writer David Itzkoff tried to make the case that Florida Governor Charlie Crist's move to have Jim Morrison pardoned may be reigniting the culture wars of the 60's.

The article mentioned the decency rally that was held at the Orange Bowl in March 1969 which was organized by Mike Levesque, then a 17 year old high school student. The rally had guest speakers on the subject of virtue; people such as Anita Bryant who would later become better known for her virulent anti-gay prejudice than her singing, or being a spokesperson for an orange juice brand.

Itzkoff rightly quoted Ray Manzarek as saying: "The battle then was the battle that's being fought today, it's the battle that America has been fighting." But the rest of the article actually pointed out, or at least implied, that a Morrison pardon may be closer than the public might expect. He (Itzkoff) quotes Katherine Fernandez-Rundle, the state attorney for Miami-Dade County as saying: "It is not worth the time, the expense or the use of precious staff resources to uphold."

The only person mentioned in the article who opposed the pardon effort was Claude R. Kirk, Jr. who was the governor of Florida during the time of Morrison's trial and who was quoted as saying: "The state didn't do anything to him. It tried him and found him guilty. Why would you pardon him then?"

Crist has *The Last Word* on Jim Morrison

November 19, 2010. The week was rife with the story that Florida Governor Charlie Crist would seek to pardon Jim Morrison from his convictions. The story and its updates appeared in the *New York Times*, and in *The Doors Examiner.* Governor Crist was on the political talk show *The Last Word* with Lawrence O'Donnell to talk almost exclusively about Morrison's pardon.

In *The Last Word* segment with Crist, O'Donnell asked why he was pursuing the Morrison pardon; were there not more egregious examples of misjustice that could be corrected? Crist responded by saying that upon reviewing the evidence it seemed flimsy, the conviction could have been a "sign of the times", and that it's "important to prosecute the guilty, but more important to exonerate the innocent."

Morrison Pardon a Done Deal?

December 9, 2010, 1 p.m. Florida newspapers began to report that Governor Charlie Crist has lined up enough votes in the morning to get Jim Morrison pardoned at that day's hearings of Florida's Board of Executive Clemency. Crist couldn't pardon Morrison (or anyone else) on his own authority, it would take the Governor's vote plus two other members of the Board.

Jim Morrison Pardoned

December 9, 2010, 3 p.m. The media began to report that Jim Morrison had been pardoned from the charges stemming from his obscenity conviction from the March 1, 1969, performance at the Dinner Key Auditorium by a unanimous vote of the Florida Board of Clemency.

The effort to pardon Jim Morrison has been actively pushed for by fans for the previous ten years with petitions being circulated and presented to former Florida governors such as Jeb Bush, and the incumbent Governor Charlie Crist. Prior to the hearings Crist had said: "What I do know is that if someone hasn't committed a crime, that should be recognized, we live in a civil society that understands that lasting legacy of a human being, and maybe the last act for which they may be known, is something that never occurred in the first place, it's never a bad idea to try to right a wrong."

Patricia Kennealy Weighs in on Jim Morrison Pardon

December 18, 2010. Amid the news that Jim Morrison had been pardoned was a dissenting voice - that of Patricia Kennealy (Morrison) – who was famous for 'marrying' Morrison in a Wicca handfasting ceremony.

Patricia Kennealy is a lightning rod in The Doors community. Many fans believe she was just another of Morrison's girlfriends, and Morrison is reported to have said the handfasting ceremony was a fun thing to do. Others whole-heartedly support Kennealy's claims and the use of the title Mrs. Morrison. Prior to the pardon Keannealy e-mailed Florida Governor Charlie Crist asking him not to pardon Morrison. Since the pardon went through, CNN interviewed Kennealy and she offered her viewpoint.

Kennealy gave the opinion that Morrison viewed the conviction as a political set-up on the part of the establishment, and that Morrison would: "hate, loathe, detest, and despise the whole idea… no doubt he would rip the pardon into tiny pieces. He did nothing to be pardoned for." Kennealy said she would have preferred the expungement of Morrison's record.

Chapter 10

The Doors Issue Statement on Jim Morrison Pardon

December 22, 2010. The Doors, in conjunction with the Morrison family, issued a press release concerning the pardoning of Jim Morrison by the Florida Board of Clemency. Here is the statement in full.

In 1969 the Doors played an infamous concert in Miami, Florida. Accounts vary as to what actually happened on stage that night.

Whatever took place that night ended with The Doors sharing beers and laughter in the dressing room with the Miami police, who acted as security at the venue that evening. No arrests were made. The next day we flew off to Jamaica for a few days' vacation before our planned 20-city tour of America.

That tour never materialized. Four days later, warrants were issued in Miami for the arrest of Morrison on trumped-up charges of indecency, public obscenity, and general rock-and-roll revelry. Every city The Doors were booked into canceled their engagement.

A circus of fire-and-brimstone "decency" rallies, grand jury investigations and apocalyptic editorials followed - not to mention allegations ranging from the unsubstantiated (he exposed himself) to the fantastic (the Doors were "inciting a riot" but also "hypnotizing" the crowd).

In August, Jim Morrison went on trial in Miami. He was acquitted on all but two misdemeanor charges and sentenced to six months' hard labor in Raiford Penitentiary. He was appealing this conviction when he died in Paris on July 3, 1971. Four decades after the fact, with Jim an icon for multiple generations - and those who railed against him now a laughingstock - Florida has seen fit to issue a pardon.

We don't feel Jim needs to be pardoned for ***anything****.*

His performance in Miami that night was certainly provocative, and entirely in the insurrectionary spirit of The Doors' music and message. The charges against him were largely an opportunity for grandstanding by ambitious politicians - not to mention an affront to free speech and a massive waste of time and taxpayer dollars. As Ann Woolner of the Albany Times-Union wrote recently, "Morrison's case bore all the signs of a political prosecution, a rebuke from the cultural right to punish a symbol of Dionysian rebellion."

If the State of Florida and the City of Miami want to make amends for the travesty of Jim Morrison's arrest and prosecution forty years after the fact, an apology would be more appropriate - and expunging the whole sorry matter from the record. And how about a promise to stop letting culture-war hysteria trump our First Amendment rights? Freedom of Speech must be held sacred, especially in these reactionary times.

Love,

The Doors

The Morrison Family

11

Book Reviews (Non-Fiction)

To most of us The Doors are history, a living history. Still, we try to assimilate the experience of The Doors and how it affects our lives. To that end, one of the ways we try to assimilate that experience is through a reading of histories of the places, persons, and events surrounding The Doors.

Canyon of Dreams

Canyon of Dreams by Harvey Kubernick is a history of Laurel Canyon and its residents from the very beginnings of Hollywood when it was a remote hideaway for stars staying at hotels such as The Garden of Allah (opened by one of Rudolph Valentino's wives). The book proves that sex and drugs and wild times existed before rock 'n' roll.

The book primarily details the stories of the famous residents of Laurel Canyon, and The Doors had an early presence. In his foreword, Doors keyboardist, Ray Manzarek recounts his first experience in the canyon with Dick Bock, the owner of Pacific Coast Records, who signed and recorded Manzarek's first band, Rick and The Ravens, and recommended the Maharishi's yoga class to Ray, where he met John Densmore and Robby Krieger.

There are a couple of first glimpses of native Los Angelites, the underage John Densmore getting into a jazz club with a fake ID he procured in Tijuana, spending nights listening and watching the jazz musicians. There's also a glimpse of Robby Krieger playing under his name at Club Lingerie.

The book is divided into easy to read chapters with a resident of the canyon relating anecdotes about the time period he lived in Laurel Canyon. Each chapter is divided into subchapters, one of which is about The Doors. Robby and John were the first to move there, then Jim Morrison came along. Morrison liked to watch the denizens of the canyon and immortalized them in the song *Love Street*. John had dinner parties followed by games of pool and Robby seems to have been a big part of the scene when he lived there, and perhaps gives a reason why Frank Zappa may have had the animus towards The Doors he had in later years. It seems Frank wanted to produce The Doors but they considered him "a weirdo" (Robby's quote), and The Doors didn't think it would work out.

Henry Diltz, who took the pictures for The Doors' *Morrison Hotel* album plays a major role in the narrative describing how he went from member of a folk band to rock photographer.

This is a great book on the history of Laurel Canyon. It is formatted in a scrapbook style, loaded with pictures and paraphernalia of the times and I urge anybody who's interested, whether they're a Doors fan or not, to get the book. There's something in there for anybody who's interested in the time period, in rock history, jazz history, or someone looking for a good oral history of the area.

Ray, Jim, John, Robby and Doug?

That's what The Doors line up could have been had Doug Lubahn taken Doors producer Paul Rothchild up on his offer to join The Doors as their bass player. Lubahn played bass for the band from the *Strange Days* album through *The Soft Parade*, but turned down the offer because he was loyal to his own band Clear Light.

This is just one of the many rock 'n' roll stories Lubahn relates in his book *My Days With The Doors and Other Stories*. The first quarter of the book is about Lubahn coming to Los Angeles from Aspen, Colorado, on the advice of Mama Cass Elliott and how he hooked up with The Doors. He details his contributions to The Doors' songs and the albums he was on. He provides some nice personal insight into each of The Doors as individuals. It's quite apparent he still has great respect and affection for The Doors and they return the sentiments as evidenced by a reunion in Florida when Ray and Robby were touring as The Doors of the 21st Century. Lubahn had a life after The Doors and it reads like a rock 'n' roll who's who of adventures. From joining Billy Squier's band, to writing the song *Treat Me Right* which Pat Benatar made a hit, to hanging with Miles Davis, John

Belushi, and Madonna, and that is only for starters! I could just list all the rock 'n' roll personalities Lubahn has known and that would make a compelling enough review for you to buy the book! The book is very nice high gloss with lots of pictures. His stories are episodic and can be read one at a time or two or three in a sitting. Each one a rock 'n' roll gem!

I Remember Jim Morrison

In Alan Graham's, *I Remember Jim Morrison*, there is an afterword by Scott Graves which says, "The statement, 'I remember,' is an existential one..." Graham has stated how he would like the reader to consider *I Remember Jim Morrison* - "... I wanted to present the book as if it were just a group of people at a gathering sitting around telling memorable stories, tales, anecdotes, jokes, etc." These states of remembrance can add shadings of their own. The hearth may provide the warm softening glow of nostalgia, or harden with bias. The picture of Jim Morrison may, or may not, be 'factual' but it is Alan Graham's Jim Morrison.

Alan Graham was Jim Morrison's brother-in-law, he married Morrison's sister Anne in 1966. He and Anne lived in close proximity to Morrison's parents and Graham met Jim in 1968 and they seemed to hit it off pretty well. Graham provides quite a few anecdotes about him and Morrison taking off and having adventures (or misadventures) that perhaps only someone like Jim Morrison was able to provide. Al Graham's Jim Morrison isn't one we're unfamiliar with, the Jim Morrison who was erudite, quick witted, the Jim Morrison who does something outrageous and laughs at the situation.

There's no linear narrative in *I Remember*. The book also strives to give us a feeling for, and some insight into, the players we haven't seen much of before; namely Jim's parents, and Anne and Andy Morrison. Each are given a synopsis of their lives and what they're like. Graham also offers the origins and meanings behind some of Morrison's lyrics. Jim Morrison may well have told Graham these anecdotes on how the songs were created, but Morrison had a habit of telling people different stories about the origins of the songs. Just about every book you read on Morrison and The Doors will have witnesses testifying about the origin or meanings of songs, some more authoritatively than others, and every story will be different!

I Remember falls into the same trap as other books that say 'the real story of Jim Morrison has never been told! Other books only tell of the drunken, sensationalized stories of Jim Morrison, this is the first book that tells the whole truth about Jim Morrison.' And they proceed to tell their Jim Morrison stories that have exactly that; the author going out with Morrison and the trouble they got into, or the outrageous situations they found themselves in because of something Morrison did. That's exactly what happens here. The first sixty pages are stories of Graham roaring off into the night with Morrison to go drinking.

A problem I had in reading *I Remember Jim Morrison* is that Alan Graham seems to have a lot of axes to grind… and grind them he does. Pam Courson seems to be nothing more than a grasping, shrewish, drug addict, which it may have seemed to Graham. At some point, if your brother-in-law is hanging around with this type of person wouldn't you ask him why? Obviously, Jim Morrison saw much more in Pam Courson than this, but if Jim ever mentioned it to Alan Graham it's not reported to us. Regarding others that surrounded Jim, Graham doesn't have a good word to say about any of them. Ray, Robby and John seem nothing more than Morrison's backing band and Graham refers to them this way even though Graham puts himself at a couple of recording sessions with The Doors. The only people who do seem to come off well are Graham, Anne Morrison, and Jim's parents who Graham seems to have a lot of respect for (especially Jim's father). Some of these family anecdotes are endearing and funny, but sometimes they left me mystified as to why they were included.

The structure of the book seems a little ad hoc; it jumps from one section to another and back without much reason. It may adhere to the spirit of the book - sitting around a table and telling stories - but Jim Morrison remains out of focus, a fuzzy silhouette of memory. It doesn't allow us to see the real Jim Morrison, or even the one Alan Graham knew.

The persona Jim Morrison presented to the world is a fictional character. Everyone who knew Jim Morrison knew a different Jim Morrison, but it is the persona Jim Morrison created for public consumption. For those of us who didn't know the living, breathing man and who try to figure out 'who the real Jim Morrison was' - perhaps it's like trying to figure out what Shakespeare's voice sounded like. Soon all we'll have left are these not so silent witnesses to Morrison and it will be left to us to puzzle which is the 'real' Jim. That proposition may only be possible through reading about the 'Jim Morrison' each author knew and coming to your own conclusions as to who Jim Morrison was.

Forever Changes, Arthur Lee and the Book of Love

"We wanted to be as big as Love." Jim Morrison

Love is a band that has had a lot of myth, lore and rumor surrounding it. *Forever Changes: Arthur Lee and the Book of Love* separates the fact from the fantasy and legend - sticking to the bones of Love due to the years, if not decades, of fan conjecture in the face of silence from Arthur Lee. Author John Einarson does this with meticulous research and interviews with family, friends, and band mates of Arthur Lee from his earliest days to his death in 2006. Einarson also incorporates the manuscript of an unfinished autobiography Lee was working on after he left prison.

Forever Changes focuses on Lee/Love's heyday in the mid 60's when Lee's band Love was the undisputed heaviest band on L.A.'s Sunset Strip. They were at the forefront of the folk-rock music scene. Love was the first house band at the Whisky a-Go-Go, and Arthur Lee may have been the sartorial model for hippies of the later 60's. Lee certainly thought Jimi Hendrix had adopted his mode of dress after meeting him.

Lee and Love (the two are indistinguishable) were one of the first bands signed by Jac Holzman of Elektra records; a record deal that culminated in Lee/Love's artistic and critical success with the album *Forever Changes*. Lee/Love were at the top of L.A.'s music scene and Jim Morrison commented that the early goal of The Doors was to be "as big as Love". Just as the other bands were breaking nationally, Lee and Love faltered. Why did the other bands succeed? And why did Love not reach a national audience? A lot of that falls on Lee. He did little national touring, he had contentious relationships with record companies, money disputes with band mates, and a mercurial habit of changing the lineup of the band.

Forever Changes doesn't fall into the trap that other rock books have of not paying enough attention to, or glossing over, what came after a band's halcyon period. You come away from reading *Forever Changes* feeling that you have a good idea of Lee's life after he was 'the prince of Sunset Strip'.

Lee was influential and admired in the Los Angeles music scene and he boasted a friendship with Jimi Hendrix, who Lee met in a recording session when Hendrix was still doing session work. The Doors, who succeeded Love as house band at The Whisky were recommended by Lee to Jac Holzman. Both The Doors and Hendrix make special guest appearances in the book. Towards the end of his life

Lee discovered that he had admirers in Eric Clapton, Robert Plant, Ian Hunter, and Robyn Hitchcock.

Doors fans will see a lot of familiar characters that were also involved with The Doors, albeit from a slightly different perspective, and their relationships to Love are different than to The Doors. People like Jac Holzman, Paul Rothchild, Bruce Botnick, and Ronnie Haran who was Love's manager at the beginning and who says her contributions to The Doors have been downplayed.

Einarson's use of Lee's autobiography is spot on. The manuscript is used sparingly but intelligently. The passages employed are like a laser on the subject at hand, and capture Lee cutting to the heart of the matter - shedding light on what may have been heretofore muddied by myth. Lee's voice stands out from Einarson's surrounding narrative and one has the feel of listening to a tape recording of Lee as he describes the times, events, and the L.A. scene.

Forever Changes is one of the best rock biographies I've read. When I started reading the book I wasn't a Lee/Love fan, but Einarson's writing pulled me right in and made me care about Lee and his life.

Jac Holzman's Adventures in Recordland

Becoming Elektra covers the years from when Elektra records was founded, by Jac Holzman in his college dorm room, to when Holzman sold Elektra to Warner Communications. In between there was a lot of music, a lot of taking chances, a folk music scene that exploded, a rock music scene that exploded, iconic personalities and albums, iconic producers, and at the center of it, sometimes barely hanging on, was Jac Holzman.

The late 40's and early 50's were a comparable time to ours for the recording industry just as today's technology is available to those who want to make a CD. The early 50's was on the cutting edge of a technology change. The young and ambitious were there to take advantage of it. Many record companies started up at this time and while some didn't survive, some did and we know them today: Atlantic Records, Chess Records, and Elektra. The first technology to make this possible was the ability to create thinner, smaller records that were more easily usable than the thick 78's. The mechanical technology to record, be portable, and be widely available to everyone was courtesy of leftover equipment from World War II.

This technological vantage point is where Holzman found himself when he started Elektra. Another was New York as the opening of coffee shops put the city at the forefront of folk music as a scene, and where Holzman was able to record the folk denizens of Greenwich Village. Later, when the music scene in Los Angeles was about to burst, Holzman had the insight to see the Sunset Strip as the same kind of focal point for music that Greenwich Village was in the 50's.

Elektra was a small company that didn't have a lot to lose but a lot to prove. Holzman was willing to experiment and let his artists experiment, from recording in a church or the artist's apartment to a club the artist was familiar with and comfortable in, to the experiments of Paul Rothchild and The Doors in the studio. His only credo was: "Just do what's right for the music."

Perhaps the easiest and best review I could write would be a review just listing all the names of Elektra's artists over the years: Theodore Bikel, Josh White, Judy Henske, Tom Paxton, Jean Ritchie, Judy Collins, Cynthia Gooding, Susan Reed, Sabicas, The Paul Butterfield Blues Band, Tim Buckley, Phil Ochs, Tom Rush, Jean Redpath, The Dillards, John Sebastian, The Doors, Love, Clear Light, Bread, David Ackles, The Stooges, MC5, Queen, and Jackson Browne amongst others. Or I could write of all the different styles of music Elektra recorded: world music, theme albums, military genre albums, ethnic music, the blues, folk, and flamenco. You would think that a compelling enough reason to buy the book.

Elektra's reputation has preceded it and earlier generations of Elektra artists have influenced later generations. Doors guitarist Robby Krieger had quite a few of Elektra's flamenco albums in his teenage record collection.

The book is absolutely beautiful, filled with page after page of high gloss pictures, album covers, people, places, catalogs, records, letters, memos, and performers. Anything and everything from Elektra's history.

An oral history of Elektra, *Follow The Music*, was published in the late 90's and it gives you the Elektra story from the point of the participants. If you already have *Follow The Music* (as I have), it's a great companion book. If you don't have it *Becoming Elektra* is a great stand-alone volume that gives you the wider perspective of the history and events. I was surprised at the new information I discovered; stories were filled out, and I gained a broader knowledge of the artists and music.

Chapter 11

The Doors FAQ

Google 'The Doors' and you will find any number of rock 'n' roll websites with rock fans wanting to know more about The Doors or have their questions about the band or Jim Morrison answered. Everything from what books did Jim Morrison read, to what really happened in Miami, or what are The Doors doing today. Rich Weidman's *The Doors FAQ* steps into that niche and answers those questions - for the casual rock fan all the way to The Doors aficionado.

As soon as you open *The Doors FAQ* you realize it's a unique book, the most obvious is that it's formatted like an FAQ (Frequently Asked Questions) found on most websites. It doesn't approach The Doors chronologically, but is divided up by subject, with short informative answers. You'll easily find the answers to who The Doors members were, Jim Morrison's literary influences, the musical influences of The Doors, how The Doors got their name, Doors singles that reached number one, and Doors songs used in movies. In short, any question a fan could have about The Doors is explored in *The Doors FAQ*.

I've been a Doors fan for thirty years and I was surprised at some of the new information I discovered in its pages, such as former members of Rick and the Ravens, Ray Manzarek's band that eventually morphed into The Doors, or the identity of the "unknown female bass player" that recorded on the nascent Doors' *World Pacific* demos. In the summaries of literary or musical influences or biographies or synopses you won't find any rote regurgitations from other books. Weidman has done his research and finds facts, quotes and other archival information, availing himself of the most recent materials available. His writing doesn't allow this material to be or seem derivative, all of which combines to make *The Doors FAQ* fresh to all except maybe the most jaded of Doors fans or experts.

Most books on The Doors are overwhelmed by Jim Morrison, not so with *The Doors FAQ*. Right from the beginning the biographies of all The Doors are of roughly equal length, and the surviving members' lives aren't relegated to the nether regions of a short last chapter or epilogue; they are included from the beginning. So if you're a fan of Ray Manzarek, Robby Krieger, or John Densmore you will read about their most recent CDs and accomplishments as well.

Doors history sometimes seems to diverge at the dividing line of the life and death of Jim Morrison, but history doesn't stop and neither have the surviving members of The Doors. Weidman tackles this later history more fully than any other book on The Doors to date. Weidman goes through the 2002 "Doors of the

21st Century" and the action and reactions of the surviving members of The Doors, which resulted in the lawsuit filed by John Densmore concerning usage of The Doors name. Weidman relates it factually and without any of the bias or acrimony that haunted the message boards of the time.

The Doors were first and foremost a literary band, even in their use of musical phrasing, and the book seems to take on a literary aspect where Weidman doesn't shy away from The Doors' literary roots. Each chapter starts with a pithy and apropos quote on the aspect of The Doors being explored in that chapter. Invariably I found the quote provided a bit of literary circularity tracking back upon the subject and providing some illumination on the topic at hand.

The Doors FAQ is an easy reference tool for Doors fans to find the answers to their questions quickly. I can see it being used as a guidebook by Doors tourists in Los Angeles, for those hitting bookstores looking for the books on Jim Morrison's reading list, and those shopping for the CDs of bands and musicians that influenced The Doors. These may be the most utilitarian of uses for the title and I feel like I've left out many more aspects of this book, but on any shortlist of Doors books to have, *The Doors FAQ* should be on there.

The Doors, Greil Marcus' Lifetime

With a cover image of Joel Brodsky's Elektra publicity photo of The Doors dressed in unexpectedly warm colors of the sun, Greil Marcus' *The Doors: A Lifetime of Listening to Five Mean Years* is an unexpected look at selected songs of The Doors and pop culture.

Marcus' book is a fan's book. He says that it started at the Avalon Ballroom when he and his wife saw The Doors play and on their way out they took a handbill of the show. After a lifetime they still have it. Marcus, best known for music criticism and pop culture critiques, is a Doors fan but an objective one. He is well versed in all aspects of music and the artists. And also the language of music. He focuses his lens on The Doors.

The Doors: A Lifetime of Listening to Five Mean Years is twenty critical essays on Doors songs. Marcus' prose weaves in and out of the songs to where his thoughts take him, either in relation to the lyrics themselves, or some aspect of pop culture. The chapter on *Twentieth Century Fox* is a take off point for an extended essay on 50's and 60's pop culture and how The Doors fit in. In the essay on *L.A. Woman* he makes the case that it could be used as a soundtrack for

Thomas Pynchon's recent novel *Inherent Vice*, and the song is a pop art map of the city. Marcus isn't an easy ride through The Doors. You'll find yourself agreeing with some of his conclusions, such as on *Take it as it Comes* which "seemed to start in the middle of some greater song." Or even disagreeing with his conclusions, such as Morrison's tribute to Otis Redding: "Poor Otis dead and gone/Left me here to sing his song…was beyond arrogant, it was beyond obnoxious, it was even beyond racism…" which always seemed a heartfelt tribute to Redding to me.

As you read *The Doors: A Lifetime of Listening to Five Mean Years* you'll find yourself wanting to listen to the songs to gauge for yourself whether Marcus' critiques are apt or not.

Dennis Jakob's *Summer With Morrison*

In times gone by there used to be small books about writers, not quite biographies, more like biographical meditations on the writer, his work and his life. The best known example of this may be Henry Miller's book on French Symbolist poet Arthur Rimbaud, a book that Jim Morrison and Dennis Jakob surely knew. In *Summer With Morrison*, Dennis Jakob, a UCLA film school friend of Morrison's, does the favor to Morrison in writing a small book of meditations. It isn't a throwback or even an homage to the form, but the best way to present Morrison to the reader. Jakob tells us stories we may not have heard before and a view of Morrison few others would be able to provide.

Summer With Morrison is divided up into two sections. The first contains Jakob's stories, anecdotes, and adventures with Jim Morrison the summer Morrison had his vision quest on top of the building Jakob was living in. Apparently, it wasn't as much of an exile as legend has it, as Jakob has Morrison coming off the roof to discuss a variety of subjects. Jakob was also there when Morrison burnt his old journals in a furnace before embarking on the notebooks that would contain the poems that would become the genesis of The Doors.

Jakob also discusses some of Morrison's ideas on things such as libraries. One afternoon Jakob trails Morrison to the public library and watches as Jim collects a huge blue book from the librarian and reads it through the afternoon. Is this what Morrison had in mind when he later said he was: "interested in activities that seemed to have no meaning"? When Jakob confronted Morrison about his library expedition, Morrison said, "The public library is one of the most exhilarating and dangerous institutions existent in our society."

Doors fans have long asked about Jim Morrison's reading list. Jakob does that one better, presenting recreated conversations with Jim Morrison on books, philosophy, film and what Jim Morrison's thoughts on each were. Dennis Jakob is said to have read more books than Jim Morrison and reading these conversations, no matter how well read you are, will make you feel like a neophyte in the literary world. Both Morrison and Jakob have command of some of the most arcane theories, but also are able to discuss them with true insight and intelligence. It seems the reading section can also be broken down by aphorisms that describe Morrison to varying degrees. The first is, "Whom the Gods favor they make die young," which the reader will instantly agree with, but there's another that Jakob thinks Morrison may have been wiser to heed, "For the mindful God abhors untimely growth."

There is also a third section of thirteen pages of Jim Morrison pre-fame. *Summer With Morrison* is an intriguing read and a very different perspective on the man. Jakob asserts Morrison was much more interesting before he was a rock star than afterwards. So read *Summer With Morrison* and get some real insight into Jim Morrison and his mind.

Jerry Scheff, Bass Player for a Classic Age

For most of us, the 1960's was the golden age of rock 'n' roll, complete with its own pantheon of gods and heroes. Some of those names bring instant recognition and we know their place and mythology in this modern iconography. Names such as Elvis, Dylan, and Jim Morrison. Jerry Scheff knew and played with his fair share of them.

In *Way Down Playing Bass with Elvis, Dylan, The Doors and More* Jerry Scheff, one of the most sought after bass and session players in Los Angeles, gives us anecdotes from his life of playing with the legends of rock 'n' roll. Scheff starts right at the top with "The King" Elvis Presley and how he went on an audition for Elvis' 1969 TCB (Takin' Care of Business) Band on a lark, never really expecting to get the job or even sure whether he wanted the job. He ended up playing with the TCB Band even after Presley's death. Scheff introduces us to other members of the band, what it was like to work up Presley's Vegas act, what it was like onstage with Presley, and even some pretty cool stories of going over to dinner with Elvis and Priscilla.

From there Scheff backtracks a bit and tells us of his formative years learning to play music on the tuba, and then getting into bass guitar. His mother took him to blues clubs when he was underage; it should be noted that this was in an era when blues clubs were all, if not predominately, black clubs. Then his time in the Navy where he met a lot of musicians that he would bump into again and again over the years; a group of individuals that created an informal musician's network recommending each other when another player was needed for a band. This network got Scheff into the early L.A. music scene and made him a staple for groups like The Association and The 5th Dimension who Scheff not only recorded with, but also toured with, during the 60's. Scheff was in the right place at the right time for playing with a lot of legendary musicians and bands, including Neil Diamond, and The Doors. Later in his career Scheff went on to play with Bob Dylan's Rolling Thunder Band, Elvis Costello (the other Elvis of rock 'n' roll), and John Denver.

Although Scheff gives us a lot of good anecdotes about his work with the various bands, some of them feel episodic and dead end right into the next anecdote. This gives *Way Down* a skimming feel, like you're auditing a class on 1960's session music.

Note for Doors fans: even though The Doors are mentioned in the title there is just over a page on Scheff's six week experience working with The Doors on *L.A. Woman.* Scheff quickly glosses over the experience. We don't get to meet The Doors in the same way that Scheff introduced other bands he played with and we don't even get any insight into the *L.A. Woman* sessions. With The Doors included in the title, I was expecting a few more pages on Scheff's time with the group.

Way Down Playing Bass with Elvis, Dylan, The Doors and More is an enjoyable read mind you. Scheff's anecdotes are interesting and he rubbed shoulders with some of the legends of rock 'n' roll. It might not be as in-depth as fans of a particular band might like, but for the casual fan who wants to have a feel for what the 1960's were like, for a working musician, this is a good read.

Jim Morrison, The Living Theatre and the FBI

I thought *We Want the World: Jim Morrison, The Living Theatre and the FBI* by Daveth Milton (published by Bennion Kearny, the publisher of this book) was going to be a sensationalized and/or a conspiracy theory that pops up on the fringes of fandom, but it wasn't. I found *We Want the World* to be an insightful look at what a lot of Doors fans think they know about Jim Morrison's performance at the Dinner Key Auditorium on March 1, 1969, and how Morrison was influenced by the Living Theatre and tried to bring their tactics to a mass audience at a Doors concert. It also covers the fallout of that performance and how it attracted the interest of the FBI and possibly even J. Edgar Hoover himself.

From the distance of over forty years The Doors' 'Miami incident' looks like a gross miscalculation on Jim Morrison's part and a minor criminal offense by an excessive rock star. Part of that may be the official trivialization of the charges by Judge Murray Goodman who denied Morrison the first amendment defense the incident deserved. Had Morrison been afforded that defense, Miami may have loomed larger in the national consciousness as a landmark case of the 1960's counter-culture and freedom of artistic expression. At official levels it may indeed have concerned the establishment, men whose names now adorn our temples of justice and jurisprudence may have felt that Jim Morrison was a real threat that had to be stopped.

We Want the World starts with a brief history of Julian Beck's and Judith Malina's Living Theatre that got started in the late 40's and which had some of the same influences that Jim Morrison would later claim, such as Antonin Artaud. Even before Morrison saw the Living Theatre, early Doors performances were approaching the same territory as the Living Theatre's *Paradise Now.* Watching the theatre group may have solidified what Morrison had been instinctively moving towards. What is clear from reading *We Want the World* is that if anybody could have brought the message of *Paradise Now* over from the avant-garde to the mainstream audience it was Jim Morrison. What is also clear is that Jim Morrison blew it in a hazy fog of only vaguely defined ideas and alcohol.

'The Miami incident' brought Jim Morrison to the attention of the FBI who were looking for a counter-culture figure or band to discredit much as they tried to do with Martin Luther King and the civil rights movement. I'm not much for conspiracy theories, but Milton makes a good case that J. Edgar Hoover's FBI infiltrated American groups to a much greater degree than we had ever been aware of or willing to admit.

Jim Morrison had envisioned the performance in Miami as his *Paradise Now*. He wanted the performance to free himself of his public image and it may have worked too well. Miami destroyed Jim Morrison and may well have been a contributing factor to his death. It also gave the FBI what it wanted, a case to discredit the counter-culture and deny them a landmark case, and to vilify and reduce to parody (not even *Rolling Stone* championed Morrison or the case) one of the perceived leaders of that counter-culture, Jim Morrison.

Chapter 11

Under television skies Jim Morrison was sure we were becoming a nation of voyeurs to our lives. Over the past forty years we have become voyeurs to The Doors story under those same television skies.

12
The Doors on Television

The Doors became famous in the generation when everyone had a television in their house. The publicity machine surrounding The Doors made the most of that medium by introducing the largest number of people in the least amount of time to the band by booking them on the music and variety shows of the day. Some of those appearances are more famous, or infamous, than others. After their legend was secured, television writers started using The Doors to set the tone or mood of an era or even added insight into The Doors experience through fictional television treatments.

The Doors Play *The End* on Toronto TV Show

There are a lot of Doors' shows, later in their career, that illustrate how different a band The Doors could be. But there are few programs that show The Doors at the height of their powers and what a truly electrifying and even scary group they could be. One such show was *The Rock Scene: Like it Is*.

The show was filmed in Toronto on September 14, 1967, at the CBC (Canadian Broadcasting Corporation) studios. It was a very stark theatre for the band, just them on stage, and the audience. The Doors played only one song, *The End*. It starts with Jim Morrison's invocation to "wake up" before the band goes into the song proper. They're a tight group; they act 'as one' in the performance and Jim Morrison almost literally looks as if a current of electricity is running through him. Diverging from the usual, The Doors omitted the Oedipal section of the song. Probably in a nod to it being broadcast although the producers didn't ask them to edit the song. Censorship was a mistake the Ed Sullivan producers would make three days later in New York when they asked The Doors to change the word "higher" in *Light My Fire*.

The Doors performance is spellbinding. Watching the video, you can't take your eyes off the band or Morrison. Much the same reaction the audience had. For the most part they stand and watch, some dance, but overall it seemed *The End* was a piece of theatre no-one could take their eyes off.

The video of this Toronto performance was included on *The Doors: Soundstage Performances* DVD and it is enhanced by the inclusion of the surviving Doors' members' recollections. The most striking is Robby Krieger's recollection of how the band was met at the airport by the Toronto chapter of the Hell's Angels and how they escorted the band to the Toronto Peace Festival.

The show aired October 16, 1967, by which time The Doors were performing in New York.

The Doors on *Ed Sullivan*

Sunday night, millions of people are huddled on the hearth around their new TV sets waiting for the *Ed Sullivan Show* to come on. Sullivan's show had been on since 1948 and by 1967 he was considered, and considered himself, to be a "star maker" in the entertainment industry. On September 17, 1967, The Doors appeared on his show.

The Doors appearance on the Sullivan show is a widely known tale. Sullivan and his staff asked The Doors to change the lyric of "Girl, we couldn't get much higher" in their hit song *Light My Fire* to "Girl, we couldn't get much better" because Sullivan feared it was a drug reference. The Doors might not have been too surprised at this because Elektra Records had censored (or edited out, if you prefer) "She gets high" from *Break on Through*. The Doors agreed to alter the lyric, but when they went onstage to perform the song (unlike most other shows the performances were live) Jim Morrison sang the lyric as Doors guitarist, Robby Krieger had written it. In Oliver Stone's, *The Doors* the moment is captured with some filmic hyperbole showing Morrison screaming the word "higher" into the camera and then somehow getting a close up of his leather pants, but the reality was more subtle. Morrison stood in front of the microphone stand and sang the word "higher" naturally with no emphasis on the word at all.

The only visible reaction by The Doors is when the camera pans over to Robby Krieger. You can see him smiling.

Afterwards, the Sullivan people were furious and told The Doors they would never play the Ed Sullivan Show again. The Doors' response was either arrogant, "Well, we just played Sullivan," or feigned over-exuberance, "Golly, we just forgot in all the excitement," depending on which telling of the story you happen upon. The incident cemented The Doors' image into legend as rebels – both in the eyes of the counter-culture and the establishment.

Sullivan's attempt to censor The Doors was nothing new. Sullivan had a habit of trying to censor acts, and if they objected or acted contrary to Sullivan's wishes he would ban them, unless of course their popularity with his audience demanded he put them on the show. This is exactly what happened with Elvis Presley. Sullivan, at first, refused to put him on the show because of Elvis' stage manner of swiveling his hips. Sullivan later recanted his position when Presley became a nationwide sensation, and Sullivan was 'scooped' when Presley appeared on the *Steve Allen Show*. Although Sullivan booked rock acts on his show he seemed to try to curtail them. He tried to censor Bo Diddley, Buddy Holly and the Crickets, Bob Dylan, The Rolling Stones, The Byrds, and, of course, The Doors. Most didn't comply and were banned by Sullivan. It's frequently mentioned that The Rolling Stones did comply and changed the words to *Let's Spend the Night Together*, to "Let's spend some time together". They did sing the song on air with the lyric changed but, immediately afterwards, went to their dressing room and changed into Nazi uniforms for their second song. Sullivan and his staff demanded The Stones change back into the clothes they had been wearing, but the band left the studio instead.

The Doors on the *Murray the K* TV Show

It had been a busy week for The Doors, but a week that would make them famous and provide the start of the Jim Morrison legend. On Sunday September 17, 1967, the band appeared on *The Ed Sullivan Show*, before which the band shot a photo session with Joel Brodsky that would include the 'young lion' photos of Morrison. Jim also sat for photos with Gloria Stavers of *16 Magazine*. On September 22, 1967, The Doors appeared on the TV show *Murray the K in New York*.

Murray the K, real name Murray Kaufman, had worked all his life in show business, mostly in public relations and as a song plugger (a piano player who played sheet music of new songs to get the public introduced to the songs). In 1958 Kaufmann became a DJ at WINS-AM radio station and made radio history by using creative, dynamic programming such as innovative segues, jingles and sound effects. Tom Wolfe called him: "The original hysterical disk-jockey." Kaufmann was the top rated disc jockey in New York when The Beatles came to America in 1964 and he gained access to the band (with the help of Ronnie Bennett of The Ronettes, later Ronnie Spector). He accompanied them to Washington D.C. (for their *Ed Sullivan Show* appearance), Miami, and later onto the set of *A Hard Day's Night*, earning himself the original title of "the fifth Beatle," bestowed upon him by either George Harrison (whom he roomed with in Miami), or Ringo Starr.

As their part of the *Murray the K in New York* show, The Doors performed *People Are Strange* around a tree in a New York plaza with Ray, Robby and John standing around with not much to do except changing position during the song to keep it visually interesting. The band also did a 'skit' where a girl in a silver jump suit approached the band on a street and snatched a medallion Morrison was wearing. The band chased her to a park. It has either a very 'James Bondish' or 'Hard Day's Night'-esque feel to it. As a contender for TV shows that added a storyline to music (no matter how loose), in the years before MTV, Kaufmann may be one of the first to lay claim to the music video.

The Doors Appear on the *Jonathan Winters* Show

The Doors had just had their biggest summer. *Light My Fire* had gone from a seven minute album cut, to an edited AM radio friendly length of 2:52, and on to being a part of the Summer of Love's soundtrack and number one on the *Billboard* charts.

With *Light My Fire* hitting number one it pushed The Doors onto the national stage and the national variety shows started calling. First Ed Sullivan, and in December the *Jonathan Winters Show.*

Winters had started his career in radio stand-up comedy in which he developed perhaps his best known character: Maude Frickert. Winters appeared on TV shows such as *The Twilight Zone*, *The Jack Paar Show*, and *The Tonight Show with Johnny Carson*, frequently appearing on the shows in character. He also appeared in movies such as *It's a Mad, Mad, Mad World*, and *The Russians are Coming, The Russian's are Coming*. His first TV show *The Jonathan Winters Show* ran from 1967 to 1969 and he later had *The Wacky World of Jonathan*

Winters on TV from 1972 to 1974. In the 70's Winters' career waned as he battled mental illness, but his career and stature in show business was revitalized in the late 70's and early 80's through Robin Williams' support.

The Doors appeared on *The Jonathan Winters Show* on December 27, 1967. The set on Winters' show was a little hipper than the predictable backdrop of the Sullivan show which featured 'doors'. *Moonlight Drive* opened with a picture of galaxies and cut to The Doors who were on risers with fog billowing out behind and around them. Jim Morrison sang wearing dark shades, and during the instrumental the show's production team added some psychedelic effects. The addition of special effects perhaps went too far during *Light My Fire* where The Doors were on a different set with some wavy frames with strings in-between them, and shadow girls dancing behind them like flames. You can tell Morrison's vocal was live as his voice broke and was hoarse when he tried to scream "fire" into the instrumental section, and that may be the reason, during the second stanza, that Morrison omitted the last scream of "FIRE!" The cameras caught Morrison tangled up, attacking the strings webbing the set, and as the music ends Morrison's body goes limp. It's hard to tell what Morrison was trying to do because the show kept adding the 'psychedelic' special effect of the wavy lines.

The Doors on *The Smothers Brothers Show*

Variety shows once ruled the airwaves of America, much like the reality shows and talent shows of today (both of which had their antecedents in the 1950's). The variety show was a smattering of everything from comedy sketches, musical groups, song and dance, animal acts, to plate twirlers. The Doors appeared on the major variety shows of the day, including *The Smothers Brothers Show*.

The Smothers Brothers were controversial because, in their comedy, they poked fun at 'the establishment' and they clearly sided with the baby boomers. They were also known for their cutting edge guests. They were the first network program to have Pete Seeger on since his blacklisting in the 50's. Seeger's appearance was also controversial because Seeger played *Waist Deep in the Big Muddy* an anti-war song that was interpreted as being an insult to President Lyndon Johnson.

The Smothers Brothers were also popular with the youth of the day because they were playing the rock groups other shows weren't: The Who, Cream, Buffalo Springfield, and, of course, The Doors. In the opening segment of the show The Doors appeared on, Tommy and Dick come out and Tommy started to put on a gas mask and motorcycle helmet. Dick asks Tommy what he's doing and he replied: "Getting ready to go to college."

The Smothers Brothers Show was also a breeding ground for a new generation of comedians. Writers on the show included Steve Martin, Don Novello (who would later become Father Guido Sarducci on Saturday Night Live), Bob Einstein (Super Dave Osborne), Albert Einstein (later Albert Brooks), and Pat Paulsen.

On December 6, 1968, The Doors videotaped their appearance on *The Smothers Brothers Show* (some Doors' sources have it as December 4, 1968). The Doors performed *Wild Child* and *Touch Me*. The segment featuring *Touch Me* is famous for a couple of reasons. The first is The Doors appeared with part of The La Cineaga Symphony - with brass and stringed instruments brought in for the recording of the *Soft Parade* album. The second, Doors guitarist Robby Krieger very noticeably has a black eye. A lot of rumors have surrounded the black eye, from a bar fight to a car accident, but Krieger recently said it was from a "tussle" with Jim. *The Smothers Brothers Show* aired on December 15, 1968.

The Doors on PBS' *Critique*

The Doors were still reeling from the March 1, 1969, performance at the Dinner Key Auditorium in Miami that brought indecency charges against Jim Morrison and effectively cancelled The Doors planned spring tour, losing what was called a "million dollars in gigs". With no new bookings to replace those shows, Jim Morrison kept himself busy as he recorded some of his poetry with an eye to a poetry album. In April, Morrison started filming *HWY* with Paul Ferrara, Frank Lisciandro and Babe Hill, and of course, collectively The Doors finished the recording of *The Soft Parade*.

Finally, there was a break in the ostracization of The Doors in the form of the PBS station WNET offering the group the chance to be on their show *Critique* where they were to be interviewed by rock journalist Richard Goldstein, who had always been an advocate in taking The Doors seriously as a band with deeper themes. The Doors would also perform new songs off *The Soft Parade* on the show. The band jumped at the chance to rehabilitate their image as an act that was out to shock its audience but which was actually a thoughtful, erudite group.

The show's format consisted of a ten minute interview with the band in which they discussed the rock star as shaman, Jim's poetry, and how audiences perceived them. It included Morrison's now famous prediction of envisioning a musician performing not with a band but surrounded by electronic instruments and tapes. The interview portion was recorded on May 13, 1969. They also performed *Tell All the People*, *Wishful Sinful*, *Build me a Woman*, *Alabama Song/Back Door Man* medley, and *The Soft Parade*. The recording session for the show was on April 28, 1969. The final portion of the show was a panel discussion moderated by Goldstein, and featured Patricia Kennealy (who was the editor of *Jazz & Pop Magazine*), Al Aronowitz (who introduced Bob Dylan to The Beatles), and a DJ named Rosko (Bill Mercer). It was included when the show was broadcast May 23, 1969.

The Doors VH-1

On November 22, 2000, The Doors appeared on the VH1 series *Storytellers*. All the surviving members of The Doors - Ray Manzarek, Robby Krieger, and John Densmore - appeared together onstage for perhaps the last time.

The Doors' *Storytellers* episode may have pushed the boundaries of the concept of the show as there was very little 'telling' of the stories behind the songs. Instead, the band were playing with a younger generation of rock stars who joined them on stage to play their now legendary songs. The *Storytellers* show was in conjunction with the release of The Doors' tribute CD *Stoned Immaculate* (released November 2000) and the new generation rock stars filled in for Jim Morrison on vocals. Almost to a man they sported leathers, some with more success than others. Those filling in the pants and place of Morrison were Scott Weiland singing *Break On Through*, Perry Farrell singing *L.A. Woman*, Travis Meeks singing *The End*, Scott Stapp singing *Roadhouse Blues*, and Ian Astbury singing the *Alabama Song/Backdoorman* medley.

Storytellers may have been one of the catalysts for Manzarek and Krieger to form *The Doors of the 21st Century* with Astbury handling the vocals. It ignited controversy among fans and lawsuits between the Manzarek/Krieger camp and drummer John Densmore over the rights to use The Doors' name.

The Doors on *Cold Case*

An episode of the TV show *Cold Case* entitled *Metamorphosis* featured Doors songs in the show. Songs included were: *Light My Fire*, *Waiting For The Sun*,

Love Her Madly, *Wild Child*, *Riders On The Storm*, *Moonlight Drive*, and *People Are Strange*. The episode centers around the 1971 death of a circus aerialist whose accidental fall may not have been so accidental after all. The episode was written by co-star Danny Pino and series producer Adam Glass.

"Both Adam [Glass] and I are definitely Doors-heads," shared Pino. "There was really no other band in our minds as our story of a case involving a traveling circus in the '70s started to manifest itself. So, we're excited that Cold Case was able to secure The Doors' music for this episode. Their haunting lyrics, mesmerizing melodies and a pulsating foreboding keyboard proved an ideal soundtrack to accompany murder in a 'one ring mud show'."

Cold Case has been on the air since 2003 and follows a group of Philadelphia homicide detectives who only investigate cold cases, murders that haven't been solved. Led by detective Lilly Rush (Kathryn Morris), the show not only solves the murder but also features story lines that focus on the detectives and their problems. *Cold Case* is noted for flashbacks in time and its use of period music to help set the era and tone of an episode. The show has included Doors songs before. The episode entitled *Revolution* (February 2005) includes a scene where two girls walk into a party and a band is covering *Touch Me*. *Cold Case* has also used other artists such as John Lennon and Bob Dylan exclusively in episodes. It also stars Danny Pino, John Finn, Thom Barry, Jeremy Ratchford, and Tracie Thomas.

The Doors on *Glee*

The April 13, 2010, episode of *Glee* featured The Doors' *Hello, I Love You*. *Glee* is the show that aims to prove that there's a whole lot of drama and melodrama in your local high school glee club, from falling in love to backstabbing, and of course, singing.

The episode titled *Hell-O* sees the glee club coach, Will, trying to bolster one of the lead characters, Finn, who is suffering a confidence problem because he isn't sure if he wants to date a fellow show choir member - Rachael. Will tells Finn he needs to connect with his inner rock star, Jagger or Morrison. Finn sees himself as the glee club's Jim Morrison and *Hello, I Love You* is given a cover.

Hello, I Love You, like the other songs used in Glee, has a music video quality. The cast jumps around in time and space in choreographed synchronicity around the school. But the songs featured in the show do move the action along, and help define the characters and act as dialog to each other.

I'd never watched the show myself or at least a whole episode, but it's a cute, quirky show, maybe like *Fame* with the ambition toned down. It is a well written show where I was easily and instantly able to identify with the characters, which may be a little clichéd in outline, but they're really drawn and filled out - even in the course of one episode. In *Hell-O* there were some laugh out loud great lines like "I'm engorged with venom", "dolphins are really gay sharks", and "most of the vocal directors I make out with are gay." If you're a fan of *Glee* I'm sure you know who said those lines, and if you've never watched it before (like me) you'll find it funny and entertaining.

Individual members of The Doors have even appeared on various TV shows, such as Robby Krieger on *Married With Children*. *Glee* isn't even the first time The Doors have gone back to high school as John Densmore appeared on *Square Pegs* in 1982. Which begs the question why hasn't Ray Manzarek ever been on a TV show?

Jim Morrison's *Dark Skies*

A mysterious crash in the New Mexico desert, only a few witnesses, a life changing event that has moved into myth, legend and which is still talked about today. Jim Morrison witnessing the crash of the Indians on the highway, and the feeling of them jumping into his soul? No, the crash of an alien craft in Roswell.

In the television series *Dark Skies*, aliens have infiltrated society, and now the government is trying to stop them while keeping it a secret from the general public. John Loengard (Eric Close) and Kimberly Sayers (Megan Ward) fight both of them in an effort to expose the truth. This is the premise of the TV series *Dark Skies* which ran from September 1996 through spring of 1997. It was NBC's answer to the *X-Files*. The eleventh show in the season *The Last Wave* featured a young UCLA film student named Jim Morrison inadvertently filming a cover-up on Venice Beach.

The Last Wave has heroes Loengard and Sayers returning to Venice Beach for the funeral of a friend who apparently committed suicide by drinking bug poison. Soon, mysterious men from a secret government agency confiscate the body and Loengard and Sayers sense a government cover-up. As they investigate the cover-up they run into Jim Morrison who is making a film around the beach and who has inadvertently filmed biological experiments by the aliens which is being countered by the government trying to stop them by polluting the water in the Santa Monica Bay.

The Jim Morrison character is kind of a caricature lifted from *The Doors* movie. The *Dark Skies* Jim Morrison is a Nietzsche quoting, poetry spouting, pretentious film school student who interjects, just off-kilter, with Doors song titles. For example, when talking to a couple of the government agents, he says: "These people are strange."

The *Dark Skies* series has been released on DVD by the Shout Factory. The episode also has a second life on YouTube.

Brett Lowenstern Takes the Sex Out of *Light My Fire*

March 1, 2011, saw *American Idol* contestant Brett Loewenstern cover The Doors' *Light My Fire*. Unfortunately, Loewenstern's effeminate, sexless cover takes all the heat and fire out of the song that Grace Slick described as: "The closest thing to sex on a record."

Loewenstern's voice has sort of a Jose Feliciano feel and lilt to it, but even Feliciano's version had the heat of fast friction in it. I think Loewenstern either doesn't understand the song, or they didn't give him access to any tapes of Jim Morrison singing the track. The best he could do to try to generate any emotion was to shake his hair around. More heavy metal than The Doors, but maybe that's the only reference point Lowenstern has of The Doors, rock 'n' roll, or the period.

Possibly the reason *American Idol* hasn't delivered on the promise of its title 'American Idol' is that the judges liked it! Randy Jackson counted fourteen hair flips during the performance. It couldn't have been that compelling a performance if he's counting hair flips.

Strange Days Have Found The Simpsons

Someone on *The Simpsons* loves The Doors. In the December 5, 2010, episode - *The Fight Before Christmas* - a parody of *Polar Express*, Bart feeds some pot into the boiler of a train engine to stoke the fire, as *Strange Days* comes on the soundtrack. This isn't the first time a Doors song has been on *The Simpsons*. As a matter of fact, Doors mentions on the program far out-distance mentions of any other rock group. It is readily apparent that a high ranking Simpsons' producer is a Doors fan.

Here is a listing, off the top of my head, of Doors mentions that have been in Simpsons' episodes. On an excursion to a beer themed amusement park Lisa goes on a tunnel of love water ride and samples some of the 'water'; her eyes get saucery and pinwheels start turning and she comes out of the ride to pronounce herself: "the lizard queen!" In another episode, Robby Krieger does a cameo where Bart has taken up grifting on a boardwalk (is Springfield near Santa Monica?) He and Homer run behind some crates to count the loot they've conned people out of and Bart finds a C-note ($100) and asks who gave them the C-note. Homer replies: "Robby Krieger of The Doors", whereupon the cartoonized Robby pops up from behind some crates with his guitar and says: "Hey, guys I'm really sorry about the cake, do you need more c-notes?" and then disappears.

The *Screamapillar* episode has a rare screaming caterpillar (The Doors "Before I sink into the big sleep/I want to hear the scream of the butterfly") in the Simpsons' yard. They find it is a protected species so Homer has to be nice to it. An episode of *Treehouse of Horror*, The Simpsons' annual Halloween special, once had Jim Morrison's headstone in the opening sequence. In another episode a suicidal Homer walks through downtown Springfield singing *The End.*

That is a very partial listing; I checked Simpsons' fan sites hoping to find a listing of all the episodes that have a Doors reference, but there is none. You would think that after twenty years someone would have put together a listing, wouldn't you? I would like to know which Simpsons producer is The Doors fan? We know Dick Wolf, producer of the *Law and Order* television series is a fan, and he produced the documentary *When You're Strange*.

Chapter 12

ර෴

Television is an ethereal medium and the images we view are ghostly in the blue glow of darkened living rooms where we invoke those images to some sort of reality. But sometimes those ghosts are summoned of their own volition and Jim Morrison's legend may be invoking the appearance of his ghost.

13
Jim Morrison's Ghost

It can probably be said that you've attained a certain level of fame and immortality if people start seeing your ghost. In recent years Jim Morrison has joined the ranks of John Lennon and Elvis (if you believe he died) in ghostly visitations. Or is it just the living resurrecting the spirits of what they want to see? I guess it's up to you to make your mind up.

Jim Morrison's Ghost Appears... Again

October 13, 2009. It seems the ghost of Jim Morrison has appeared, or rather reappeared. The photo which shows rock critic Brett Meisner standing at the grave of Jim Morrison is typical of the thousands of the same type of picture taken at Morrison's grave every year. The difference with this one is that it seems to show, in the background, the translucent figure of a lithe man in a white shirt and presumably leather pants with his arms outstretched in a pose reminiscent of Morrison doing his 'high wire' walking on the edge of a stage.

Meisner said the picture was taken in 1997, but he didn't discover the ghostly image on the film until 2002 and it hit the internet in 2007 (at least that's the first time I heard the story). As pointed out by other Doors pundits, the image shown of the young, leather clad, daredevil is one Morrison became uncomfortable with in life. Why would he return to it in death? It is also not the Jim Morrison that was in Paris. The Jim Morrison that haunted Paris in the last five months of his life was the heavier, and at first bearded, Morrison. If he were to continue his Paris haunt, wouldn't that be the image he'd leave behind?

The reemergence of Mr. Meisner's picture is in conjunction with the release of a new book, *Ghosts Caught on Film 2: Photographs of the Unexplained*, which claims that the picture of Morrison's ghost has been authenticated stating, "Researchers rule out both lighting and image manipulation and conclude that the photo is simply 'unexplainable'."

Of course they don't explain what tests the photo has undergone to authenticate the ghostly image, nor do they explain why the image can't be or hasn't been faked. I did check out *Ghosts* author Jim Eaton's website, Ghoststudy. While it does differentiate between authentic and faked photos it doesn't explain the process used to prove either assertion. Maybe it is explained in the book.

Meisner now says he wishes he: "never stepped into the graveyard in the first place." He's looking for an archive to donate the photo and negative to. As for the photo itself? To me it looks photoshopped. I tend to lean towards being a skeptic (with an open mind), but if you tend to believe in such things it is best to examine the evidence and make your own conclusions. Whichever way your opinion leans, I suppose, like a ghostly apparition every two or three years, the photo will make another 'appearance' for future Doors board debates.

The Return of Jim Morrison's Ghost

July 1, 2010. It looks like Jim Morrison's ghost is back. Back in the news that is. The building that used to be the Doors' Workshop is now a Mexican restaurant called Mexico. Chris Epting of *AOL News* paid a visit to the restaurant with the intention of writing a story on the building being the recording place of *L.A. Woman* and the bathroom that was Morrison's vocal booth. As he spoke with the owner and the employees he discovered Jim Morrison's ghost in that bathroom.

Mr. Epting considers himself a bit of skeptic, but as he talked with the employees for the story he believed they were sincere in their belief that Morrison's spirit still lingers on the premises. How do they know? Well, lights pop on and off at weird times, and the door handle in the bathroom (where Morrison sang) jiggles. Restaurant general manager Christina Arena says: "His presence hangs very heavy here."

Larry Nicola, the owner of the restaurant is a Doors fan, and has decorated the restaurant with a lot of Doors memorabilia. He even got Robby Krieger to visit the restaurant and reminisce. For now, the restaurateurs and their customers are content to share the premises with the ghost of Jim Morrison.

Now Appearing in Arlington, VA, The Ghost of Jim Morrison

May 12, 2011. Is Jim Morrison still on tour? It has been said old soldiers never die they just fade away. But do dead rock stars just keep on touring? A current resident of one of the homes the Morrison family lived in is claiming the ghost of Jim visits her on her bed in his old bedroom.

The Arlington, Virginia, home at 4907 N. 28th Street is now owned by Gertrude Baron. Her daughter Rhonda claims the ghost of Jim Morrison started visiting her in the room when she was in college about ten years after his death. Rhonda said she could see Morrison, he had long brown hair, and he laid down next to her on the bed, although he was transparent. She thinks the spirit may have been trying to help her through a bad time with a boyfriend.

This story has been growing on the internet, starting from just a blurb in a longer article 'Our Man in Arlington' by Charlie Clark of the *Falls Church News Press*, and it kept on rolling until it was picked up by *WUSA9 News*. The news story interviews Baron, but the video has its lighter moments as the reporter in the field sang Doors songs to people and asked if they knew who Jim Morrison was.

Is Jim Morrison as Big as Jesus or John Lennon?

September 7, 2011. Jesus and Elvis have shown up on toast and tortillas, but so far Jim Morrison hasn't manifested himself within the contours of food or in swirls of wood or some other Rorschach medium, until now that is.

Recently, a picture of a garage door with an image on it, said to be Jim Morrison, has surfaced on the internet. At first it looks like a garage door with the shadows of leaves falling on it. Then, if you look long enough you can discern the face of Jim Morrison from his 'young lion' period. The image ostensibly created by the interplay of light and shadow, the sun casting shadows and peeking through creates an image of Jim Morrison.

The picture first surfaced on a site called imgur.com, which is a photo uploading site, and only included a caption that he thought the face looked like Jim Morrison but there is no story with it nor does the photographer say where it's from. That leaves a lot of open questions. Is it a photoshopped image? A photo manipulated in some other way? The power of suggestion from the caption that it is Jim Morrison? Or could it be Jim Morrison peering through from the other side?

It is said that a photograph steals one's soul. If so, the soul of Jim Morrison may not be haunting our world through physical manifestation, but through visual manifestation, photographs.

14
The Doors' Photographers

Photography walks a fine line between every picture being worth a thousand words, and stealing your soul. The photographers of The Doors have shot endless rolls of the band that tell, if the adage is correct, how one picture is worth a thousand words, and millions of words tell The Doors story. Each picture has revealed some part of each band member's soul to us. Some of the photographers' stories have made it into the public eye, along with their photos.

Bobby Klein: The Doors Through the Lens

Many Doors fans will recognize the pictures taken by Bobby Klein. He was the first official photographer of The Doors and his most famous pictures of the band includes them 'handling' the sections of the billboard Jac Holzman put up on Sunset Boulevard, and the shot on Venice Beach where Morrison (perhaps) has a noticeable erection.

There are other photographs you'll recognize including The Doors at the Bronson Caves and on Venice Beach. What makes Klein's pictures unique is the access he had to the band from their earliest moments. Klein has a story behind each picture. It may not be a thousand words, but they are short stories that most fans will recognize. Klein, in a video on his website, says the hardest part was getting the band up at seven in the morning for the Sunset Boulevard photo shoot. Klein also relates the story around the Venice Beach picture of the group and how Morrison snuck off behind a tree then came back and Klein never noticed Morrison's erection until he developed the pictures. There are pictures of

Morrison and Pam Courson when they lived in Laurel Canyon, but one story Klein doesn't have a picture for is one of the least known incidents of Jim Morrison's life. Klein lived behind Jim and Pam on Laurel Canyon and one morning Pam was pounding on his front door because Jim had set fire to the closet. This tale, of course, was later illustrated in the Oliver Stone movie *The Doors*.

Like many rock photographers of his time, Klein wasn't a professional. He was in the right place at the right time and he took pictures, put together a portfolio and started taking it around to record companies until he convinced an art director to hire him. With his career started he would go on to take pictures of Jimi Hendrix, Janis Joplin, Dennis Hopper, Igor Stravinsky, and Steve Martin. The pictures for Steve Martin would later find their way into Martin's book *Cruel Shoes*.

Klein is one of the many photographers whose pictures will be telling The Doors' story for a long time to come.

Jim Marshall Rock Photographer

Rock photographer Jim Marshall died on Wednesday March 24, 2010, at age 74. Most famous for his photographs of the San Francisco music scene, including Janis Joplin, The Grateful Dead, The Beatles, and perhaps most famously Jimi Hendrix burning his guitar at the Monterey Pop Festival, he was also at Woodstock and Altamont.

Marshall never really took pictures of Jim Morrison or The Doors except on one occasion and that produced a near iconic picture of Morrison. Taken at the Northern California Folk Rock Festival in San Jose in 1968, Marshall described how the picture came to be taken. "I don't think I ever spoke three words to Morrison. We were on the side of the stage and I was shooting with just one frame left on the roll, and Jim said, 'Hey Marshall, you want a photo?' and looked right into my camera. He was one of those guys in his own space. I never got close to him. My impression of Morrison was that he was like C.S. Lewis, spiritual without being religious."

Marshall also shot journalistic photographs. He took photographs of the civil-rights movement, the poor in Appalachia, and was taking pictures in Dallas on the day JFK was shot. He worked for magazines such as *Look*, *Rolling Stone*, *Life*, and the *Saturday Evening Post* as well as magazines like *Teen-Set*.

Marshall also published a lot of books of his photographs on singular subjects such as books on Johnny Cash, jazz musicians, as well as overall retrospectives of his work. Some of his titles include *Not Fade Away*, *Pocket Cash*, and *Trust*. Marshall was part of a generation of photographers that had unprecedented access to musicians and bands, and who shot 'real' photographs of the musicians and not posed pictures that press agents or PR people wanted - to present a band's 'image'. Photographers of Marshall's talent and stature are literally a dying breed and photographers like him will be sorely missed, not to be recreated.

Henry Diltz Photographer of Morrison Hotel

For those of you who already know a little something about Henry Diltz, it's that he's as interesting as the subjects he photographs. Henry Diltz, who is responsible for the iconic 'Morrison Hotel' photographs, was born September 6, 1938.

When Diltz started taking photographs of bands, like every other rock 'n' roll photographer of the era it was more of being in the right place at the right time. There were no press passes and if you showed up with a camera at the back door it was assumed you were a professional photographer. Henry Diltz was the king of being in the right place at the right time.

Diltz didn't want to be a photographer, he wanted to be a musician. In the early 60's he was a member of the Modern Folk Quartet that had a bit of mild recognition, releasing two albums in 1963-1964 and was later produced by Phil Spector. Diltz started taking photographs when the band made a little bit of money. He bought a second hand camera and started taking pictures of his friends and the first picture he sold was of Buffalo Springfield in front of a psychedelic mural. A few days after he took the picture, a magazine called to ask to publish it and they would pay $100. Diltz has been a working photographer since then. Over the years Diltz has taken pictures of Crosby, Stills and Nash, Steppenwolf, Joni Mitchell, he was the official photographer of Woodstock, David Cassidy, and The Monkees. Diltz is quick to note that he doesn't work for the record companies but for the artists themselves.

Doors' keyboardist Ray Manzarek, along with his wife Dorothy, had discovered the Morrison Hotel as they wandered downtown Los Angeles in late 1969. The Morrison Hotel was a cheap $2.50 a night transient hotel, a skid row hotel. Jim Morrison liked Diltz's work, so Diltz was suggested as the photographer and Morrison Hotel as the site for the shoot. When they arrived at the hotel, they at first asked permission to shoot in the lobby, but the receptionist wouldn't allow it without the owner's permission. Diltz and The Doors retired to the outside of the hotel. As they were discussing what to do next, Diltz noticed the receptionist go upstairs, so he told The Doors to go inside and sit in the front window. He went across the street and shot a roll of film. Diltz said The Doors hit their marks and they were gone before the receptionist returned. Guerilla photography was born.

Afterwards they went farther into skid row and discovered a bar called the Hardrock Café, and took pictures there with the clientele (seemingly with less managerial interference than at the Morrison Hotel). Photographs were also shot at the Lucky U, the film school hangout of UCLA film students. A few days later Elektra asked for publicity photographs and Diltz went out to the Venice Beach boardwalk and shot not only stills, but a Super 8 film of The Doors.

Diltz still seems the prototypical 60's photographer. He doesn't have different kinds of cameras draped over his body, when he's out on shoots he seems almost unobtrusive with his one camera and a soft spoken humility that belies his talent and the influence he's had on rock 'n' roll over the last forty-five years.

Linda McCartney: Band Member with a Camera

In the mid-60's rock 'n' roll as an industry was still in its infancy, borders hadn't yet been solidified between fan, band, and photographer. If you were a fan with a camera you could be mistaken for a photographer, or with a notebook it would be assumed you were a journalist (see the movie *Almost Famous*) and were given access to the band. As has been noted with other Doors photographers – many individuals weren't professional photographers and didn't intend to be, they just were around the bands and were taking pictures of their friends. Linda Eastman got her start as a rock photographer in the same way.

Eastman, from the start of her life, was involved in music. Her father Lee Eastman was an attorney (and not George Eastman of Eastman Kodak fame) who represented artists and musicians. She grew up in an environment that included Willem de Kooning, and a songwriter, Jack Lawrence, who wrote a song *Linda* in 1942 for the one year old Eastman.

The baby boom generation came of age with rock 'n' roll and Eastman had an early interest, sneaking out of her parent's house to see Alan Freed's rock 'n' roll shows that included Buddy Holly and the Crickets, Little Richard, and Fats Domino. In college, Eastman majored in art history and developed an interest in black-and-white films from Italy and France. It wasn't until after college, when she was living in Arizona, that she attended a photography course at the local arts center that had a showing of the Depression-era photographers, Walker Evans and Dorothea Lange, that Eastman was inspired to take photographs.

Eastman's early photographs were of her daughter (from her first marriage to Joseph Melville See Jr.) and of nature. When she moved back to New York she was supporting herself working at *Town and Country Magazine* and on her lunch hour she would hang out in the photography section at the Museum of Modern Art. Her first music photographs were of The Dave Clark Five, and during a Rolling Stones party on a yacht she was the only the photographer allowed on board (it probably didn't hurt that she was a cute blond) - her career as a rock photographer had started.

Eastman first met The Doors at Ondine in the winter of 1966 before the first album had been released, when they were just trying to make a living as a band hoping to make it. It wasn't until March of '67 when The Doors returned to New York to play Ondine and Steve Paul's The Scene - on the verge of stardom - that Eastman got to know Jim Morrison well. They'd go to bookstores, Chinatown or just hang out in Eastman's apartment. Eastman's photographs of The Doors in this era hardly resembled a wild rock band. In most of the photographs The Doors are all dressed in brown or black clothing, Jim Morrison hadn't yet graduated to the leathers that would make him almost as famous as the music. And the band seen onstage in Eastman's photographs still looks a little unconfident, although Eastman noted that what they lacked in confidence they all made up for in creativity.

Eastman would also have close relationships with most of the 60's rock royalty such as Jimi Hendrix, The Who, and Janis Joplin. She credited her success as a photographer as not posing her subjects and likened herself to: "a band member whose chosen instrument was the camera." Eastman's most famous subject was Paul McCartney, and most people will remember Eastman as Linda McCartney. Eastman and McCartney were married in March of 1969 and raised Eastman's daughter from her first marriage, as well as having three children together. Eastman-McCartney would play in McCartney's band Wings, would write vegetarian cookbooks, start a vegetarian food line, and sadly died of breast cancer at age 56 in 1998.

Chapter 14

O. Bisogno Scotti: Morrison Hotel Today

We like to fool ourselves about the permanence of the landscape we operate in. We console ourselves that geography or landmarks don't change or only change very slowly over time, but the front of buildings are called facades, or false fronts that can be changed and that speaks to the very nature of the impermanence of our surroundings.

Pictures are snapshots, one frame, a still life out of the film of our lives, but Doors fans can find comfort in the fact that at least one Doors landmark still exists in its almost pristine state, and that is the Morrison Hotel today.

Many would be surprised to know the building still exists at all. It is at 1246 S Hope Street in Los Angeles. And you may be surprised that the Morrison Hotel is still drawing the attention of artistically inclined L.A. photographers, such as O. Bisogno Scotti. He took a photo of the Morrison Hotel building in 2010, and although the building no longer houses the Morrison Hotel, if you were to walk past it you would probably recognize the building because its facade has changed so little.

Comparing Scotti's picture to the classic Diltz original you can line up the pictures. The light pole that is visible in Diltz's photos is still there, and the window The Doors posed in is still there, to the left of the light pole. It hasn't been altered since the 60's.

Scotti is a long time Los Angeles resident. In the past he's played in bands and taken photographs on the side. But that equation has flipped and now Scotti is a photographer that occasionally hooks up with a band. He has taken photographs of landscapes, cityscapes, people, still lives, and digital photographs. Looking through his portfolio you notice that Scotti has an eye for finding the unusual in everyday things which we might ordinarily take for granted. His photographs of buildings capture the curving lines and sweep of the architecture. One of his pictures that I found really amazing - pushes the boundaries between photography and painting. Check out the photographs of Bisogno Scotti and you will find yourself on the ground floor of discovering an emerging artist who's ready to break through to a larger public consciousness.
Scotti has a blog at: http://blog-bisogno.com

Some Doors fan ought to buy the building, paint Morrison Hotel in the window, and charge fans to sit in the window and have their picture taken a lá The Doors. It would be The Doors version of Abbey Road.

From the reality of photographs to what reality fiction writers try to find and create in their books… The Doors and their legend have given fiction writers enough fodder to create new worlds that again open the doors of possibility as well as nightmares.

15
The Doors in Fiction

A rock star as a character in a book may be an indicator of how far that person has gone beyond life and entered our collective consciousness. How we see that person, and how we perceive the image of that person, may reveal more insight about ourselves than the star we're purporting to add some insight to.

Lewis Shiner's *Glimpses*

For the first three years after discovering *Glimpses* by Lewis Shiner I read it once a year, which I don't do with books very often.

Ray Shackleford is a stereo repairman with problems and a career as a rock star that never got started, much less went anywhere. His father, with whom he had a contentious relationship, has died under mysterious circumstances. His marriage is unraveling like a ball of string in his fingers and he can't quite grasp the threads to pull it back together. He also has a burgeoning drinking problem. But he has discovered a means of escape by retreating into the past, and not just any past. He retreats to the 60's to help the idols of his rock 'n' roll dreams reclaim what they've lost, their lost albums. Brian Wilson's *Smile*, Jim Morrison and *The Celebration of the Lizard*, and Jimi Hendrix's *The First Rays of the New Rising Sun*.

I first read this book because I was looking for a nice escapist story to lose myself in for a few hours. I found that. The more I read the more I found myself drawn in, especially to Ray's trips to the past, getting drawn into Brian Wilson's family, living the rock 'n' roll lifestyle with Jim Morrison as his guide, and Ray's truly heartbreaking attempts to keep Jimi Hendrix from dying. The question is - will these trips to the past help Ray heal the same issues he has in his life?

There is the element of time travel in this book. Is Ray really going back into the past and meeting his idols? Or is he suffering a series of strokes? *Glimpses* offers evidence of both, giving the reader the choice of which is truly occurring.

On each reading of *Glimpses*, I found something new in it, some nuance previously undiscovered. I guess one could say that this is due to the changing circumstances of *my* life. But isn't that the mark of any good book? That we can find something new from whatever perspective in life we come at it?

Turn the Page: The Lost Letters of Jim Morrison

I'm somewhat hesitant to review *Turn the Page: The Lost Letters of Jim Morrison* by Victoria Williams because it brings the book to the attention of an audience that might not ordinarily run into it. But if I didn't review it I would be remiss in my duties as The Doors Examiner. One of the purposes of a review is to let people know what they're getting and let them make an informed decision.

The synopsis for the book states it's: "a gripping chronicle regarding the involvement of a mysterious French count in the greatest mystery in rock 'n' roll history - how did Jim Morrison actually die?" That blurb turns out to be a masquerade for what is a series of 'letters' from Jim Morrison from beyond the grave to his true 'cosmic mate' Rebecca. The story turns out to be nothing more than bashing Pam Courson for actually murdering Jim. Williams, in the authorial voice, withholds no invective for Courson calling her Morrison's "toxic mate". Morrison is characterized as having no will of his own in the matters of Pamela and is cast as her unwilling puppet, completely contrary to the Jim Morrison I've read about.

I'm not adverse to books being written that fictionalize Morrison or The Doors, even those purported to be 'true'. Novels that make use of the literary device of communications from the beyond represent a legitimate form of literature that can be highly revelatory of a subject when in the right hands. But *Turn The Page* doesn't engage any of the techniques that would make this anything more than a monograph, if not a diatribe, against Courson.

The 'letters' in question, whether this book is meant to be fiction or non-fiction, are letters dictated by Morrison to "Rebecca" - at first detailing his murder at Courson's hand, then of his eternal love for her (Rebecca). We're told that Rebecca was six years old when Jim Morrison died and it may be that Rebecca is a stand-in for Williams' own fantasies or wish-fulfillment. There are also letters from Anais Nin, Michael Hutchence, Heath Ledger, Jeff Buckley, and Kurt Cobain to Rebecca on Jim's behalf. These letters should add some insight into Morrison's character and/or the characters of the person speaking. However, these letters are redundant in theme and seem more like fan letters the author would like to have received from her idols. In the end, Williams goes on to disparage The Doors'/Morrison's fans and friends, even going so far as to have a list of people Morrison reveals 'the truth' about. And unlike Courson, who isn't here to defend herself, some of the people named are very much alive.

If you're of the same opinion of Pam Courson as Williams, then this book may be of interest to you. For other Doors fans, it doesn't shed any insight on Morrison, Courson, or The Doors.

Anthology Features Jim Morrison in Story

Classics Mutilated is an anthology of thirteen short stories that 'mashup' genres, characters, and the lines between them.

Mutilated is kind of a misnomer for these stories, there's nothing mutilated or even stitched together about these tales, they're a seamless fusion of genres. Like alternate histories, in writing a good mashup you have to have a strong command of the material, balanced with a respect for the original while maintaining a sense of irreverence about it. Hopefully, the new story, besides being entertaining, will also provide a better understanding or insight into the original, and these are well written stories.

Quoth The Rock Star has Jim Morrison entering the world of Edgar Allan Poe and *The Raven* as they battle it out for possession of a soul. The author of *Quoth*, Rio Youers, writes one of the best descriptions of a Doors concert I've ever read. A tyro mistake of novice writers is in creating an homage to their literary heroes through the use of obvious imagery to the detriment of their original work. But Youers interlaces Morrison's lyrics into the prose to create effect, tone and even real power utilizing Morrison's motifs and imagery in the telling of the story that will give Doors fans a rush of recognition.

A couple of other stories that stood out for me leaned, again, towards the poetic. It has been said of Emily Dickinson that she courted death in her poetry. In *Death Stopped for Miss Dickinson*, author Kristine Kathryn Rusch changes that figurative assessment of Dickinson's work into the literal. In *From Hell's Heart* Nancy Collins has Captain Ahab from Moby Dick fused with H.P. Lovecraft. I was never a big fan of Lovecraft when he was big in the mid-70's because he always backed away from describing the horror, but Nancy Collins takes that extra step and describes Lovecraft's indescribable. *Frankenbilly* meshes *Frankenstein* with the B-movie *Billy the Kid Versus Dracula*. For rock fans who want to continue in the vein of *Quoth The Rock Star*, Mark Morris' *Vicious* has Sid Vicious on tour in the U.S. meeting up with a Voodoo priestess or two.

Should you buy *Classics Mutilated* for one story? I did. All the stories have a quotient of fun in them, a joie de vivre in the writing that you can see even in the titles like *Anne-Droid of Green Gables*. Who knows, a reading of *Classics Mutilated* may even send you back to the original.

Jim Morrison Jesus Complex

Poetry is the fine painting of literature, you have to dare to tread where only masters like DaVinci, Van Gogh, Picasso, or Dali have trod before you. You must paint the words thickly, they must have two or more meanings to capture the moment when physics becomes metaphysics, when science becomes magic, the alchemical moment when words become the stone of a truth within a statement well written. Jim Morrison wrote: "There are continents and shores that beseech our understanding," and Wayne Grogan in *Jim Morrison Jesus Complex* attempts to breach those continents and shores in our understanding of Morrison.

Jim Morrison Jesus Complex is an extended poetic meditation on Jim Morrison that has two stated goals: "The shaman/Jesus trope he danced with has always been a fault line in need of perspective. His own intellectual integrity would have demanded it," and "A larger horizon that contains this divergence is the Blake statement from which derived the inspiration for The Doors name. There would have been a time for Jim to drill deeper into that quote."

Morrison has been bent to Christ like poses almost since the beginning by observers, but like Morrison said in his poem *As I Look Back*: "I rebelled against church/after phases of/fervor." A line that all the biographies have missed or overlooked. So there is the possibility we're all missing something in Morrison's message. Grogan's *Jim Morrison Jesus Complex* may not be too far off the track in its exploration, only just missing the third rail.

One of the places Grogan misses is by interjecting himself into the action. Writers frequently embark on meditations of other writers (usually one that influenced them) and with whom the writer feels a kinship. The writer interjects himself into the poet's life noticing the similarities of their lives in the hope we will too, such as Henry Miller's study of Rimbaud. In places *Jim Morrison Jesus Complex* seems more like how Morrison informs Grogan's existential experience. Using some of the same tropes as Morrison, the reader has instant identification and recognition of Morrison, but Grogan isn't as accessible in his use of them as Morrison was.

Jim Morrison Jesus Complex plays better when Grogan concentrates on Morrison and there are things Grogan gets right. We're always changing states, becoming something else. Morrison understood this when he explained The Doors' music is about sex, death and travel, everything is beginning and ending at the same time. Grogan hits upon that near the end, and a little earlier in the book, when he explores *When The Music's Over*.

An extended poetic meditation isn't for everybody and may only be for the heartiest and/or most poetically adventuresome of Morrison's/Doors fans. And yes, *Jim Morrison Jesus Complex* has its excesses, but that's also one of the charges that have always been leveled against Morrison's life and poetry. It has its moments of hubris. But creation, the mere act of scribbling down a few words that you think others will be interested in, that you have the nerve to think you have something to say to the world, is an act of hubris and self-indulgence in itself.

Mr. Mojo Risin' (Ain't Dead)

Rock 'n' roll fiction books are rare, good ones are rarer. Ron Clooney's *Mr. Mojo Risin' (Ain't Dead)* falls into the rarer category.

Mr. Mojo Risin' (Ain't Dead) follows journalist "Ron Clooney" after he encounters a man at a bar outside of Père LaChaise Cemetery whom he believes is a still alive Jim Morrison. Ron then sets off on his journalistic quest to find Jim Morrison. He first visits all the French archives then he starts to meet people whom he thinks might be Morrison, but he discovers he might be seeing Morrison's face in the face of everyone he meets. Then he meets an alcoholic street musician, Doug Prayer, who claims that he recorded an album with Jim Morrison in Paris, and who offers him a tantalizing bit of evidence, in a note in Jim Morrison's handwriting dated 1976, before disappearing. Ron tracks down and befriends Prayer and slowly cajoles the story of Jim Morrison out of him as well as his own story, which is inextricably entwined with Morrison's.

In the category of rock 'n' roll books, there might be the sub-genre of 'Jim Morrison is still alive' (that includes non-fiction as well as fiction) which includes Doors' keyboardist Ray Manzarek's novel *The Poet in Exile*, which for the most part is a novel of lost opportunities. But Clooney in *Mr. Mojo Risin'* makes full use of those opportunities and doesn't shy away from themes that you have to deal with in a book that looks at Jim Morrison, such as fathers and sons, existential issues of life and death, and the inner self.

Clooney also does something almost unheard of, and unique in *Mojo Risin'*, he includes photographs of Morrison's haunts, both the known and speculative. The first novel I ever saw this used in was *From Time to Time* by Jack Finney (a time travel book of another sort). I don't know if Clooney is familiar with Finney's book but he uses the device to great effect. It helps the reader to picture the environments Morrison frequented and adds a level of verisimilitude to the 'Morrison is alive' storyline, instantly putting you in the world Jim Morrison would have experienced.

Mr. Mojo Risin' also considers what most other books about Jim Morrison don't, or examine only peripherally, and that is Pam Courson. Courson who was Jim Morrison's 'cosmic mate' and part of Morrison's life from almost the beginning of The Doors until Paris July 1971, is intimately a part of the story more than she is usually given credit for. Clooney demonstrates a rare insight into Pam Courson. There's a muscularity in the writing that belies the conclusion, which is startlingly different for this type of novel. *Mr. Mojo Risin' (Ain't Dead)* is a book that Doors fans of all stripes will want to read.

Jim Morrison and The Doors' ability to influence doesn't end with the written word. The Doors were musicians that created an original, legendary, influential and provocative body of work and that influence can be seen, felt, and heard in one of the most original and provocative musical forms to come along in the past fifty years: rap music.

16
The Doors Take the Rap

As the present becomes the past it moves into the future, and The Doors have moved into a future they helped create. Looking to their past they want to ensure their future legacy, and so have embraced rap music. Over the last decade more and more rappers have sampled The Doors' music and have even admitted to The Doors as a musical influence. The Doors themselves have been returning the favor in the last few years and have worked with the rappers.

Cypress Hill Samples The Doors

Artists have long paid homage to other artists who influenced them. Jim Morrison paid homage to his literary heroes in Doors songs. "Realms of bliss/Realms of light" from *End of the Night* is from William Blake's *Songs of Innocence*. The Doors also covered a lot of songs from their musical heroes including Bo Diddley's *Who Do You Love*, Willie Dixon's *Back Door Man*, and John Lee Hooker's *Crawling King Snake*.

The Doors have influenced groups as diverse as Echo and The Bunnymen who covered *People Are Strange*, Duran Duran *The Crystal Ship*, and even Weird Al Yankovic. As The Doors CD *Stoned Immaculate* demonstrated, when The Doors called, groups such as the Stone Temple Pilots, Creed, Days of the New, Perry Farrell and Marilyn Manson contributed covers (which featured The Doors playing with the groups) and showed up to rub elbows with their rock 'n' roll heroes.

In today's cut and paste world of sampling, mashups and remixes - homages also started showing up. Blondie did a mashup of their song *Rapture* blended with *Riders on The Storm*. Snoop Dogg also covered *Riders on The Storm* and Cypress Hill sampled part of *Break on Through* on their song *Take My Pain* off their CD *Rise Up*. Admittedly, *Take My Pain* may not be a 'true' sampling, as the group uses the phrase: "Night destroys the day".

According to the *Toronto Sun*, members of Cypress Hill met and played with Ray Manzarek, Robby Krieger, and John Densmore in the past. It may not be that surprising that they added a tribute to The Doors in their song.

Did The Doors Reunite in the Studio?

October 6, 2011.

A lot of Doors fans have been hoping for a reunion of Ray Manzarek, Robby Krieger and John Densmore on stage. A new project by Skrillex may be the closest fans can get to that reunion. Doors keyboardist Ray Manzarek told *Rolling Stone*: "I like to say this is the first Doors track of the 21st century," and 'the reunion' will appear in the 2012 documentary film *RE:GENERATION Music Project*.

RE:GENERATION will explore music through the eyes of five modern DJs with each DJ embarking on a musical odyssey working outside of their usual genre to create new music inspired by a more traditional genre such as Jazz, R&B, Country, Classical and Rock. The Doors (as they're being billed in the film) are matched with DJ/Producer Skrillex, aka Sonny Moore, a twenty-three year old electronic musician and music producer. Other matchings include DJ Premier trying his hand at classical music, Pretty Lights doing country, Crystal Method covering R&B, and Mark Ronson with Jazz. Other guests participating in the project include Lee Ann Rimes, Martha Reeves, and Erykah Badu.

The question for Doors fans is: did Ray, John and Robby play in the studio together?

The Doors in the Studio with Skrillex

October 13, 2011.

As reported previously the surviving members of The Doors did play with DJ Sonny Moore, aka Skrillex, who counts The Doors among his earliest musical influences.

The Doors played on a track called *Breakin' a Sweat* (still a tentative title) and will be part of the documentary *RE:GENERATION Music Project*. The documentary is directed by Amir Bar Levy (*The Pat Tillman Story*) and is produced in association with the Grammys (National Academy of Recording Arts and Sciences), and is scheduled for a February 2012 release.

Although all three surviving members of The Doors did participate in the recording, they weren't in the studio together. Jim Southwick, the moderator of John Densmore's board reports that John went in and did some hand drumming. While Ray Manzarek and Robby Krieger came in for one session, and as Krieger reports in an *L.A. Weekly* article, Skrillex "seemed like a mad scientist". The pictures in the Weekly prove there still is a rift between Manzarek, Krieger, and Densmore as they had their pictures taken separately.

Would Jim Morrison 'Love' Skrillex?

January 21, 2012.

Billboard Magazine published an article *Jim Morrison Would 'Love' Skrillex + The Doors, says Ray Manzarek*. In the article Manzarek says Morrison was no purist, he wouldn't want anybody touching his words, but he'd be fine with new adaptations. In fact, this experience with Skrillex has inspired Manzarek to pursue more electronic experiments in the future. He is quoted as saying: "What I'd like to do and what might happen is to do some electronic treatments of the songs, of the multi-tracks we have, Robby (Krieger) and I are working with different people. That would be a lot of fun. That's the new realm of music, electronics…" When Jim Morrison predicted, in the 1969 interview with Richard Goldstein, that he could envision a person in the future playing an instrument surrounded by tapes and electronic equipment, could he have envisioned those people might be his own bandmates?

The article also reveals that The Doors were asked to perform *Breakin' A Sweat* at this year's Grammy's, but aren't able to because of the long standing estrangement of Manzarek, and Krieger from Doors' drummer John Densmore. *Re:Generation Music Project* is scheduled to hit theaters February 16, 2012.

Skrillex has been nominated for five Grammys including Best New Artist, Best Dance Recording, Best Dance/Electronica Recording (*Scary Monsters and Nice Sprites*), Best Remixed Recording, Non-Classical (Cinema, Skrillex remix), and Best Short Form Music Video (*First of the Year*).

The Doors and Tech N9ne

The Doors are doing it again! First the collaboration with Skrillex and electronic music for the recently released *Re:Generation Music Project* movie with the song *Breakin' a Sweat*, now hip hop artist Tech N9ne has announced that he is working with the surviving members of The Doors.

The news was released via Twitter and Facebook, but not much information has been released as to what the song recorded is, or when it will be released. In a recent podcast, Tech N9ne alluded to his working with The Doors, and hit Twitter about his collaboration with The Doors. The new announcement confirms that Ray Manzarek, John Densmore and Robby Krieger are appearing on the song. It will also include the vocals of Jim Morrison on *He Wasn't Missing.*

Tech N9ne also posted a picture of John Densmore in the studio with him and producer Fred Wreck. No word, as of yet, on the song or when the CD will be released.

L.A. Woman Meets Dog Town

On the heels of recent collaborations with Skrillex and Tech N9ne The Doors are reaching out yet again to a new generation with a video of *L.A. Woman* that is meant to appeal to the younger skateboarding audience.

The *L.A. Woman* video features professional skateboarders Kenny Anderson, Alex Olson, and Braydon Szafranski skateboarding through Doors heavy environments including Venice Beach, the Sunset Strip and downtown L.A. The video also has the skateboarders meeting up with Doors' drummer John Densmore, Doors' guitarist Robby Krieger, and in a special cameo the skateboarders stop for Elektra Records' founder Jac Holzman coming around a corner on his scooter. There is a rack on the back to carry albums, a reference to how Holzman actually went around selling Elektra albums in his early days. The video was directed by two-time Emmy nominated Matt Goodman.

The Doors Takin' the Rap?

How do you get some hip cred nowadays? How do you let your fans know you're on the cutting edge? That you're a rebel? Or even get noticed on the internet? Wear a Jim Morrison t-shirt for that hip factor, Paris Hilton did it, Ashlee Simpson did on SNL. Websites that are looking for search engines to pick up them up include Jim Morrison in their meta-tags. Now rappers are enlisting The Doors both in mixes and enlisting the surviving members of the band to collaborate on projects.

The newest contender is Clipse with a new mashup CD titled *Keys Open Doors*. The track listings are titled with Doors songs and subtitled with a Clipse title. The songs seem to include a sampling of Doors' songs. Perhaps the legal limit that can be sampled without having to pay royalties? No word on whether The Doors collaborated with Clipse on the songs or granted permissions for usage of the songs.

Although The Doors have ceased to exist as an active creative band since 1974, they have not stopped making the news. While Jim Morrison certainly courted controversy during his lifetime, sometimes controversy adheres to a person or persons. The Doors with their legendary status have courted controversy intentionally or unintentionally and continue to show up in our news reports.

17
The Doors in the News

Our fascination with legend and celebrity is marked by their newsworthiness and our interest in the stories that come out about them. The Doors are still newsworthy whether they're courting controversy, the news media covers their appearances, or because of our own fascination with the legend of Jim Morrison. The Doors are still able to capture columns in the newspapers and online. Here are some news stories The Doors Examiner was able to capture.

The Doors Name on Trial

Most of us know The Doors as history, but there's a living history, not only in the members of the band, but also the living history fans participate in. There's a generation of Doors fans who saw the band in the 60's, and there's also the generation of fans that lived through The Doors history and who *virtually* participated in it when Doors drummer John Densmore filed suit on February 4, 2003, against The Doors of the 21st Century.

The Doors are famous among fans as a band that operated as a democracy where any one member of the band could veto any of the business decisions of the others, such as Jim Morrison's objection to The Doors allowing *Light My Fire* to be used for a Buick commercial. In March of 1971, The Doors documented this arrangement in anticipation of Jim Morrison going to Paris, and it is unclear whether this was an attorney's idea to safeguard all members of the band or if the other members of The Doors feared Morrison would try to form a new band called The Doors once he was in Paris.

The rift leading to the lawsuit started because of Ray Manzarek's and Robby Krieger's appearance at the 100th anniversary celebration at the Fontana Speedway on September 6, 2002. Encouraged by their appearance on the TV series VH-1's *Storytellers* (November 22, 2000) in which they appeared with many different lead singers, everyone from Perry Farrell, Scott Stapp, Scott Weiland, and Ian Astbury (which also coincided with the CD release of *Stoned Immaculate*), Ray and Robby appeared with Stewart Copeland on drums. John Densmore either didn't want to appear because of tinnitus or he wasn't asked, and Ian Astbury of The Cult handled the lead vocals. The band was billed as "The Doors of the 21st Century" but was introduced as "The Doors". Then in January of 2003 the band appeared on Jay Leno's *The Tonight Show*, and again were introduced as "The Doors". John Densmore filed a lawsuit seeking to stop the band from being billed as "The Doors" as he had not agreed to it.

As with any lawsuit, the accusations, countersuits and counteractions soon became complicated. By June of 2003 Copeland was also suing the band for breach of contract, claiming Ray Manzarek and Robby Krieger had promised to use him on a tour and studio album (Copeland and Manzarek and Krieger later settled the case). The estate of Jim Morrison and Pam Courson joined Densmore in the suit and asked for compensation from Manzarek and Krieger for their being unfairly compensated by using The Doors name. In May 2005, the court ruled in favor of Densmore and the Morrison/Courson estates and since then, Manzarek and Krieger have appeared as "Riders on the Storm" (which was taken as a slap at Densmore who had titled his autobiography as the same) and have gone through a string of singers, and now appear as "The Manzarek-Krieger Band" with Dave Brock from The Doors tribute band "Wild Child" handling the vocals.

Palestinian Group Asks Manzarek-Krieger to Cancel

March 20, 2011.

The Doors were never a band to avoid controversy, they seemed to court it. They were never an overtly political band either. *Unknown Soldier* was designed to be an anti-war song as opposed to an anti-Vietnam War song. For the most part The

Doors were happy to be 'erotic politicians' and let people read their own connotations, political or otherwise, into their lyrics.

It seems controversy is following The Manzarek-Krieger Band's scheduled July appearance in Israel. The Palestinian Campaign for the Academic and Cultural Boycott of Israel (PACBI) has issued an open letter to Ray Manzarek and Robby Krieger asking them to cancel their July 5, 2011, concert in Tel-Aviv. The letter appeals to Manzarek and Krieger as alumni of a band that suffered at the hands of "police brutality" and compares the Israel-Palestinian situation to South Africa's Apartheid. The letter also goes on to list the human rights violations against the Palestinian people by Israel, and artists who are honoring the asked for cultural boycott.

As of this writing, the Manzarek-Krieger Band's appearance in Israel is still scheduled and there's been no official response to the letter.

John Densmore Occupies L.A.

October 18, 2011.

Occupy Wall Street is in its first month. In the past few weeks, more and more of America has become occupied. City after city is met with protestors. But few of the Occupy rallies have had a rock legend such as John Densmore supporting them.

Densmore has been involved in charitable and protest movements for quite some time, having been arrested with Bonnie Raitt in Chicago in 2001, and having lent his name to any number of charities from saving horses to appearing and playing for alternative schools.

Densmore appeared at the Occupy L.A. rally looking very urban-post-tribal in a top-knot and carrying a hand drum. He related how his family, when he was a kid, was a lower middle class family who had to move to make room for the freeway and he's never forgotten that he came 'from the 99%'. He read from *The New York Times*, which told the occupiers they were "unsophisticated" and hippies. Densmore countered by telling onlookers how the hippies ended the Vietnam War, threw a monkey wrench into the "industrial/military complex", and then recited a poem by Etheridge Knight.

Chapter 17

Jim Morrison's 'Love Street' House Damaged in L.A. Fires

December 31, 2011.

In *L.A. Woman* Jim Morrison sang, "I see your hair is burning/Hills are filled with fire", referring to the annual Santa Ana winds that blow small fires in the Hollywood Hills into conflagrations that threaten the houses. This year, arsonists have decided to add to the yearly number of fires, having already set thirty-five fires in the last two days of December mostly between the hours of midnight and six a.m.

One man has been arrested in connection with the fires, but other fires have been set since, leading authorities to suspect other conspirators or copycat arsonists are taking advantage of the situation. In response, the Los Angeles Fire Department has stationed fire trucks around the city, as well as set up a tip line to expedite reports of new incidents.

One of the houses damaged in the fires was the 'Love Street' house of Jim Morrison and Pam Courson at 8021 Rothdell Trail. Built in 1922, the house has been part of Hollywood Hills' history due to Morrison's and Courson's residence there. The house overlooked the Country Store, all of which Morrison incorporated into The Doors song *Love Street*. The house has been empty for a few years and the owners have recently been looking to rent the property. The house was also included in the closing credits for season two of the television show *Entourage*.

The common element among the fires seems to be that they started from cars set ablaze. Authorities speculate it would have to be the work of a "superman" to have set all the blazes at the times and places the fires had started although not impossible if the arsonist were traveling by car or motorcycle. The total amount of damage cannot yet be estimated, but about $350,000 worth of cars have been torched.

'Love Street' Arsonist Arrested

January 3, 2012.

Harry Burkhart, a German national, was taken into custody on Monday, January 2, 2012, in connection with the Los Angeles fires that officials have estimated to have caused $3 million in damages including the Laurel Canyon house that Jim Morrison and "cosmic mate" Pam Courson lived in during the 60's.

The exact motivation for Burkhart's arson binge isn't known. His mother was arrested last week on fraud charges stemming from incidents in their native Germany. At his mother's hearing, Burkhart broke out in an expletive filled rant against the United States. While he made no specific threat to either person or property, the fires started within twenty-four hours of the hearing.

Burkhart was identified by federal authorities after seeing a video of the arsonist taken at a carport where one of the fires broke out. He was later picked up by a Los Angeles County Sheriff's deputy who saw him driving a van similar to one reported in the area of the fires. He was arrested on suspicion of arson and is expected in court Wednesday January 4th.

Doors fans have been following this case with acute interest because the 'Love Street' house at 8021 Rothdell Trail was damaged in the fires. No fires have been started since Burkhart's arrest.

Will Jim Morrison Play with The Doors Again?

April 17, 2012.

Welcome to the future!

John Densmore has said he wouldn't play with former bandmates Ray Manzarek and Robby Krieger, as The Doors, unless Jim Morrison was singing with the band again. That was an impossibility until Sunday night when Tupac Shakur 'appeared' at the Coachella Festival in the form of a hologram. The video of the performance has made its way onto YouTube and the Tupac hologram is a very realistic imaging of the dead rapper. The Shakur hologram performed a couple of his songs, and did a shout out to the Coachella Festival itself (Coachella's first festival was three years after Shakur died). 'Tupac' even interacted with Snoop

Dogg and there were no obvious glitches and no obvious incursions of technology on stage. So, did Tupac's appearance herald in a new age of concert going?

With the technology to create realistic images now, seemingly, within our grasp, can long dead rock stars appear 'live' in concert again? That's the question bouncing all around the internet and the music world. Suddenly a lot of names of legendary dead stars have been bandied about as being next for holographic resurrection. Elvis, Jimi Hendrix, Janis Joplin, Michael Jackson and, of course, Jim Morrison. Will The Doors cancel Jim Morrison's cancellation to the resurrection or renew his subscription to a holographic resurrection?

For the last decade Ray Manzarek and Robby Krieger have been appearing in various incarnations; from the controversial (e.g. The Doors of the 21st Century, which caused the public rift between Densmore and Manzarek and Krieger), down to the present Manzarek-Krieger Band. All iterations of the band have featured lead singers seemingly moving down the food chain from lead singers of bands on hiatus, to a singer of a relatively unknown band, and finally to a lead singer from a Doors tribute band.

So, what does this mean for Doors fans? Fans who have always lamented being too young to have seen The Doors will no longer have that regret. Older fans would be able to relive a concert of their youth, or see it for the first time… maybe they had indulged in too much of something the first time around? For the band, the holographic Jim Morrison may be easier to appear with. They would not have to worry about Jim being drunk or stoned, unless they programmed it into the show. Jim also couldn't expose himself, or be arrested onstage. Would a controllable and totally predictable Jim Morrison be faithful to an actual Doors concert?

What do you Doors fans think? Are you going to buy a ticket? Or would it be the ultimate betrayal of Jim Morrison? Would you prefer the leonine dangerous Jim Morrison? Or the bearded poetic Jim Morrison? So many questions to be answered.

The future is uncertain, this may not be the end, but the beginning?

The Doors Welcome the Digital Resurrection?

April 29, 2012.

Since Tupac Shakur's holographic resurrection at the Coachella Festival it seems a lot of estates of dead rock stars and/or their families are expressing an interest in resurrecting dead rock stars. It looks like the revolution is upon us.

The very lifelike hologram of Shakur is causing not ripples through the concert touring industry, but waves. Who knows if those waves will turn into tidal waves. *Rolling Stone Magazine* ran a poll asking readers who they would like to see in digital concert; Jimi Hendrix won the poll with Jim Morrison coming in fifth. Since the Coachella Festival the families of Michael Jackson (or at least Michael's brother Jackie) have expressed interest in a holographic Michael, as have the estates of Kurt Cobain, and Elvis Presley. Mysteriously one of the members of The Beatles has 'expressed an interest' in a virtual Beatles reunion with a holographic George and John. The estate of Jim Morrison is taking initial steps into investigating the possibility of a holographically resurrected Jim.

It even seems the technology is conducive to having a lot of holographic rock legends appearing in concert again. It's being reported the technology for a holographic anybody is fairly cost effective. The Tupac hologram was created by Digital Domain who have created special effects for movies such as *Apollo 13* and while they haven't released the exact amount the Tupac hologram cost, they have said it cost under $100,000, a figure that would be well within the budgets and justify the cost of virtual concert tours that would be virtually guaranteed to pull in millions of dollars! Whole new generations could say they saw Jimi Hendrix play 'live' or The Doors with Jim Morrison.

A couple of days after the Coachella Festival article, I asked fans if they would go to see The Doors play with Jim Morrison again, and most said yes. While such a question would have been academic until recently, every day that goes by sees more bands and estates expressing an interest, and I wouldn't be surprised if, in the coming period, we hear a definite announcement of a coming virtual tour of a dead rock star. But how will fans react to their favorite star raised from the dead for profit? Fans of Kurt Cobain seem most vehement that Cobain would loathe the idea, but faced with the 'reality' of Cobain in concert, would they go? Jim Morrison also had strong ideas of how his image was portrayed and he became disillusioned when the use of that image escaped him. How would he react to a hologram of himself? It seems the future is here and now, and included with it is the question of: should we do it just because we can?

Chapter 17

Jim Morrison 'Resurrection' Coming Soon?

June 13, 2012.

As predicted, the estates of Jim Morrison and Jimi Hendrix are looking into, or have been looking into, creating holographic recreations of their dead rock stars.

Billboard Magazine is reporting that Doors' manager Jeff Jampol has been looking into creating a 3-D experience for the past eight years with British music video/commercial director Jake Nava in the hopes of creating a show where: "Jim Morrison will be able to walk right up to you, look you in the eye, sing right at you and then turn around and walk away."

The technology seems there for the scenario Jampol described. Ed Ulbrich, chief creative officer of Digital Domain, the people who brought you the Tupac Shakur hologram at the Coachella Festival in April, says: "This is not repurposing old footage the world has already seen. We're making totally original and exclusive performances so that fans can have new experiences." Digital Domain has signed an exclusive deal with Elvis Presley Enterprises to produce virtual Elvis images for a variety of Elvis projects.

Jeff Jampol also manages the estates of Janis Joplin, Otis Redding, Peter Tosh, and Rick James. Could Jampol and company be planning a whole slew of 'resurrected' concerts?

John Densmore on the Death of Vaclav Havel

Sometimes news and entertainment intersect, such as with the life of Vaclav Havel. The Doors' drummer John Densmore has long taken public stands on issues and lent his name to causes. With the news this weekend of the death of Vaclav Havel (February 2003), the first president of the Czech Republic, John Densmore released this statement:

"Havel was a hero of mine. While in the communist prison for his writing, he listened to rock 'n' roll to keep his spirit alive, waiting for the 'Velvet Revolution' (named after the 60's group the "Velvet Underground") to happen. I hope he is Resting In (Disturbed) Peace. One of his book titles, *Disturbing the Peace,* was about fighting complacency under communism."

Vaclav Havel was a poet, playwright and essayist whose work turned increasingly towards politics, and after the 1968 'Prague Spring' he became increasingly active in politics until his *Charter77* brought him international fame and imprisonment in Czecho-Slovakia. The 1989 'Velvet Revolution' led to his presidency of the Czech-Republic, his policies brought multi-party democracy and radical change in the nation. Havel was 75.

Doors fans-cination with the group have led to, arguably, one of the most artistically active fan bases of any rock band. Following Jim Morrison's lead, Doors fans have explored many artistic outlets and launched many projects that explore Jim Morrison, The Doors, and their influence on our lives.

18
Fans-cination with The Doors

Fascination: to attract and hold spellbound. Jim Morrison has done that and his fans are very fertile in imagination and creation. They've created and celebrated that fascination in any number of art forms.

Jim Morrison in the Theatre

High on Jim Morrison's reading list was Greek Mythology and theatre. When Jim Morrison put the Oedipal section in *The End* he entered the song, The Doors, and even his life into the purview of Greek tragedy. Annie Herridge, a writer/director with the Golden Goat Productions theatre company in Dorset, England, saw the connection between Morrison's life and Greek tragedy and had the idea to do a modern retelling of Euripides, *The Bacchae*, in Morrison's story, *An American Prayer.*

Herridge describes her production, *An American Prayer*, as: "It's late 1960's and America is experiencing a social and cultural revolution. At its heart Jim Morrison - who with The Doors and female groupies are setting the world on fire. The authorities in the guise of the Governor of California, a man who upholds the law and the principles of the American dream. In this wild raucous musical we experience the highs and the lows of the era through music of The Doors and the poetry and song of Jim Morrison."

Herridge's vision of *An American Prayer* was inspiration that came like the proverbial bolt of lightning from the Gods, borne on the wings of a divine messenger. When she decided that *The Bacchae* was going to be her second production, it was going to be a more traditional telling of the story, but then she put on The Doors' *Peace Frog* and it was as if: "Jim had leaped in and showed me that 'The Bacchae' was right, but to set in 1960's America with him returning as Dionysus."

Through a grant, Herridge was able to mount a preview of the show to an enthusiastic audience reaction. Herridge would like to expand the show and hopefully open it in London and eventually in America. Herridge is currently seeking investors for the show to bring her vision of *An American Prayer* to full fruition.

Jim Morrison in the Ballet

The Doors were conceived as a band with the idea that they would explore music with poetry and theater. All that was missing was interpretive dance, and maybe Morrison's shamanic dance moves filled in that void. But now the theatre arts are catching up with The Doors. The Leipziger Ballet opened a show in May of 2011 entitled *Jim Morrison*, which married interpretive dance with The Doors' music and angst of Jim Morrison, poet.

The plot of the ballet seems to follow Morrison's life and career as a rock star. The trailer of the ballet doesn't give away too much, but there are characters based on Pamela Courson, Patricia Kennealy, and the shaman. From the Leipziger Ballet's website is a synopsis of the piece (translated from German).

"A rock legend, but also a torn personality who captured the world's stage and is lost in the struggle with himself. Jim Morrison - a magnificent artist, rebel, poet, sensual, dancing shaman, traveler in the endless night. The press called him "lizard king", a "black leather demon". Mario Schröder steers his ballet in search of the man, his biography, and his sensitive poetry and his music.

Even before the curtain opens, the audience is in tune with the drama the charismatic star will face. Yes, Jim Morrison is dead, but the myth of the "King of the Lizards" lives. In expressive and energetic images, the breathtaking way the life of this enigmatic figure in rock history idol is real, until it finally says: "This is the End."

"Similar to Morrison in the balancing act of his life over the abyss, the dancers catapult in rapid capers, pirouettes and breakneck beats. Mario Schröder's moving creation goes beyond a celebration of an enfant terrible of rock music, formulated in the drama of the rock egomaniac, narcissist and surprisingly current in its insights." (Hamburger Abendblatt).

This isn't the first time that The Doors have inspired a ballet. In April, the Savannah Danse Theatre put on a production of *Giselle* that included a section titled *Pere LaChaise* and a *Tribute to The Doors*.

Jim Morrison's Bust

Sean Joyce was twelve years old when The Doors' *Light My Fire* came out, and even at that age he immediately recognized The Doors were on the cusp of what was going on. He saw Jim Morrison as a superhero, or at the least a "heroic looking dude".

Joyce who has had an artistic bent all of his life, remembers doing sculptures when he was three! He worked at Industrial Light and Magic (George Lucas' special effects company) and worked as a matte painter and storyboard artist, but didn't feel the artistic accomplishment in realizing someone else's vision. So, for the last twenty years, he's been a struggling artist creating paintings and sculptures of his own vision, including those of Jim Morrison.

Joyce started sculpting busts of artists he found "heroic and transformative" in his life including Henry Miller, Beethoven, Einstein, and Rodin. Ten years ago he started working on a bust of Jim Morrison and emailed (then) Doors' manager Danny Sugerman who loved the idea of the bust. Sugerman asked Joyce if he could finish it for the forthcoming 30th anniversary of Morrison's death, but it was only a couple of weeks before the anniversary and the bust couldn't be completed on time.

In the years since then Joyce has placed some of his busts in prestigious venues. The Henry Miller Library bought the bronze of Joyce's Miller. His former boss, George Lucas, showed some interest in a bust of himself. Joyce recently revisited his bust of Morrison.

Seeing Morrison as "heroic", Joyce's bust of Morrison is a cross between the 'young lion' era Morrison and classical Greek style. Joyce has created a double life sized bust of Morrison, and he would like to have a bronze of this piece placed at Venice Beach and/or Père LaChaise Cemetery. Joyce also feels Rainer Maria Rilke's poem would be a good epigram for the base that would hold the bust:

He was summoned like the ore from a stones silence.
His mortal heart pressed out a deathless inexhaustible wine.
Whenever he felt god's paradigm grip his throat, the voice
Did not die in his mouth.
All became vineyard, all became grape, ripened on the hills
Of his sensuous South.
Neither decay in the sepulcher of kings nor any shadow that has fallen

From the gods can ever contradict his glorious oration.

For he is a herald that is with us always, holding far across the doors of the dead.

A bowl ripe with praiseworthy fruit.

L.A. Woman Tours

History still exists in the buildings and the locales where famous events happened or persons hung out, even in a new city like Los Angeles. L.A. Woman Tours takes guests on tours of the Los Angeles homes and hangouts of Jean Harlow, Marilyn Monroe and The Doors.

L.A. Woman Tours is run by Elisa Jordan, a Los Angeles born resident, who realized that many of her idols had lived nearby. She took to exploring the sites of the city, researching the homes and haunts of the famous. Soon she realized she had information and enthusiasm that she could share with others and L.A. Woman Tours was born.

Jordan became a Doors fan in the 1980's when MTV would run *Closet Classics* of old bands and The Doors performing *Light My Fire* on *Ed Sullivan* soon became one of her favorites. Jordan thinks The Doors are unique to Los Angeles because: "a lot of bands are from Los Angeles. They either start here, or move here to get their careers going. The Doors not only started here, they're really one of the few bands that are of the city. They are inspired by it, they write about it, it's part of their identity."

Her "Strange Days: A Tour through The Doors' L.A." starts at Venice Beach and the building where Jim Morrison wrote the rooftop poems/lyrics that would become the backbone of The Doors' repertoire throughout their career. Also included on the tour is the Sunset Strip, The Doors' offices, the recording studios and of course some of Jim Morrison's favorite hangouts. You can visit her website, L.A. Woman Tours. Elisa Jordan also writes the Marilyn Monroe Examiner.

Stephen Beauvais' Doors Portraits

I may be a little biased, but Doors fans seem to be one of the most creative groups of fans to produce creative works. Maybe it's because of Jim Morrison's interest in poetry and art and his well-known attempts to support artists, but Doors fans seem to produce more works of art than fans of other rock 'n' roll bands. The latest Doors fan artist to rise out of the mists is Stephen Beauvais.

Beauvais is a visual artist with a unique style that sets him apart from other artists, and instantly grabs your attention and invites closer examination of his subjects (mostly portraits). Beauvais' portraits of Jim Morrison and The Doors were inspired by Morrison's UCLA film school friend Paul Ferrara who took a picture of Jim Morrison with a wreath of laurel on his head and Beauvais expanded on it adding his own touches of a Picassoian primitive sort of style. Beauvais adds images that at first might seem separate from a portrait. Beauvais makes them a part of the portrait and while the portraits aren't pointillist in style, you'll want to give each work a closer examination that you might find only in admirers of pointillism. While not acknowledging it, perhaps a bit of his style has also been inspired by some of Morrison's more naturalistic poetry.

The Quest to Find Jim Morrison's Long Lost Cobra

Christian Mixon is making a documentary with a unique and interesting angle on Jim Morrison.

In *Vision Quest to find 'The Blue Lady,'* Mixon is in the process of creating a documentary film on his quest to find Jim Morrison's car, 'The Blue Lady'. The car was given to Morrison when Elektra Records owner Jac Holzman asked each of The Doors what present they wanted after *Light My Fire* became a gold record.

Morrison asked for and received a 1967 GT500 Shelby Mustang. Morrison was later involved in a crash with the car and it is thought the car was scrapped and disappeared from history. But Mixon isn't so sure, "In the age of the internet, many registries are filling in most of the blanks and some entire production runs of rare cars are accounted for. Add to the fact that the owner was a celebrity at the time of the car's disappearance, and I feel strongly that it is still somewhere."

Mixon is a lifelong Doors fan, avid reader, car collector, and actor/director/producer. He was the owner of Collector Car Central in Temple, Texas, and it was his research headquarters until the economic downturn closed its doors. All of these interests have coalesced into producing *Vision Quest*. He became interested in the project after reading Stephen Davis' *Jim Morrison: Life, Death, Legend* book. He doesn't want to create a documentary focused on just one aspect of Morrison or the car, he wants to create an all-around overview of Morrison, "Too many people write Jim Morrison off as a drug and alcohol fueled madman who just did crazy things and probably abandoned the car. But if you dig anywhere past the surface, you find that Jim was a man driven by deep passions and big appetites. 'The Blue Lady' was the embodiment of an icon for him and he would not let her go easily." Mixon is planning on talking to people from the Sunset Strip crowd of the time, he'll talk to Shelby Mustang owners, and he'll be interviewing friends of Morrison about what the car meant to him.

The project to find 'The Blue Lady' is still in the research stage of production. Not only is he contacting people to interview, but at the same time he's trying to find the car itself. Mixon says, "a few 'possible' cars have shown up, but nothing has panned out." So far.

A Night to Remember

It was 32 hours, 1000 miles, 10 readers, 1 film, and 1 Doors tribute band to make it *A Night to Remember*.

A Night to Remember: Jim Morrison in Poetry, Film and Song was held last Saturday night at Rutledge's in Nashville. I had the opportunity to attend the festivities and had a very good time.

The Trip. We left suburban Chicago at 8 a.m. Saturday morning heading south, chasing the fleeing horizon, passing through the urban areas of Indianapolis, and the rolling hills of Kentucky. We had to skip the Bourbon Trail, and finally arrived into Nashville where we noticed that everyone seemed to be leaving!

Thanks to Mapquest we quickly found The Rutledge where *A Night to Remember* was being held. We were early so we went next door to a Mexican restaurant, had dinner and a couple of Margaritas. When we went into The Rutledge we found a nice brick building, that had once perhaps been a house, but which now had a nicely sized bar, and an adjacent room where the bands play. It was an intimate setting for a band. The farthest seat from the stage was not more than sixty feet (and as we would find out the acoustics were great!). We were so early we got directions to Broadway, which is the Sunset Strip of Nashville's music scene.

Broadway was a lot of small Depression-era brick buildings close together with dive bars pressed into the buildings and their 50's neon signs glowing over the sidewalks. The bands playing in the bars blared for the attention of the passing crowds. Walking up and down Broadway I noticed that, in Nashville, cowboy boots are a must, but you can get away with not having a cowboy hat. It seemed that only about 25% of men on the street had a cowboy hat. We had a drink in a bar which, we were told, was frequented by Hank Williams before he had a Grand Old Opry gig, and we made our way back to The Rutledge for *A Night to Remember*.

The Reading. About ten of us got up to read selections from Jim Morrison's poems. The readers were a wide variety of people from a Nashville DJ Proud Mary to Craig Krampf. Craig saw The Doors when they were still at The Whisky (they were pointed out to him because his band also didn't have a bass player), and he told of how Jim Morrison scared him. Jim Johnston read *The Lords*, and *Connections*. I was asked to read *Ode to Brian Jones, Deceased.*

The Film. *Dawn's Highway*, Brad Durham's film about the accident a young Jim Morrison witnessed driving with his parents in New Mexico while en-route to his father's assignment at Los Alamos was shown. Mr. Durham tracked down, through New Mexico highway records, what he believes was the accident the Morrisons witnessed, and even found the survivors of the accident. Afterwards, a few of us discussed the implication of this event on Morrison's life. Jim Morrison's mother, before her death, said that Jim may have exaggerated the incident or was dramatizing it more than what really happened. Which may be true from her perspective, but from Jim's perspective the experience was mystical. From the account of Frank Lisciandro in the film, Jim told the story as a factual happening and how it had affected him greatly. If *No One Here Gets Out Alive* can be believed, the event may have been reinforced in young Jim Morrison's mind when his mother tried to convince him: "It was all a dream Jimmy."

The Band. The Sideshow (who usually play as The Lost Sideshow) are one of the best Doors tribute bands I've seen. Lead singer Chris James wears leather pants like Morrison, tight and shiny. They were loud, but the 'good loud' that a band does when burning out a song without it being hard on the ears. There was a sense of timelessness to the band but not of the songs themselves. You lost yourself in the music and didn't care where you were, or if you would ever get out. James as Morrison did great renditions of The Doors' songs with Morrison's stage theatrics adding poetic touches at just the right moments with just the right poems.

A standout moment in the show for me was during *Riders On The Storm* when James added the poem that starts "A vast radiant beach". It fitted into the song perfectly. The Sideshow is a great band made up of some of Nashville's best session players, and they know how to play the instruments and get a huge sound from them. The Sideshow probably has a better lighting set-up than The Doors ever did and it added a dramatic element to the show that The Doors never had, but which they might have used had they gone into the 70's as a touring band.

Brad Durham plans on taking his film *Dawn's Highway* to film festivals before releasing a DVD. Here's hoping that he'll host other nights to remember.

Jim Morrison, Poet?

Daniel Nester's essay *When You're Strange* on his Poetry Foundation blog, asks whether Jim Morrison was a great American poet, or not, and has been going around the internet. While I thought it was going to lead to the usual conclusion that Jim Morrison's pretensions at being a poet were greater than his ability, it didn't reach that conclusion, but it still didn't give Morrison the credit as a poet he deserves and instilled in me the urge for a response.

Naturally, as Doors fans we're more predisposed than non-Doors fans to consider the poetry of Jim Morrison at least pretty good. Before I was a Doors fan I was reading poetry and wanted to be a poet myself. Jim Morrison provided a modern day model of a poet for me.

It's a very strange question that Morrison's status as a poet is consistently called into question, but Bob Dylan was given almost immediate poet status upon releasing his first album, and named as the voice of his generation. Not to piss off any of Bob Dylan's fans, the poetry in Dylan's *Tarantula* seems more self-consciously obscure and pretentious than Jim Morrison's poetry though.

In an interview, Anne Morrison, Jim's sister, said the family thought Jim would be poor all his life, and Jim knew that most poets didn't make a living by their writing. They usually teach, and many poets don't receive much recognition outside a small coterie of academics, small presses, other poets, and readers. Morrison took a shortcut to becoming a poet; he took the path of rock 'n' roll (also not a guaranteed path to success but the possibilities of a wider audience existed). If Morrison had pursued the usual path of poetry he might not have been recognized during his lifetime. The poets of Morrison's generation, for the most part, didn't start getting recognized until the late 70's, almost a decade after Morrison was dead (although if Morrison had taken another path he would, of course, have altered the events and the course of his life, but that's something for *Back to the Future*).

Jim Morrison really brought poetry to the mass audience of young people that constitute the 'baby boom generation'. In works like *When the Music's Over* and *The End*, he brought concepts, themes, and phrasing over from poetry. "Screams of the butterfly" or even "Cars stuffed full of eyes" and introduced poetry to people who were listening to their radios, watching TV and who might have not, ordinarily, responded to the poetry if they had been presented with a book of 'Poems' by James Douglas Morrison. The Doors are still doing it to this day.

Nester's essay claims that only academia can anoint someone as a poet. This, in itself, is an elitist position. Doesn't readership and listeners add credibility to the claim or title of poet? Doesn't the act of writing make you a writer? Or writing poems make you a poet? If there is some other criterion, I've never heard of it.

Morrison's poetry has a disadvantage most other poets don't have. In *Wilderness* and *The American Night* the reader is seeing a much rawer book than other poets or even Morrison would have released if he had lived to see them through to publication. The poems that were gleaned from Morrison's manuscripts and journals and published in *Wilderness* and *The American Night* weren't recognizable final versions or even in a state Morrison may have considered to be worthy of publishing. This isn't the fault of Columbus and Pearl Courson, Jim Morrison's 'in-laws' who, through Pam Courson, inherited the rights to Morrison's poetry, or Frank and Kathy Lisciandro who helped in the pre-publication preparation of the books. It's just the nature of Morrison dying at an early age. He didn't seem to have prepared any manuscripts of completed works of poems. In fact, as stated in the notes of *The American Night* the poems weren't dated and they often had to figure out which version of a poem seemed to be the latest version or what Morrison considered completed. If you want a good idea of the quality of Morrison's poetry or even a glimpse of where his poetry could have gone, read *An American Prayer* and compare it next to Allen Ginsberg's *Howl,* or T.S. Eliot's *The Wasteland.*

That the question of Morrison's qualification as a poet is still even being asked smacks of some elitism or snobbery, that poetry is for a more refined sense and erudition to be enjoyed and understood, and that people as unrefined or unsophisticated or maybe uncivilized (uncivilized, in its original meaning, living outside of the city or community) as rock 'n' roll fans couldn't possibly understand real poetry. But the academics and keepers of the gate at the walls of civilization will always be taken back by some new punk-poet such as Rimbaud, or Morrison himself walking on a Venice Beach in sandy jeans, holding a notebook stuffed with poems, snatching that snobbery from the jaws of academia and the expert voices, and writing for all people willing to read and understand what he's trying to say.

Today rock 'n' roll is the predominant musical form and is recognized as so by the Grammys, MTV, and the Rock Hall of Fame. Bands of varying talents and degrees receive awards and encomiums easily. The Doors as elder statesmen of the music industry are today receiving awards they weren't recognized for in their heyday.

19

Not Quite The End

"And death not ends it", a quote taken out of context from Jim Morrison's *An American Prayer*. It is also a truism; Ray Manzarek, John Densmore, Robby Krieger and The Doors go on.

Ray and Robby Music Producers

After rock bands break up, especially acclaimed ones, the band members usually try their hand at producing other acts. When I first became a fan of The Doors I always wondered why none of the members of The Doors went on to become producers. They had already dipped their toes in the producing waters when they co-produced *L.A. Woman* with long time engineer Bruce Botnick, and their unique vision and the experimental nature of The Doors suggested they would translate well to producing other bands. The answer turned out to be they did produce other acts, it just took a little research.

In the 80's Doors keyboardist Ray Manzarek produced the band X and their first four studio albums. Manzarek discovered X at The Whisky a Go-Go where The Doors had been discovered ten years earlier by Elektra Records' Jac Holzman. Manzarek and wife Dorothy were sitting in the club listening to the band when Manzarek's wife leaned over and said to him: "Do you recognize that one?" and he said no, and she said "Listen carefully." It was only then that Manzarek recognized the song as being The Doors' *Soul Kitchen* played at high speed.

From there Manzarek went on to produce X's debut album, the critically acclaimed *Los Angeles* which Manzarek also contributed to through some of his keyboard playing. With Manzarek's influence, X eventually went to Elektra Records and although they never reached the popular acclaim and visibility The Doors did, they had their cult and critical acceptance. For the past few years Manzarek has sat in with X in Los Angeles venues.

Doors' guitarist Robby Krieger is the most low-key member of the band and stays under the radar for the most part, so information is hard to come by. Krieger had one of the most unique sounds in all of rock history, one that other bands over the past forty-five years haven't even tried to reproduce. It seems natural that this creativity for creating a unique and identifiable sound would lead him to producing. Krieger generally is the member of The Doors that maintains the lowest profile. He's the only one that hasn't published a memoir (although he has stated that he has worked, or is working, on one), but he too has had his time as a record reproducer producing The Mau Maus in 1983. He produced their first and only studio album as well as playing the guitar solo on *(I'm) Psychotic*. The Mau Maus are releasing a CD *Scorched Earth Policies: Then and Now* that will feature the 1983 Krieger produced album (that was remixed in 2010) as well as new songs.

John Densmore in the Twenty-First Century

John Densmore has also been keeping himself busy with new projects, one of which is a long awaited book on his experience with the lawsuit that has put a rift between him and his former bandmates Ray Manzarek and Robby Krieger. Another is a movie which he's producing; coming to a DVD near you in the future.

John Densmore's long awaited book *The Doors: Unhinged, Jim Morrison's Legacy Goes on Trial* will finally be published April 17, 2013. It details his efforts to stop former bandmates Ray Manzarek and Robby Krieger from using The Doors name for use in advertising campaigns or personal gain without the full consent of all the members of The Doors, including Densmore himself and the estate of Jim Morrison.

One of the things The Doors were known for was being a group of equals, all the publishing rights to The Doors songs were shared equally amongst The Doors, with the idea that all the band members were important in the creation of the songs. This 'all for one' ideal was later codified in a formal document before Jim

Morrison left for Paris in the spring of 1971. Although, the formalization of the agreement might not have started in the most idealistic conditions, the agreement was drawn up and signed because Ray Manzarek, Robby Krieger, and John Densmore feared Jim Morrison might go to Paris and start a European Doors - this document was the seed of the internecine battle that would plague The Doors thirty years after it was signed, and ironically what proved the decisive document in the court case.

The Doors: Unhinged promises to take fans into the courtroom as it details the three month long trial, and the surrounding crash and roar of Doors fans on both sides of the issue. The book also includes some unknown aspects of The Doors, the trial, Jim Morrison and his estate, including how Morrison's career as a rock star hindered his father's naval career.

John Densmore has long flirted with producing movies. He produced (along with Mark Wahlberg) the documentary *Juvies* and in his post-Doors career has focused on the theatre appearing in his own one man show *Skins* and producing and acting in theatre productions such as *Waiting for Jack*. Densmore is combining those interests in a forthcoming feature film *Window of Opportunity*.

Window of Opportunity was a play which Densmore produced and as a producer he's now bringing the project to movie screens as a feature film. *Window of Opportunity* was written and directed by Samuel Warren Joseph based on his play. The story follows corporate executive, Roger Sizemore, who takes a couple of his junior executives up to a hunting cabin for a weekend of drinking. Sizemore also invites a couple of hookers up to the cabin and over the course of the weekend one of the hookers ends up dead. Sizemore then enlists his underlings in the cover up of the murder. Densmore has released a statement on the film: "I am very proud to have produced a new feature film, Window Of Opportunity, a suspenseful, darkly comic thriller. The themes in the movie are ones that I've been concerned about for a long time; primarily the corporate greed that has so damaged our country and world, and the CEOs who have been in charge. Please take a look at look at the trailer and let me know what you think."

The most visible cast member is Oliver Muirhead who is widely recognized from his roles in movies such as in *National Treasure: Book of Secrets*, *The Social Network*, *Austin Powers: The Spy Who Shagged Me*, and TV shows such as *The Big Bang Theory*, and *Seinfeld*. *Window of Opportunity* is still in post-production. A release date for the film is still unannounced at this time.

Chapter 19

Père Lachaise July 3, 2011

July 3, 2011, was the commemoration of the 40th anniversary of Jim Morrison's death, held at Père Lachaise Cemetery. Every newspaper and online media outlet from the *L.A. Times* to the *India Times* found angles on the story. But they just reported on the factual events and didn't give you a feeling for what it was like to be there.

Walking through the gates of Père Lachaise you're struck by the sense of the autumnal, the shades of trees, a quieting of the day from the world outside the gates. The cemetery slopes upward, and it's not like a cemetery, but seems more like a necropolis, a city of the dead. The small mausoleums line avenues and side streets, and lanes of the city inside a city. The stone of the graves and mausoleums can be old and rough-hewn to the newest polished marbles. As you ascend into the cemetery, the section of the cemetery where Jim Morrison is buried is on a sloping hill and it was easy to find; just follow the flow of people coming and going to the site. I didn't have a map of the cemetery and I didn't have any problems just following The Doors t-shirts on these Paris pilgrims.

As I got close to Morrison's grave you could hear a thrumming sound of a lot of people talking. It wasn't loud. A deep thrumming sound that created its own sense of reverence like the lingering reverberations of chants and songs in a cathedral. Morrison's grave creates its own natural clearing. Immediately across from his grave is a fenced off section of wildflowers. The grave itself is small, you can see why John Densmore would say he doesn't think Jim is buried there because it doesn't look big enough. Of course, the grave is under the framing bed and headstone. Standing at the barrier fences surrounding his grave (they're not much of barrier, anyone with the slightest inclination can hop them) is a reflective moment. Do you say a prayer? Would Jim want that? Would he understand this rock 'n' roll pilgrimage at all? Most people stood next to the grave only briefly, quietly paying their respects, taking a picture of the grave, and the nearby tree that bears the scars of graffiti messages from fans. They then seemed to fall back to the nearby lane, sit down for a while, play some music, meet other Doors fans, smoke a joint, or have a drink in Jim's memory.

A friend of mine said he doesn't want to go to the cemetery because he can't go any further with Jim. Being there, I was overcome by a sense of that, a sense of the anti-climactic. Jim isn't there, but he's everywhere else, in the music, in his poems, his films, he's alive in the memories of the people who knew him, and dances on in the imagination of fans.

The Classical Music of the Future

For a decade The Doors have been in search of making sure their music goes on; so that they have a legacy to leave to the future. It's not a new search for the band either; Jim Morrison asked publicists that if he died would he and the band have accomplished enough to secure the group's name into the future. That legacy was secured in 1971. With the death of Jim Morrison he became legend and The Doors as well. However, The Doors were never just Jim Morrison. The Doors were the sum of all their parts.

Ray Manzarek, who met Jim Morrison in film school, and then again on the beach in the hot July of 1965, had vision enough to see the poetry and music in the sandy figure before him. A man who had just spent six weeks on his own personal vision quest; a man who many had written him off as being too undisciplined or erratic. Manzarek took Morrison in and together they created the basis of The Doors. Morrison, who had witnessed a "fantastic rock concert in his head" took notes, his words sometimes the only link to a melody he heard.

Manzarek was a few years older and more experienced in worldly terms. Up until then he had been in bands that mostly covered others and while they had some original material - it was derivative and imitative. Manzarek was facile enough to not only see the future, but hear the future, and he worked out with Morrison the melody and structures of those first few songs that made up The Doors. Had Morrison not chosen that all writing credits go to 'The Doors' surely the credit of Manzarek/Morrison or Morrison/Manzarek would be as recognized, revered and canonized as Lennon/McCartney?

Drumming is said to be a chaotic art because you can't chart what a drummer plays in the way you can a piano or guitar player. The drummer is the heartbeat of any band and John Densmore provided the crash and cacophony for Morrison's own chaos and discord. Densmore was a confluence of influences (as were all of The Doors). Because of his background in jazz, he added the punctuation to Morrison's poetic statements which otherwise might have sounded like slogans or non-sequiturs without the context the band added.

When The Doors formed, Robby Krieger had been playing electric guitar for only eighteen months! He is a guitar player so distinctive that no other guitar player or band has successfully recreated the sound he did with The Doors. In Krieger, The Doors also discovered a second songwriter for the group. Krieger is credited with most of The Doors' hits including: *Light My Fire*, *Touch Me*, and *Love Her Madly*. Morrison encouraged him, gave him themes and imagery, and it was

Morrison who pushed Krieger to his creative limits by creating a competitive tension in the band that ultimately brought them to a national audience.

Jim Morrison said: "There's the known and the unknown and in between are The Doors." What is known is that The Doors and their music will go on, and five hundred years from now people will be playing and speaking of The Doors just as we still talk of Beethoven and Mozart in reverential tones.

Acknowledgments

This is the part where the writer fesses up that he couldn't have done it alone. First, I would like to thank The Doors, Jim Morrison, Ray Manzarek, John Densmore, and Robby Krieger. Jeff Jampol has also been very helpful early on with baseline information on The Doors, helping with contacts as well, and throughout the life of The Doors Examiner.

I would to thank Jason Elzy at Rhino Records, Carol Kaye at Kayos Productions for their help in advance promotional materials for The Doors, as well as Backbeat Books, Oglio Records, Jaw Bone Press and any others I've forgotten for providing review materials over the past three years.

I would like to thank Mr. Anthony Funches for the great foreword, and Messrs. Robert Rodriquez (also, thank you Robert for catching errors), Michael Anthony and Rich Weidman for their encouragement and blurbs they supplied to this volume.

I would be remiss not to mention the books and websites I used to research articles.

Break on Through by James Riordan and Jerry Prochnicky, No One Here Gets Out Alive by Jerry Hopkins and Danny Sugerman, The Doors FAQ by Rich Weidman, Moonlight Drive: The Stories Behind Every Doors' Song by Chris Crisafulli, Becoming Elektra and Follow the Music by Jac Holzman, Light My Fire by Ray Manzarek, and the The Lizard King: The Essential Jim Morrison by

Acknowledgements

Jerry Hopkins. There are books both old and new in my bookcase that I occasionally reference but these are the books that are out when I'm writing The Doors Examiner.

The websites Doors History.com, Mild Equator.com, Other Voices message board, and a new one I haven't used much but seems like it's going to a great website for resources, The Doors Guide.com.

The personal notes, special thanks to Mr. James Lumsden for editing this volume and having to put up with the best and worst of a temperamental artist (probably one and the same!), My sister and mother, the Connie Cherry's squared, Charles and Barbara Post for their continued support.

All of the books, CDs, DVDs and Blu-Rays mentioned in reviews in this book are available at Amazon. Tell them The Doors Examiner sent you!

If I've missed anybody, or any website, I do apologize - it is the proverbial sin of omission.

We Want The World: Jim Morrison, The Living Theatre and the FBI by Daveth Milton

Jim Morrison was a songwriter, film maker, poet and singer with The Doors. His opponents saw him as a criminal. And more. In an escalating confrontation over the freedom of America, he was up against men who used law to block justice and fear to halt social change. Those men included the FBI's infamous director, J. Edgar Hoover.

Inspired by true events, this imaginative recreation of history re-opens Morrison's secret FBI dossier to reveal his Establishment opponents. Moving between Jim's image, influences and brushes with the law in Phoenix and Miami, Daveth Milton uses meticulous research skills to assess the extent of the conspiracy against the singer. Part meditation, part rock in the dock exposé, We Want The World provides the ultimate account of Jim Morrison's awkward encounter with the Bureau.

The Hidden Whisper by Dr JJ Lumsden

Want to learn about the science of parapsychology and paranormal phenomena? Follow the exploits of fictional parapsychologist Dr Luke Jackson as he seeks to uncover a poltergeist outbreak in Southern Arizona. Along the way, learn all about paranormal phenomena such as Extra Sensory Perception, Psychokinesis, Ghosts, Poltergeists, Out of Body Experiences and more.

This book works on many levels, an excellent introduction to the concepts current in the field of parapsychology... at best you may learn something new, and at worst you'll have read a witty and well-written paranormal detective story. **Parascience**

...a ghost investigation novel that has all the elements of a good detective mystery and spooky thriller...an engrossing haunting tale... an informative overview of the current theories on the phenomena. **paranormal.about.com**

An extremely well-written and suspenseful page-turner from real life parapsychologist JJ Lumsden. **Yoga Magazine**

Around the World in 80 Scams: an Essential Travel Guide by Peter John

Every year, thousands of people fall victim to various travel scams, crimes and confidence tricks while they travel. Most people escape having simply lost a little money, but many lose much more, and some encounter real personal danger

This essential book is a practical, focused, and detailed guide to eighty of the most common scams and crimes travellers might encounter. It is packed with real-world examples drawn from resources across the globe and the author's own travels. Being aware of scammers' tricks is the best way of avoiding them altogether.

Chapters cover all sorts of scams including: Hotels and other accommodation scams, Transport scams, Eating, drinking and gambling scams, Begging and street hustling scams, extortion, blackmail and fraud scams, and more.

Bryan Adams: A Fretted Biography - The First Six Albums by Mark Duffett

Bryan Adams is a one man rock'n'roll success story: he went from washing dishes for $2.50 per hour to becoming a multi-millionaire by making music that people liked. Adams' 'Reckless' album sold over 10 million units globally whilst his ballad 'Everything I Do (I Do It For You)' cleared an impressive 7 million copies. He remains one of the world's most popular rockers and a Canadian national hero.

In this detailed but accessible biography Mark Duffett explores Adams' meteoric recording career, 'ordinary guy' persona, and unfolding political commitment. The supporting activities of his manager and record company are included to complete the picture. As a well-informed story of maximum rock 'n' roll it constitutes essential reading material for true fans.